THE
ALCATRAZ ROSE

A Lawrence Kingston Mystery

ANTHONY EGLIN

LARKSPUR
HOUSE

This is a work of fiction. All of the characters, events, and places described herein (other than Alcatraz Island, Kew Gardens and Dobells) are either products of the author's imaginations or are used fictitiously.

ISBN 13: 9781502707031
ISBN 10: 1502707039
Library of Congress Control Number: 2014913779
Larkspur House, Sonoma CA
First Edition: November 2014

ALSO BY ANTHONY EGLIN

The Blue Rose

The Lost Gardens

The Water Lily Cross

The Trail of the Wild Rose

Garden of Secrets Past

For Dave Stern

1

Cheltenham, England

WHY DOES SHE keep staring at me?

At first, Kingston had shrugged it off as a maddening teenage quirk, but now, ten minutes into the panel debate, it was becoming distracting. And that was a problem.

Public discussion groups such as this one, to which he was no stranger, required one hundred percent of his concentration and intellectual faculties. Even more so this afternoon because the other distinguished scientists on the stage with him were considered among the best in their respective branches of academia, and he had a reputation to uphold.

Yet under the girl's constant gaze, innocent as it was, he was finding it increasingly difficult to focus. Her get-up didn't help matters, either. For all he knew it might have been fashionable, but to him, the gelled short hair and layered grunge outfit, topped by a red-and-white football scarf, bordered on the comical.

Luckily he was on one end of the table. Unnoticed by most, he shifted his chair slightly, to face his colleagues more than the audience. Though she'd now faded into the periphery, he could still feel her presence. And why was she alone? he wondered. *Why not?* a steadying voice inside him murmured. *What's so unusual about a twelve-or thirteen-year-old attending a science fair symposium?* Yet it still didn't sit quite right.

The event, in the Queen's Hotel Regency Room—part of Cheltenham's annual Science Festival—was billed as a panel discussion on topics related to the environment and green-energy programs. Lawrence Kingston, University of Edinburgh professor emeritus, had been invited mostly in recognition of his standing as one of the country's leading botanists. But—as the program chairman must have been all too aware—it was common knowledge among his peers and the media that Kingston didn't shy away from taking a contrarian stance now and then, and was often an outspoken critic of certain aspects of the "green" agenda.

Kingston's erudite and witty presence made for good box office. No matter what side of the aisle you were on, fireworks were guaranteed. But what had helped make this event a sellout was the sizable contingent of mystery and crime aficionados in attendance, who were far more interested in Kingston's spare-time exploits as an amateur investigator than they were in saving the planet.

The closing Q&A part of the program finally arrived, and Kingston now had no choice but to shift his chair and face the audience full on. To his surprise, the girl's seat was empty. She must have become bored. He couldn't blame her. Why had she made him so uneasy in the first place? he wondered. Now he would never know what had motivated her to attend, not that it mattered anymore.

The program officially concluded, Kingston and his colleagues left the stage to mingle with the audience. He was midsentence, attempting to answer a three-part question from a garrulous gentleman in the back of the group milling around him when, out of the corner of his eye, he once more caught sight of the young girl and her unwavering stare.

"Damn," he muttered under his breath, quickly stuttering an apology of sorts to the man, gathering his thoughts sufficiently to finish answering him. Though partly hidden among the adults, he realized by her steady gaze that she wanted him to notice her. She was closer now than before, and he could see—magnified by her round John Lennon glasses—that her eyes were ice blue and unusually large for her age. Either that or her vision was so bad it needed a lot of help.

At least she has none of those wretched tattoos or piercings—at least no visible ones, he mused. Was she waiting to ask him a question or request an autograph? What other reason could she have for being there?

One by one the admirers and autograph seekers departed, leaving the two of them alone. As if each was waiting for the other to speak, they stood separated by no more than a dozen feet, an awkward and unlikely couple. She looked even smaller now, more vulnerable, in a way he couldn't explain. For a few seconds the only sound was the hum of a vacuum cleaner from the other side of the room, and then, finally, she spoke. Not in a voice that matched her age and appearance, but in a manner incongruously self-assured and fluent.

"Hello," she said, eyes unwavering. "Could I please have a word, sir, just a few minutes—you and me?"

"Of course you can." He smiled, eager to put her at ease. "I couldn't help noticing you in the audience. I was thinking how gratifying it was to see one so young at a science fair, particularly at such a serious discussion."

"I didn't come to hear about the science, sir. Though I liked what you said about endangered animals—you know, making a comeback, mysteriously reappearing—that stuff," she added hastily. "I really came to ask you a favor."

"And what kind of favor would that be?"

She paused, pursing her lips, as if thinking about her answer. She blinked several times before answering. "If it's all right with you, sir, could we go somewhere quiet, where we can sit down and talk about it? It's . . . complicated. I mean, it might take some time to explain, you see."

"I don't see why not," he replied, knowing that he couldn't refuse, at the same time wondering what he was letting himself in for. "And there's no need to call me sir. Doctor will do fine."

"All right." The girl smiled. "Doctor's cool."

"And what's your name?"

"It's Letty. Letty McGuire."

"Short for Leticia?"

She shook her head. "Lettice. Let-TEECE," she repeated, exaggerating the pronunciation.

"It's unusual."

She made a face, wrinkling her nose. "My grandma's middle name. I hate it. They used to call me lettuce in school."

Kingston grinned. "All right, Letty. Now, are you here alone? With your parents, or—"

She shook her head. "I don't have any parents. But don't worry, my foster parents know where I am and why I came here." She patted her skirt pocket. "I'll call them when we're done, and one of them will come get me. We live ten minutes away. Anyway I *am* thirteen, you know," she said, with a tinge of resentment.

Kingston smiled. "Of course," he said, pausing. "There's one more thing, though. My friend Andrew is waiting for me in the lounge, and I don't want to keep him too long, he gets impatient. So why don't we go get him first, then find a place where you can tell us both what's on your mind?"

She beamed. "That would be brilliant—Doctor."

Five minutes later, the three were seated in a quiet corner of the hotel's lounge. Kingston had ordered a Coke for Letty and glass of white wine for himself. Andrew was nursing the remainder of his beer from the bar, looking as though he'd still not yet recovered from the sight of Kingston sauntering into the lounge with a teenager in tow.

Kingston's neighbor and longtime friend had accompanied him not for the sake of science but rather the Stratford Festival of Motoring that was taking place nearby that same weekend. Three hundred classic cars, paraded along the streets of Stratford-upon-Avon, was an event that neither wanted to pass up.

When Kingston had introduced Letty, all he had told Andrew that she'd simply asked for a favor. Now he turned to Letty.

"So what's this all about, then? This mysterious favor?" he asked, with a twinkle in his voice.

"I want you to help me find out what happened to my mother."

Her eyes shifted from Kingston's to Andrew's, as if knowing what kind of reaction her words would elicit. "She went missing eight years ago," she added softly.

Kingston's expression changed abruptly to frowning consternation. "Disappeared completely?"

She nodded. "She left one morning when I was little and never came back. No message, not a word. Nothing," she said, her voice showing no trace of emotion.

"You said you didn't have parents. But what about your father?"

"He was killed in a motorbike accident when I was little."

Kingston glanced at Andrew, who showed no inclination yet to join in the conversation. He returned his gaze to the girl. "I'm truly sorry."

"That's all right," she replied stoically.

"What about your foster parents?"

"You mean, who are they?"

Kingston nodded. "Yes."

"They're Richie and Molly Collins, friends of my mum and dad. Uncle Richie—that's what I call him now—used to work with my dad a long time ago. Auntie Molly used to babysit me."

"And you've lived with them since your mum disappeared, I take it? In Cheltenham?"

She nodded.

"I'm curious why you chose to seek me out," Kingston said. "Why do you think that I might be able to help? After eight years, surely the police must have done everything in their power to find her."

"They have. But they came to a dead end a long while ago. They told us that unless they come across new information or new witnesses, the chances of finding out what happened to her are next to none. My foster parents even hired a private detective for a while. I believe it cost them a lot of money. But that went nowhere, too."

"What about the Missing Persons Bureau?"

Letty shook her head again. "We've pretty much given up on them. There's been no change since the case was first reported."

"What about your aunt and uncle? What do they think, after all this time?"

"They say I shouldn't give up hope. But I know they're just trying to be nice." She shrugged.

"So how did you learn about me?" Kingston asked, sipping his wine.

"The *Gazette*, our local paper. There was an article about you and the Science Festival. At first, Molly didn't think it was a good idea for me to come here, particularly by myself." She paused, gave a quick smile. "But I finally persuaded her."

"It seems that you're quite good at persuasion."

"Sometimes," she replied, wrinkling her nose again. "Anyway, in the article it said that you were a famous professor and had also solved several crimes that the police couldn't." She sucked on the straw of her Coke. "Molly said that you're not a real detective. But I think she said that just to put me off."

Not a real detective. At those words, Kingston exchanged a glance with Andrew, who was finally taking an interest in the conversation. And Kingston knew why.

His friend had never entirely approved of Kingston's amateur sleuthing. Andrew, in fact, had spent a great deal of time trying to deter him from "playing detective." But a year ago, when Kingston was involved in an investigation that threatened to become dangerous—and, indeed, at the end Kingston received a serious gunshot wound—Andrew insisted that in the future—should Kingston consider any more ventures or inquiries—he would take a more active role in what he described as Kingston's "ill-advised activities."

Kingston was glad to agree and promised to take Andrew's opinion and advice more seriously. And he would try, as best he could, to curb his tendency to jump into any future such situation without considering the ramifications. In turn, Andrew assured his friend that he would do his best to collaborate and to find ways to help Kingston instead of treating him like a bullying nanny and second-guessing.

That was why Kingston was glad that Letty was talking to both of them. He could see by the look in Andrew's eyes that he, too, was taken in by the girl's story; her composure and tenacity for one so young were irresistible. Even after eight years, Letty was determined not to accept that her mum was lost forever. That was much longer than most adults would persevere.

"Letty," Kingston began in the most avuncular tone he could muster, "your aunt Molly is not entirely wrong about the detective thing. Let me explain. After I retired from teaching in Scotland and went to live in London, I fell into solving crimes more by accident than by design. Over the last few years, my reputation has been blown way out of proportion." He smiled reassuringly. "Don't misunderstand me, I'm not making excuses and I do want to help you, but you need to realize that my influence is not as far-reaching as you might have been led to believe. Not anymore, anyway. I mention this because trying to find out what happened to your mum will require working with the police, trying to persuade them to part with information that they've gathered on the case over the years. It will be essential for us to know, exactly, not only what they've done in the course of their investigation, who they've interviewed, et cetera, but more important, what they might not have done."

Letty nodded and remained silently attentive.

"Here's what I'm going to suggest as a start," Kingston said. "Before I do, it's only fair to tell you that I no longer have the time or the energy to conduct a full-blown independent inquiry into your mum's disappearance. Furthermore, it's what the police call a cold case, which makes it even more difficult." He paused, returning her steady gaze. "That said, let me tell you what I will do. Collaborating with the police over the last few years, I've got to know a number of high-ranking officers and I'm prepared to write a letter to one of them asking if he will help on the case. I'll also ask the Gloucestershire police about the standing of the case and learn as much as I can about why it remains unsolved: anything and everything about her disappearance. This doesn't mean they'll cooperate, though. I don't expect for one moment that they'll hand over their files, or anything like that, but whatever I can get my hands on, I promise to comb through it, to see if there are instances where a second look, a fresh inquiry, would be justified. I don't want to raise your hopes, Letty, but sometimes it's the little, seemingly inconsequential, things that are overlooked in these cases. As thorough as the police are—and they don't miss much—they're not infallible."

For the next ten minutes, Letty told them everything that had happened leading up to and following her mum's disappearance. For one so young, she was unexpectedly composed and lucid. When she finished, she took a small envelope from her pocket and handed it to Kingston.

"These are photos of Mum and a couple of Dad. Molly put dates on the back so you'll know when they were taken."

"Excellent. I was going to ask if you could find some," Kingston said, impressed with her preparedness.

Andrew produced a pen and a folded program and proceeded to jot down notes on the blank back page as Letty gave them her mother's first name—Fiona—her address, her home and mobile phone numbers, and her e-mail address. She also remembered the name of the senior investigating officer on the Gloucestershire Police in charge of the case, another indication of her resolve.

Looking satisfied and animated for the first time, Letty pulled out her mobile and called her foster mum, asking for a lift. The three walked to the hotel's entrance, where they said brief goodbyes. Kingston and Andrew offered to stay until Molly showed up, but Letty insisted that she was okay waiting for the five or so minutes it would take, so they parted company. A few moments later, heading for the car park with Andrew, Kingston glanced back. Letty was still standing there, waiting patiently for her ride.

"That's a determined young woman," Andrew said, echoing Kingston's own thoughts.

"Indeed. Determined, engaging, and resourceful."

"Remind you of anyone?" Andrew asked.

Kingston smiled.

At that instant, he vowed to do his best not to let her down.

2

THE NEXT AFTERNOON in his study, Kingston sat tapping his fingers idly on the desktop alongside his iMac keyboard, looking at the spread-out photos that Letty had given him. When he'd first studied them, he was immediately taken by the attractiveness of her mother, Fiona. Letty had inherited her wide and mesmerizing eyes and affectionate smile. It wasn't so much her pretty, photogenic quality, but more a natural warmth, a calm contentment and kindness that seeped from the oft-fingered photos. He looked away momentarily. An uneasy pause, stifling a fleeting thought that she was someone he might once have known, perhaps in a dream or another life. Not in just one or two photos, but in each and every one. He slid them aside gently, thinking nothing more of it.

He'd had plenty of time to think about the letter he'd promised to write, but he was now struggling to find not so much the right words but, more, the right tone. Of the several inspectors with whom he had collaborated, he'd decided to write to Detective Inspector Sheffield of the Thames Valley police. He'd chosen Sheffield because Oxfordshire bordered Gloucestershire, where Letty's mum had disappeared. But despite what he'd told Letty, he knew it was highly unlikely that any letter, no matter how much bowing and scraping he did, or how persuasive he was, would result in reopening the case. After eight years, the odds of a break now were slim. Only new, compelling evidence would achieve that. He realized now that he had perhaps been far too indulgent and should have been more honest with her from the start.

Combing the Internet, he'd managed to find barely a handful of reports on the disappearance of Fiona McGuire, all brief and none revealing anything worthy of note. Given the modest press coverage and the passage of time, he wondered if Sheffield would be familiar with the case. And even if he was, would he be able to recall any details? The more he thought about it, the more he realized that if his letter fell on deaf ears, his request politely dismissed, it might not be such a bad thing. To the best of his ability, he would have fulfilled his promise to Letty. Staring at his ghosted reflection in the blank screen, he realized how petty and self-serving the thought was. He shook his head and started typing.

Dear Inspector Sheffield,

Recently, I had a chance meeting with a thirteen year-old named Letty McGuire. A bright child with an admirably persistent nature, she asked, innocently, if I would help to put her mind at rest by trying to find out what happened to her mother, who disappeared eight years ago. It grieved me to tell her that I was no longer active in such affairs and could not conduct an independent inquiry of any kind. However, in a moment of vulnerability in the company of one so young, distressed, and determined, I made a hasty promise: that I would break a self-imposed principle by contacting you, to ask for advice.

I realize that the Fiona McGuire case (the mother's name) was handled by the Gloucester police and will be filed by now. Nevertheless, I am bound to ask you for any help you could provide, no matter how trivial or inconsequential, that could shed more light on the case, if nothing else, to give Letty a thread of hope to cling to or, at worst, confirm my suspicions that no proverbial stone has been left unturned to solve the case and that nothing more can be done.

The investigation started in the autumn of 2003, and the senior investigating officer on the case was Detective Inspector Endersby of the Gloucestershire Constabulary. If he is still on the force, and it doesn't violate internal procedures, perhaps you could drop him a letter of inquiry, mentioning my request, asking his opinion, thoughts, and any advice that could be passed on to the child to bring closure, after all these years of uncertainty and grief.

I wish you well and appreciate your collaboration and consideration in this matter.
Sincerely,
Lawrence Kingston

He read the letter twice, making a few minor changes. While he would have preferred it to convey a more earnest and overtly compassionate plea for help, he knew that such a request would be considered presumptuous. He was satisfied, however—knowing the inspector as he did—that, if nothing else, the child's long struggle with grieving and frustration over the loss of her mother would appeal to Sheffield's sense of decency and justice. He checked it one last time, signed it, and tucked it into an addressed envelope ready for posting.

The days that followed continued in much the same predictable, though agreeable, pattern as they had since Kingston's release from the hospital in Staffordshire almost a year earlier, after his brush with death in his last escapade. Outside the usual household chores, home maintenance and day-to-day demands of a domesticated existence, the tedium was relieved by the occasional lunch at the Antelope, and dinner now and then with Andrew, usually at the new restaurant du jour. One warm and cloudless afternoon a week ago, he took off alone on a spur-of-the-moment midweek walk through Kensington Gardens, and attended a West End play with his friend Henrietta—a bohemian artist type who had a habit of becoming brazenly amorous after a couple of gin and tonics—who had "scored" the tickets. He hadn't asked how.

On this particular morning, a former student of his, one Evelyn Cotter, in London for two days, had called unexpectedly and, even though Kingston had no recollection of her, he agreed to meet her for a late lunch. He spent the entire meal regretting his decision. Barely stopping for a breath—even while eating—she droned on and on about her children, dragging out awful photos of them—her children, for heaven's sake. She didn't seem much older than a child herself. Kingston was shocked to learn she had just celebrated her fortieth birthday and relieved when, after more than two hours, she ran out of banal conversation. Never again, he swore to himself, as he walked home.

Back at the apartment, he found a stack of e-mails waiting for him, including one from his daughter, Julie, confirming details of his upcoming trip to America: that she would pick him up at SeaTac airport, advising him of how to dress for the weather in Seattle, et cetera, which reminded him to send her a note later that evening confirming the arrival of the plane tickets and thanking her again for the gift. He continued to scroll down his messages, finding next a notification from one of the online journals he still subscribed to: news of an unusual chance discovery of a new plant species in Costa Rica, which he flagged for further investigation. Following, were four e-mails from friends and, of course, the usual spate of junk mail.

His evening was planned. An early dinner: crab cakes, already prepared by his housekeeper, Mrs. Tripp and in the refrigerator, a crusty baguette, and a Waldorf salad accompanied by a chilled bottle of Savennières, his favorite Loire Valley chenin blanc. Afterward, he would stretch out, feet up, in his wingback and watch a new rented documentary about a year in the Burgundy vineyards and wineries. He'd finish off the night with the late TV news, catch up with day's headline events, and then it would be off to bed.

Despite this sybaritic and citified lifestyle that most would envy, Kingston couldn't help thinking of all this as a precursor, a paradigm for permanent retirement. Would it be like this from now on? If so, he knew it would quickly become intolerable, and he would soon be hankering after a new pursuit, a substitute for his years of crime solving. He also knew, of course, that nothing could replace the cerebral challenge and self-satisfaction derived from hunting down and bringing criminals to justice—the challenge of investigating.

Two weeks passed and still no word from Sheffield. Kingston was now starting to worry that Letty would think that he'd forgotten her, which was the last thing he wanted. He was thinking about phoning, when a letter finally arrived bearing the Thames Valley police insignia.

Dear Lawrence,

It was a pleasant surprise to hear from you after so long. Your recent exploits in Staffordshire gave me cause for concern, so it was gratifying to learn from your letter that you are none the worse for wear and had chosen to hang up your deerstalker, turning over the pursuit of the miscreants to us. I think I can speak for my colleagues in commending you for your prudent decision.

Were it not for an unexpected occurrence, I would have sent you a polite reply, informing you that your inquiry is strictly a matter for the Gloucester police and nothing more can be done—for they have informed me that the case is now filed as undetected. For better or worse, such a reply would have resolved your dilemma and you would no longer feel beholden to the child and could start planning that round-the-world cruise.

There is, however, an alternative and perhaps a more satisfactory solution to your dilemma. The aforementioned "occurrence" concerns a detective sergeant who was transferred to the Thames Valley force several years ago. By a stroke of serendipity, the policewoman, Emma Dixon, was formerly with Gloucestershire Constabulary CID and had worked on the McGuire case. She has since retired, after an automobile accident left her permanently disabled.

Lawrence, none of us wish to be complicit in either encouraging or enabling you to continue an active investigation into this case. To the contrary, I would urge that you seriously consider not doing so. However, it occurred to me that with Emma Dixon's cooperation, the two of you might be able to arrive at a resolution that would satisfy everyone's best interest, particularly that of the child. If Emma Dixon were to explain, one on one, to Letty McGuire everything she knows about the mother's disappearance, there's a good chance that the child would accept the word of a policewoman intimate with the case. If nothing else, she might be persuaded, once and for all, to abandon her search for the truth, realizing that to continue could only mean further pain and, quite possibly, long-term psychological damage. Most of all, she should be persuaded to focus instead on her own future.

I have discussed this with both Emma and a senior officer on the Gloucester force, and she will be expecting to hear from you. She lives in Winchcombe. Her phone number is 01386-796-4300. For the sake of both the child and you, I hope that the matter reaches a satisfactory conclusion.

Regards,
M. K. Sheffield

Kingston smiled. He was pleased not just to hear from Sheffield but also to learn about Emma Dixon. He put the letter aside, recalling the time, several years ago, when he was sitting across from Sheffield in the interview room at Oxford police station being grilled and excoriated at the same time for "meddling" in police matters.

Sheffield could be officious, and sometimes supercilious, but as they got to know each other, Kingston had grown to respect the man. It would have been easy for Sheffield to have withheld all information about Emma Dixon's involvement in the McGuire case and left it at that. But he understood that Kingston was searching for something more than just a convenient resolution and had been thinking more of Letty McGuire than the letter of the law.

He was even more pleased after speaking with Emma Dixon. He had reached her right away, and she had sounded both pleasant and genuinely interested in trying to help. They agreed to meet at her home in the charming town of Winchcombe, Gloucestershire, two days hence, which pleased him no end. The Cotswolds were one of loveliest parts of England, and it would be a respite to get out of London for a change of scenery, if only for a day.

Coincidentally, he had been thinking about taking a trip to that part of the country for several days now. He had an old friend who worked not too far from Emma's whom he hadn't seen for several years, so the timing couldn't be better. He picked up the phone to invite Andrew.

3

The phone call that would give Kingston's rather humdrum existence a second shot in the arm within a few days came the following afternoon, after he had just returned home from lunch with Andrew at the Antelope pub. Over excellent pasta, they had discussed, among other things, their upcoming jaunt to Winchcombe to talk with Emma Dixon about Letty's plight and, time permitting, a visit to nearby Belmaris Castle to see the gardens—especially the antique roses. Of the two, Andrew had shown more interest in the first—but Kingston knew Andrew well enough to know that what had really persuaded him to go along for the ride was the prospect of both lunch and dinner in the same day, gastro pub or up-and-coming restaurant.

Kingston picked up the phone. He recognized the voice right away.

"Hello, Lawrence, It's Clifford. Glad I caught you. I imagined you off on another of your escapades. Held hostage in a drafty mountain cabin somewhere in Wales." He chuckled.

Clifford Attenborough, a longtime friend and former colleague of Kingston's at Edinburgh University, was director of horticulture at the Royal Botanic Gardens at Kew. His only daughter was named after Kingston's late wife, Megan.

"What a nice surprise to hear your voice, Clifford. It's been far too long."

"It certainly has. How are you? Still driving the coppers crazy?"

"Not really. After that episode in Stafford, everybody's telling me to pack it in. They're probably right, I suppose."

"Good advice, I'd say."

"So what's going on at Kew?"

"A couple of things, actually. The main reason I'm calling concerns a directive I just received from the top brass. It deals with a letter from "Whitehall" describing a series of upcoming meetings and conferences between top-level government officials and leading scientists from a variety of specialties. The reason for the conference is the growing concern of homeowners, landowners, and some businesses over the proliferation of land acquisition by environmental agencies in the name of critical habitat—endangered species, that sort of thing. Some cities and counties have got into the fray, too, apparently. Anyway, your name was put forward as one of the potential botanists on the committee."

"Interesting."

"I thought it would be right up your alley, Lawrence. Great crested newt, Glanville fritillary, creeping marshwort—all that sort of stuff. Particularly since you're now at a loose end, so to speak."

"To tell the truth, Clifford, I'm not—"

"Oh, I forgot to mention, for a government project, the compensation and expenses are generous, to say the least."

"Well, I was about to say I'm not doing anything in particular in the coming weeks, so—what the heck?"

"Excellent. I know you'll liven things up, which is what these people need. That's only my personal opinion, of course. I'll send you all the details, dates, et cetera, in the next few days."

After talking for another five minutes or so, about Clifford's upcoming retirement after forty years of service to Kew and personal and trivial matters, Kingston was about to say goodbye when Clifford interrupted.

"There was one other matter that will pique your curiosity, Lawrence."

"Right. You said 'a couple of things.'"

"It's about a recent discovery in the United States."

Not another new plant species, Kingston was thinking.

"It's not at all what you're thinking. It's about a rose they've just discovered, growing on Alcatraz Island, of all places."

"You mean the former prison?"

"Exactly."

"What about it? What makes it special?"

"Two things. First, it's over two centuries old and was last known to have grown only in England. And second, it was declared extinct over fifty years ago."

"I'm having trouble believing this."

"Indeed, but it's true. I'll e-mail you a copy of the newspaper report that I received from our friends at Ravenshill Botanical Garden in Sonoma County."

After hanging up. Kingston stared into space for a moment. What had started out to be just another ho-hum day had certainly gone topsy-turvy.

For the better, or to make life more complicated? He wondered.

When Kingston went into his office the next morning, Clifford's e-mail was in his in-box.

Two-Hundred-Year-Old Extinct English Rose
Shows Up on Alcatraz

BY DOUGLAS LEE CHAMBERS

San Francisco, CA—A rare, now extinct, rose that grew for 200 years in a famous English garden but perished 50 years ago was discovered last month in an overgrown patch on Alcatraz Island, former site of the infamous prison in San Francisco Bay. The inexplicable reincarnation has led some to speculate that Al Capone might have once sniffed its fragrance.

The red-and-black rose was first cultivated in the 19th century by Samuel Cavendish, an English grower. It is named the Belmaris Rose, after Belmaris Castle in Gloucestershire, once home to Katherine Parr, the last of Henry VIII's six wives.

Thought to be lost forever, and considered among the rarest of the some 100,000 known rose varieties, it was discovered by a team of Bay Area rosarians from the Heritage Rose Group visiting the island to search for and take cuttings of rare roses. Greg Robinson, a member of the team, spotted the diminutive Belmaris in a weedy, overrun area that was once part of the head warden's garden. "There it was. A tiny blossom, waving in the breeze above a thicket of brambles," Robinson recalled, noting his astonishment at the rose's ability to survive all these years in the wild, in a climate inhospitable to all but the hardiest native species.

Alcatraz historian Andy Harris was similarly puzzled, though for different reasons. "The real mystery here," Harris stated, "is how the rose traveled over 5,000 miles, from the shores of England all the way to Alcatraz."

Harris went on to say that one of the Alcatraz wardens was known to be a keen gardener and cultivated a rose garden behind the house. Only on rare occasions were inmates permitted outside the confines of the prison walls. Among the very few awarded that privilege were model prisoners who worked in the warden's garden and two or three other cultivated areas on the island. This would rule out the Al Capone flight of fancy.

Robinson, who owns Past Perfect, a Sebastopol, California, nursery specializing in old garden and species roses, took cuttings of the errant rose and will eventually be sending a shipment to Belmaris Castle, where a special ceremony is planned to welcome it home after its globetrotting travels. He will also be introducing the distinctive dark crimson rose, with its pronounced yellow stamens, to his inventory.

Kingston's thoughts had turned instinctively to the hoax of the century—the infamous Piltdown Man fraud. The discovery, in 1912, of a skull and jawbone in a gravel pit at Piltdown in East Sussex, set off a worldwide clamor, when the remains were certified by paleontologists and other experts as belonging to a hitherto unknown form of early man. Even the British Museum was unwittingly complicit, helping to reconstruct the skull. In time, this led to a scientific "consensus" that the Piltdown Man represented an evolutionary "missing link" between ape and man.

It took forty years for the discovery to be exposed as the deliberate work of a master forger and prankster, who remains to this day unknown. It was finally determined, beyond all doubt, that skull fragment was human, from some time in the Middle Ages. The jaw was from an orangutan and the fossilized teeth from a chimpanzee. Perhaps the most confounding aspect of the deception was that it was perpetrated purely as a hoax, with no motivation for material, financial, or other gain.

To all appearances, so it was with the Alcatraz rose. But there, Kingston concluded, the comparisons ended. He found nothing in the newspaper report, no red flags or anything to hint at chicanery or twits playing games. Clifford had been right.

Kingston knew that the average reader would likely find the story of a transatlantic-hopping rose nothing more than mildly curious, but to scientists, horticulturists, rose aficionados, and serious gardeners, it was the equivalent of finding a mummified English rose in King Tut's tomb. How on earth could a rose that to all intents and purposes had ceased to exist, that had been classified by botanical authorities worldwide as extinct, suddenly pop up on, of all places, a wind-swept, barren rock jutting out of the frigid waters of San Francisco Bay? Roses were much hardier than they were given credit for, but as a survival test in the wild, this, by all standards, would be cruel and unusual punishment.

As familiar as Kingston was with the genus *Rosa*, his knowledge of Alcatraz Island and its notorious penitentiary was passable at best. On their one visit to San Francisco, back in the early eighties, he and his wife Megan had taken the Alcatraz tour. Back in those days, however, visitors were permitted to tour only the prison itself, and all other areas of the island were strictly off-limits. The areas surrounding the buildings had been a tangle of wild vegetation, a survival of the fittest. Their guide had made no mention of gardens or plant cultivation—why would he? Least of all a rose garden of any kind. That, Kingston would certainly have remembered.

Yet the more he thought about it, the more he become convinced that the only possible explanation for the rose's appearance on Alcatraz was that it had been brought there when the prison was in operation. But by what process? And brought by whom? The warden? One of the prison staff, perhaps, or even a civilian worker? If so, what would have motivated someone to acquire such a thing? More important, who would have been able to supply him with the rose's seeds—or, more probable, cuttings?

The rose had been first cultivated at Belmaris Castle. What an amazing coincidence. Clifford would have been gobsmacked to learn that Kingston was going there that very afternoon and that the head gardener was a close friend. What a strange world, he thought.

Getting ready to leave—Andrew would be ringing the doorbell any moment—he hoped that the trip to Belmaris might provide answers to some of those questions.

4

BEHIND THE WHEEL of his racing-green TR4, the top down, Andrew in the passenger seat alongside, Kingston was in a chipper mood. Much of the reason for this bonhomie had to do with the prospect of meeting Emma Dixon. An equal measure had to do with their visit afterward to Belmaris. And the cornflower blue skies and warm sun that bathed the green and pleasant countryside of the Cotswolds made it all the more agreeable.

Andrew appeared to be in a similar state of geniality; he'd been in fine humor all morning. Not surprising, perhaps, since the day had started off with a smile. They'd met at nine o'clock to take off for Kingston's garage, only to find that they were wearing near-identical clothes: navy blazers with tan slacks and open-neck check sport shirts. After flipping a coin, Kingston had popped back into the flat to swap his blazer for a suede jacket.

It was several years since Kingston had been in the Cotswolds Hills, considered by natives and tourists alike as the most quintessentially British region in the isles. The clusters of small towns and villages tucked into folds under steep-sided hills; picture-postcard houses, shops, old inns, and tearooms of local stone and black-and-white timber had remained unchanged over the centuries and were a magnet for tourists. On a day like today, the Triumph was one with the road as it tooled through the winding muddle of minor roads that meandered through sheep-flecked pastures, hemmed in by ancient drystone walls that crossed humpback bridges over bubbling streams, with names like Windrush, Evenlode, and Churn.

After a break for a plowman's lunch at the Angel, in the market town of Burford, they arrived in the village of Winchcombe. Driving at a crawl through the absurdly narrow high street, flanked on both sides by half-timbered medieval and honey-color limestone buildings, Kingston pointed out to Andrew examples of the traditional architecture, trotting out his knowledge of Cotswolds trivia by commenting that wall-mounted signs were no longer permissible because of damage to buses and other large vehicles. Andrew did not appear to be overly impressed. He'd wanted to stay for a second pint at the pub.

They soon arrived at Emma Dixon's modest Vine Street bungalow. "You can't miss the pillar-box-red front door," she'd said when they'd talked on the phone. At the time he'd detected a dry wit in her conversation, reasoning that anyone who chose to paint her front door bright red could hardly be a crashing bore.

As she opened the door, smiling, Kingston's first thought was how unlike a policewoman she looked.

"Dr. Kingston?"

"Yes, indeed."

"Emma Dixon."

They shook hands.

Emma was considerably smaller than he'd expected—five four at the most. Police height requirements must now be a thing of the past, he suspected. Her shoulder-length dark hair was tied in a ponytail and, other than a pale shade of lipstick and a judicious touch of mascara, she wore no discernible makeup. Didn't need to, Kingston thought. She had dark brown inquisitive and restless eyes that reminded him in some ways of a hummingbird—hovering for a while, then darting off to gather more nectar: another thought, another observation or witticism. He judged her to be in her late thirties or early forties.

"A pleasure to meet you," she said.

She turned to the man with Kingston. "And you of course are Andrew."

"That's me," he said, leaning forward to shake her hand, too.

"I recognize you from the TV interview in Staffordshire after your friend broke the code and survived the shooting. It was very impressive."

Andrew looked embarrassed. "I thought it was awful."

"Nonetheless, I'm glad you're here. Won't you come in please, gentleman?"

"They followed her inside. "We work as sort of a team," Kingston added.

Emma's smile was playful. "Holmes and Watson, eh? Except, you're the doctor."

"I wouldn't go that far," he replied with a broad smile. "First of all, I want you to know that we greatly appreciate your going to all the trouble of helping, Emma. That's what this is really all about."

Emma nodded, looking more earnest. "I wanted to do it, because the case is still important to me—it always will be. The way I look at it, it's still an unsolved incident—and for all we know, a criminal case—and, frankly, if I were still at that desk in Gloucester, I would be working day and night looking for ways to solve it. I wouldn't go as far as to call it an obsession, but it's cost me a lot of sleepless nights, and the more clever brains that can be put to work to help solve it, the better—official or unofficial. And, I confess, retirement isn't as interesting as I'd hoped."

She led them into a sunny living room where they sat in chintz-covered chairs in an alcove by a bay window. On the phone, Kingston had told Emma that Andrew would be accompanying him and of their plan to stop for lunch on the way down, so she'd forgone the courtesy of offering tea or cold drinks. Tea later would be welcome, they agreed.

Out of the corner of his eye, Kingston noticed that some of the books piled on one end of the coffee table were related to gardening; he wondered what kind of garden, if any, might be behind the small bungalow. That led him to wonder how someone with the temperament of a policewoman would take to the slow, let-nature-take-its-course pace of gardening, and what nature of policewoman she had been. Despite knowing that it was blatantly chauvinistic, he couldn't suppress the thought of being arrested by her. Would all that warmth and amiability suddenly evaporate, to be replaced by a humorless and authoritative nature? Or would she simply smile benignly while placing a hand on his head as he was eased into the patrol car? He banished his musing as Emma told them briefly of her accident—a side-impact collision involving a drunk driver when she was returning home one night after working late on an interview. That segued into her many months of recuperation and therapy, adjusting to early-age retirement and life in the slow lane, the pros and cons of living in Winchcombe, closing with a customary peroration about the merits of the Cotswold climate.

All this gave him a several minutes to quietly size her up, to picture her and Letty together and visualize how they would get on; if Letty would be persuaded that this might be her last chance to reach some kind of closure; and, perhaps most important of all, if she would accept the advice and judgment offered by a woman detective who probably knew and could recall more about the case than anyone else.

The niceties over, Kingston got down to the matter at hand.

"When Inspector Sheffield told me that you'd worked on the Fiona McGuire case and that you were prepared to talk to me—and possibly to Letty as well—it was a big load off my shoulders. I couldn't have asked for a better outcome. That said—and not knowing police regulations in these matters—I wondered how much information on the case you would be allowed to disclose. I certainly don't want to be responsible for your exposing yourself to censure, or future problems, for divulging information about a criminal case that's filed as undetected. That's been worrying me. The last thing I want is for you to risk losing your pension or anything like that."

"It's not a problem," she said with a shake of her head.

"Good. I brought it up because in his letter Sheffield stated only that he'd discussed the matter with a Gloucester senior officer. It struck me as being uncharacteristically vague for him. So, before we start, I just want to make sure you can talk freely about the case and not have to worry about repercussions. Also, if any aspects of the case are still officially off the record."

Emma smiled. "That's very thoughtful of you, Doctor, but don't worry on my behalf, it's a nonissue."

"Please call me Lawrence," Kingston interjected.

Emma smiled. "Thank you. I didn't want to appear too presumptuous. Lawrence is much better. So, to continue, I spoke at length with Charlie Endersby about it. He was the SIO on the case back then, and he has no worries about my 'spilling any beans.' In any case, the rules are more relaxed now. There's more latitude. We're obligated to disclose much more information to victims and families than in the past. It's all spelled out in what's aptly, if a little grimly, called 'the Victims Charter,' yet another Home Office masterpiece that lays down rules and regs for crime victims' rights. Essentially, we're still an institutionalized lot and like to do things with some degree of permission, after which we are masters at bending that permission to suit."

This brought a smile from Kingston as well as from Andrew, who was only too well aware of his friend's penchant for bending the rules.

Emma continued. "By the way, Endersby wanted me to stress that during the investigation, the foster parents were provided with detailed information on all aspects of the case and that, as far as he knew, nothing was withheld. If the truth be known, from my involvement, there wasn't much to divulge in the first place."

Her expression had shifted, now more thoughtful and purposeful.

"I cannot imagine how it must have eaten away at Letty over the years, the frustrating lack of information. Her mother vanishing overnight and not a shred of evidence to explain why or how."

"Impossible to," said Kingston.

Emma nodded. "It's truly heartbreaking. I did meet Letty once, but only briefly. It was on our first visit. Molly—her foster mother—had warned me that Letty was still confused, crying a lot, asking why her mum had left and when she was coming back. Molly told me that Fiona had dropped off Letty that morning, as usual, and everything appeared normal with her. She wasn't able to provide any clues whatsoever. She was at a complete loss to explain it."

"You do know, of course, that Letty's foster parents hired a private investigator?" Kingston said. "Apparently that ended up costing them a lot of money and sod all to show for it."

Emma nodded. "That was several months later and, yes, we were informed. Not that it makes much difference because"—she gave Kingston a knowing look—"we always find out eventually if someone else is out there playing detective. It was frustrating for everyone. There was literally nothing to go on, hardly anyone to talk to, no eyewitnesses whatsoever. There's pretty much an established procedure in missing person cases: conducting interviews with anybody and everybody who had, or might have had, contact with the missing person. In most cases we end up with a laundry list of contacts, and it takes weeks, sometimes months of plodding and knocking on doors to interview everyone. It was different with the McGuire case, though. We quickly ran out of potential contacts, credible witnesses. Naturally, we started with Molly and her husband, Richard—Richie—Collins. We'd hoped that they could provide some useful information and contacts, but that wasn't the case. Richie and Terry McGuire—Fiona's husband—had worked together at one time. That's how they first met." She paused. "Some of this you probably know already."

Kingston nodded. "Some, but please continue."

"After Terry McGuire's death in the accident, Fiona and Molly's friendship became closer, to the point where Molly was like an aunt to Letty and often took care of her."

"What kind of work did they do—the men?" Andrew asked.

"They were both drivers, delivering for McLendon's, the car parts people."

"Any police records?"

"Terry McGuire had had some minor brushes with the law as a teenager but nothing since, and Richie was clean."

"What about income? Accident insurance?"

"Molly said the accident was entirely Terry's fault. Too many drinks, rainy night, excessive speed—you know the story. I recall her saying that, at one time, both Terry and Richie were making decent money, with lots of overtime. As for income, Molly had a suspicion that Fiona might have inherited some money when her mother died. Fiona had never spoken of it, though. Until Letty was born, Fiona worked part time, in the local supermarket, as I recall."

"What about Fiona's father?"

"He died soon after she was born." Emma looked up to the ceiling. "That was way back in the late fifties, I believe."

"Sorry to keep asking so many questions. It's an incurable habit, I'm afraid," Kingston said with a little smile.

She smiled back. "So I'm told. I don't mind one bit, actually. It helps me remember. Besides, if you didn't, you wouldn't be living up to your reputation." She paused, her smile vanishing, then continued with a trace of policespeak creeping into her voice. "Anyway, after that, we followed standard procedure: checking phone records, bills, the post, computers, e-mails, et cetera; talked to the immediate neighbors, her doctor, tradespeople and delivery persons, the beauty shop she frequented, her bank, shopkeepers, the fish-and-chips shop where she was a regular—always haddock and chips with mushy peas—the train station, bus and taxi drivers—and on and on."

She paused for breath, then continued in a more pensive tone. "The sad part is that Fiona didn't appear to have many friends, or even acquaintances, for that matter. She was a homebody, and with the exception of the Collinses she knew her neighbors only on a nodding basis. I got the impression that she preferred it that way. Some people are just like that." She shrugged. "Others have reasons for that kind of behavior that they'd prefer not to discuss. In rare situations, maybe it's something that they want to hide, but we found nothing whatsoever in her background to suggest that was the case with her."

"Did you conduct most of the interviews?"

"I did. Not that there were that many. Though, in the beginning, Endersby was hands-on, running the show. Don't misunderstand me. He was all along. He's a damned good policeman. It was very much his case but, for the best part, I was—shall we say—chief cook and bottle washer."

A brief pause followed, then Andrew joined in. "What about the Missing Persons Bureau? Letty said that had gone nowhere."

Emma shook her head. "They're always among the first to be informed. But if you mean have we heard anything from them since, the answer's no. At least, up to the time I left the force. You might want to check, though." She looked over at Kingston. "Have you ever been there? The bureau?"

"I haven't."

"It's in Hampshire, at Bramshill, a five-hundred-year-old redbrick manor house. Couple of hundred acres, I believe. You strike me as being someone who would love it. The grounds are gorgeous, and it's got a library that's located in the oldest part of the rambling building, with a winding staircase and hidden rooms. All very Agatha Christie."

"Sounds a bit like Bletchley Park, where the Enigma code breakers were sequestered. I wonder why government offices and headquarters often end up in places of historical interest. Chicksands, the Defence Intelligence Centre, in Bedfordshire, is another one. It's on the grounds of a twelfth-century Gilbertine priory, for heaven's sake. A beautiful place, if you can turn a blind eye to the barbed-wire fencing and camouflaged guards toting nasty-looking weapons."

"I've never thought too much about it, but you're right."

"Probably rent 'em on the cheap," Andrew chipped in.

Kingston leaned back and glanced at his watch. "I have one last question. Were you able to look at Fiona McGuire's personal belongings, what she left behind at the house: photographs, letters, documents, her computer, CDs, e-mails, and the like?"

Emma nodded. "You're right to ask. Often, these things can provide clues or further insights into a person's lifestyle—friendships, habits, and even secrets that open up new lines of investigation, but in her case we found nothing whatsoever. We turned the place upside down. As I remember there were some photos in a shoe box and a couple of albums. Most were old, but Molly was able to identify most of the people in them. But there wasn't a single one that appeared unusual or out of place, nothing to warrant following up. As you might expect, there were no letters per se." She leaned back and sighed. "Sadly, people no longer write letters. Handwriting, too, that's another casualty of the technological age. You should see some of the rubbish we get from young people. Unintelligible." She paused and shook her head, pursing her lips. "Sorry. I didn't mean to fly off the handle like that. Getting back to your question, she did have a laptop. We had our computer forensics chaps search the hard drive, but again, nothing raised any red flags. We went through every e-mail, of course, but they were of no help."

"What about books?"

"Books?"

"Well, what I mean is that often you can tell quite a lot about people by what they read, particularly nonfiction."

Emma smiled. "You mean if they have the *Communist Manifesto* or *How to Make an Atom Bomb in your Kitchen* on the shelf for all to see? Pressed flowers?"

"You never know," Kingston said, smiling back, recalling an experience involving a highly poisonous flower.

"Now that you mention it . . . I do recall a small bookcase in the living room. One of our young chaps, a bookish type, took a quick shufti at them, joking that there were no first editions. Anyway, it may be moot, because I honestly can't recall what happened to them—if they were given to Letty's foster parents, the library, or simply thrown in the rubbish bin."

"I'd still be curious," Kingston said.

The phone rang before Emma could respond. She excused herself and headed for the kitchen to answer it. She walked slowly, with a pronounced limp, which Kingston hadn't noticed when he'd first arrived. A result of the accident that had caused her to leave the force, he presumed.

While she was gone, Andrew got up and stretched, looking out the window, while Kingston thought about their conversation so far, encouraged with the way it was going. When Emma returned he would ask her about the specifics of when and where she planned to meet and talk with Letty. And, even though he knew the answer, he'd ask what she thought the chances were of it working. Would she really be able to persuade Letty to give up tormenting herself and accept the painful truth: that unless new evidence presented itself, her search was in vain. For what it was worth, more for curiosity's sake, he would ask if she had any thoughts outside the scope of the official investigation, if she could and would be willing to speculate about the case in general. As he was thinking on it, she returned.

"Sorry about that," she said, easing herself slowly into her chair. "Where were we?"

"I was thinking about your meeting with Letty. Have you decided how you want to set it up? Where and when?"

"At her home, I would think. Wherever is most comfortable for her—and alone, of course. As for when, I can do it almost anytime. I'll let her choose. Whoever dreamed up the phrase 'luxury of time' obviously never experienced it." She sighed. "Sometimes it's anything but a damned luxury."

"After police work every day, I can well imagine."

Kingston was about to get up, sensing that they'd reached a conclusion, when Emma spoke again. "There's something I want to give you."

Kingston said nothing, thinking it was perhaps a jar of homemade marmalade, scones, something like that. She got up slowly and limped to a carved bureau against a wall on the other side of the room.

She returned holding a large manila envelope, sat, and placed it on the coffee table. "You don't have to open it now. I'm going to tell you what's in it."

Kingston frowned. "Mysterious."

"When DI Endersby called to tell me about your inquiry and your coming here, I made some notes about the case. It wasn't that organized, but I found it good therapy of sorts. It gave me something constructive to do on rainy days, other than watching *Footballers' Wives* and reruns of *The Big Fat Quiz of the Year*. I no longer have access to the files, of course, but, as I explained, it wasn't that complicated. There weren't hundreds of contacts and interviews, as with some cases. So this envelope contains a summary, if you will, of what I can remember of the case. Names and places are reasonably accurate, but the time frame may be a bit off in places."

Kingston was puzzled. Why, if her mission were to convince Letty, once and for all, that the case was closed, probably for good, would she want to hand over such information? What was the purpose?

"Thank you, Emma, I appreciate that," he said.

A trace of a smile appeared. "I can see you're already wondering why I would go to that trouble."

"The thought had crossed my mind."

"Well, when Endersby told me about you and your interest in the McGuire case, I did a little bit of sleuthing of my own. I'm sure you know that your reputation's hardly what you'd call a secret, Doctor—Lawrence. I gave up after wading through the first six paragraphs of your Wikipedia life story. What I'm getting at is this. It's very clear, and speaks highly of you, that your interest in the case is centered on helping Letty straighten out her life by convincing her to give up trying to find out what happened to her mother. That said, I couldn't help wondering if there wasn't perhaps also a mild curiosity on your part, shall we say, about specific details of the case and why it's remained unsolved. If it might have criminal implications?" She smiled. "Am I wrong?"

Kingston took his eyes off of Emma to glance at Andrew, who had been quietly listening and was looking amused.

"Not entirely," he said, looking at Emma again. "It would be out of the ordinary for one to think otherwise, wouldn't you say?"

"Maybe. But then I asked myself, if it hadn't been for that close call you had up in Staffordshire, you might have given serious thought to promising Letty that you would conduct an independent inquiry. But I'm sure that other forces are at work here, urging you and reminding you not to become involved in such situations."

Kingston could reply to this innocent-looking yet percipient police-woman only with a forced smile and a shrug.

Five minutes later, at Emma's crimson front door, Kingston and Andrew said goodbye and walked up the street to his TR4. The fine weather was holding and the sun was still high in the sky and hot enough to cause an "ouch!" when Kingston gripped the chrome door handle. They took off their jackets and placed them behind the seats and got in the car.

"Okay, Andrew, now for some fun, something more relaxing," he said, buckling his seat belt. "The head gardener is a friend of mine—"

"No surprise there," interrupted Andrew.

"—and he's expecting us. He'll probably have a pot of tea waiting."

"Tea?" Andrew was less than enthusiastic. "Maybe he'll have beer in the fridge?"

"You'll like him. One of the most genuine, good-natured, and inspiring men I've ever met." He started the engine, glancing at Andrew. "There's also a small matter we need to discuss. "I've promised to help him out with a bit of a mystery that concerns his own backyard."

Andrew raised an eyebrow. "A mystery, eh? Why am I not shocked?"

"Here." Kingston reached into his pocket and pulled out a photo-copy of the newspaper clipping and handed it to Andrew. "Take a look."

Andrew glanced at the clipping and frowned. He read the head-line aloud—"Two-Hundred-Year-Old Extinct Rose Shows Up on

Alcatraz?"—then took a sideways look at Kingston. "This is the real reason we're visiting your friend, isn't it?"

"That's not possible, Andrew. I received Clifford's e-mail only this morning, and we've planned this for three days, now. It's just an extraordinary coincidence, that's all. In any case, everybody at Belmaris Castle will certainly know about it; the article mentions a homecoming ceremony for the rose having taken place. We would have come here, regardless. I want you to see the gardens. But read the rest of it."

As Andrew went back to reading, Kingston smiled, then stabbed the accelerator a couple of times before driving off.

5

AFTER READING THE clipping yesterday morning, Kingston had spent an hour or so pondering its implications and scouring the Internet for additional information. There were a number of stories from both sides of the pond—a few providing additional local interest but nothing more. He soon realized that, generally, the media was using the original story by Chambers as the source. He'd purposely waited until now to tell Andrew, knowing that a mysterious back-from-extinction rose would elicit a long sigh, and could also have been a distraction at their meeting with Emma. He kept his eyes on the road while Andrew was reading.

Kingston parked under an enormous horse chestnut tree in the grassy parking area, then he and Andrew took off on the short walk to the castle and gardens. Yesterday's storm had long since passed, leaving the skies an unaccustomed clear blue and the air sweet with the fragrance of freshly mown grass. The lawns flanking the wide gravel paths were still beaded with the last drops of rain, and a muffled calm lulled the senses. In every direction, as far as the eye could see, the lush green parkland was speckled with red deer grazing under the black-shaded canopies of towering chestnut, oak, plane, and copper beech trees that had stood for centuries, stoically witnessing history unfold at the castle in their midst.

On his first visit to Belmaris many years ago, Kingston had taken the recommended guided tour of the castle, finding it educational, impressive, and essential in setting the stage for a walk through the extensive gardens and grounds. His subsequent visits to Belmaris—three or four, over time—had been solely to view the award-winning gardens' magnificent collection of antique roses. But his hands-down favorite sight was the remains of the fifteenth-century Tithe Barn, used in the Middle Ages to store one-tenth of a farm's produce for the church. The tableau of the ruined shell of the great stone barn destroyed by Cromwell in the Civil War was abundant with beauty. The high, roofless stone walls followed the path of a long reflecting pool, stocked with carp and draped with living curtains of old climbing roses interwoven with wild clematis and wisteria. In Kingston's opinion, in the height of summer there was no lovelier floral sight in all of England.

At the impressive main entrance, Jimmy Cosworth, the head gardener, greeted them with smiles and handshakes. He was a lanky man with wispy silver hair, ruddy cheeks, and a deeply wrinkled face, tanned from forty-plus summers spent nurturing the castle's gardens as if they were his own, as in a sense they were: central casting's vision of an English gardener. Easygoing, good-humored, and immediately likable, this kindly man made everyone feel at ease.

The three sat at a pine refectory table in a small kitchen in the back of the castle used only by the staff. As coffee—alas, no beer—was being poured into thick-rimmed mugs, a roly-poly woman wearing a frilly white apron entered. Wobbling across the room in a determined beeline, she planted a large Cornishware plate of muffins on the table, and after a booming, "There you go, loves, 'ot from the oven," disappeared as quickly as she'd arrived.

Kingston gingerly took a sip of the steaming coffee and looked at Cosworth. "So, Jimmy. What do you make of this globetrotting rose of yours?"

"'Ard to fathom," he drawled, in his West Country accent, shaking his head. "I don't know what to make of it. Mrs. Fitzwarren is dealing with all the phone calls and inquiries now, thank God."

"The castle's manager?"

"She and her husband, Adrian, are the new owners—relatively new, that is."

"A climbing rose, right?"

Cosworth nodded. "And a rambunctious one, at that."

"I understand it became extinct in the sixties. Is that correct?"

"That's about right, according to our records, anyway. I came 'ere in the mid-eighties and remember being told that the Belmaris rose had been classified as extinct twenty years prior—as you say, sometime in the sixties. It was a big deal at the time, and all the garden staff was provided with information on its pedigree. A conversation piece."

Kingston scratched his forehead. "Where in the garden was it growing?"

"In the Tithe Barn ruins. Well out of reach of the public, fortunately. But if you're wondering 'ow easy or difficult it would have been for someone to 'ave filched cuttings, I think you know the answer to that."

"Impossible to prevent."

"Right. When you think about it, growing there for two hundred bloody years, you'd have to be a bit thick to think that some silly bugger with secateurs in 'is pocket won't snip off a couple of bits while no one's looking. Even our own people might 'ave been tempted. Though I'd prefer to think not."

"I have a question," Andrew said, looking across the table at Cosworth.

Kingston wondered what kind of question he could possibly ask. Roses were not one of Andrew's particular interests.

Cosworth nodded. "By all means."

"Who—what authority—decides whether and at what point a rose is classified as extinct? If, as you say, they're so easy to transplant from cuttings, how can anyone possibly know that a rose has disappeared from the planet forevermore?"

Cosworth frowned. After a moment of thought, he replied, "To tell the truth, Andrew, though I've spent most of my adult life gardening, I've never given that question too much thought. Guess that's because I spend more time tending to the living plants in front of me than thinking about what isn't there. You're right, though," he said, nodding. "And it's a fair question." He paused and reached for a muffin. "How can we be so sure? Well, the short answer is, we can't. It's the word 'extinct' that's the problem. It's a semantic problem. A lot of historians, growers, plant authorities, and so on use the word to signify that a plant or seed is no longer commercially available or not generally known to exist for purposes of propagation. This doesn't mean that somewhere in the world there's not more than one Belmaris rose growing in obscurity, as it were, admired and nurtured by its uninformed owner who hasn't the foggiest idea of its provenance or rarity, just thinks it's pretty. So the idea of a bunch of rose experts and botanical authorities decreeing a plant extinct isn't really accurate. 'Become a rarity' might be a better way of putting it." He looked at Kingston. "What do you think, Lawrence? You know a lot more about these technical things than I do."

"I think your explanation is spot-on. I would only add that many native plants, somewhat like endangered animals, are suffering serious threats to their survival. As our planet undergoes changes with population density, industrial development, overharvesting, deforestation, habitat loss, and so on, more plants are being pushed toward extinction in the true sense of the word, and no longer will their species be found anywhere in the wild. However, there's a distinction when it comes to roses. What makes them different is that, while they've been growing in the wild in many parts of the world since time immemorial, much of that time they've also been cultivated and hybridized by man. In fact, references to Chinese floriculture date back to the eleventh century B.C., and Chinese floral encyclopedias indicate that by the fourth and fifth centuries A.D., rose culture was widespread in China. I'd venture a guess that under controlled and ideal conditions, using advanced propagation techniques and technology, rose cultivars today now number in the many thousands worldwide. So Jimmy is correct. It's not accurate to state that any given rose is truly extinct."

Andrew still appeared a little perplexed. "So if, as you say, the possibility exists that there could be any number of this particular rose growing in different parts of the world, one could have easily been growing in the States, somewhere out of the public's eye, for many years. If nothing else, that would account for the transcontinental question."

"That's true," Kingston said. "But when and how it ended up on Alcatraz remains a big puzzle. One way or another, it had to cross the Atlantic and then another twenty-five hundred miles overland across the North American continent."

Andrew didn't look altogether convinced and simply nodded.

"Who was the head gardener when you first came to Belmaris, Jimmy?" Kingston asked.

"Hmm." Cosworth's watery eyes looked up to the ceiling. "That would be Arthur Purseglove. Otherwise known as Percy. Quiet sort of bloke, but 'e was a bloody encyclopedia when it came to plants. What 'e didn't know wasn't in any book I know of. Why do you ask?"

"Nothing, really. I was wondering if he'd seen the rose in bloom."

"He must 'ave." Cosworth nodded. "'E was 'ere for twenty-five years before me."

As the three drank and polished off the muffins, their conversation gradually drifted away from the rose to the gardens and life in general, finally petering out after Jimmy announced that he would soon retire— "throw in the trowel"—as he put it. After handshakes outside the kitchen door, Kingston and Andrew headed to the gardens. They'd gone only a dozen steps, when Kingston heard Cosworth shout his name. He stopped and looked back.

"Lawrence, I've just remembered someone else who probably saw the rose growing 'ere," Jimmy said. "Reginald Payne. Local bloke, used to 'ang around a lot when I first came 'ere. 'E's a bit of a cagey sort, but 'e knows 'is stuff when it comes to gardening, that's for sure. 'Aven't seen 'im in quite a while, come to think of it. As a matter of fact, I believe 'e was quite chummy with Graham Stewart Thomas at one time."

"Really? Graham Stewart Thomas?"

"Who's he?" Andrew asked.

Kingston looked pensive. "A legendary horticulturist, author, garden designer, and much more. He's probably best known for his knowledge and love of old and new shrub roses. Among other achievements, he designed the National Collection of old-fashioned roses at Mottisfont Abbey. It's still considered to be the best of its kind in the world."

"You knew him, too, didn't you Lawrence?" Jimmy asked.

"I did. I had the privilege of meeting him at the abbey's opening of the collection, back in . . . 1974, I believe. I'll never forget it."

"Of course." Andrew rolled his eyes.

Kingston ignored the gesture. "Any idea where this Payne chap lives, Jimmy?"

"Last I 'eard it was in Middle Cheverell, outside Cheltenham. The village is small, so you won't have trouble finding 'is place. Ask at the Rose & Thistle, they'll know it."

"Rose and Thistle. We'll do just that. Thanks, Jimmy."

Kingston and Andrew strolled around the lush grounds. Kingston managed to stifle his inner professor, and they ambled about in companionable silence, enjoying the beauty and tranquillity rarely found in London.

6

KINGSTON STARED AT the oak door. No response.

He rapped the brass dolphin knocker a second time. He waited for another minute, then stepped back off the porch and took in the front of the two-story redbrick Edwardian house with shiny white trim on symmetrically spaced windows. Flanked on both sides by eight-foot-high blocks of yew hedging, it appeared far too large to be called a "cottage," so described by the barmaid at the Rose & Thistle, where he'd inquired after Reginald Payne on arriving in Middle Cheverell.

What little garden there was in front had been masterfully planted by someone with an understanding of horticulture as well as a practiced eye for design, texture, and color. The splendid herbaceous borders were crowded with a who's who of carefully chosen perennials, backed by gracefully arching old shrub roses that reached to the top of a drystone wall behind. Properly trained climbing roses and clematis fanned the walls of the house and even the upstairs windows. A weathered wooden sign hanging by chains from a post bore the name BEECHWOOD.

Two cars were parked in a gravel area off to his left, an old khaki colored Land Rover and red VW convertible. Save for the omnipresent bird chatter and the distant lowing of cows, all around was a genial stillness. No barking of dogs inside and no signs of habitation. He was about to head back down the front path, back to the car where Andrew was waiting, when he heard a bolt being withdrawn and the big door creaking open. He turned to see a woman, thirtyish, he guessed—fairly attractive, slim, longish blond hair—standing half hidden behind the partly open door. She looked at him suspiciously, tension evident in her body language.

"Good afternoon. I'm awfully sorry to bother you. My name's Lawrence Kingston—Doctor Kingston," he added. The title, he found, had a way of putting people more at ease. "I've just been visiting Belmaris Castle inquiring about their rose collection, and it was suggested that I also talk to Reginald Payne who, I'm given to understand, is also something of a rose fancier. If he's home and it's not too much trouble, I'd like to have a word."

His words were met with a blank stare, as if she'd already made up her mind that she didn't want to talk to him, that she might close the door at any moment.

"This is his residence, is it not?" Kingston asked, trying to pry at least a sentence from her.

She nodded. "It is," she said in a near whisper. "Or was."

Kingston stepped back a couple of paces, trying to look as friendly and nonthreatening as he could. It was clear that she was uncomfortable with him standing a mere few feet away on her doorstep. It began to look as if she was about to slam the door in his face at any moment. "I'm not quite sure I understand. Perhaps it's best if I leave?" he said, searching for words that would keep the conversation alive.

His comment had a slight mollifying effect. For an instant she relaxed her tight grip on the door, and her unblinking eyes now met his more with curiosity than caution.

"He no longer lives here?" Kingston asked.

"He's dead." The two words held no emotion, no hint of underlying sorrow.

"I'm terribly sorry."

"That's all right. You weren't to know. Sorry, I must go. Goodbye," she said, slowly closing the door.

As if to punctuate her "goodbye," the inside bolt slid shut with a metallic thud. Kingston stared at the door momentarily, then turned and went back to the car.

"I think you're wasting your time," Andrew said, glancing sideways at Kingston, whose eyes were glued to the road ahead, his thoughts clearly elsewhere.

After they'd left Payne's house, Kingston had described the brief encounter with the taciturn woman, admonishing himself aloud for not having handled it more diplomatically and, worse, for having come away with no information on the late, reclusive Reginald Payne or his roses.

"Why's that?" Kingston asked, shifting into second as they approached a busy roundabout.

"Even if you had gotten to chat with this Payne chap, what did you hope to achieve? At best, he would have told you the same as Cosworth told us: that he'd seen the rose growing at Belmaris."

"I suppose," Kingston said.

"Suppose?" Andrew frowned. "You don't think for one moment that he would've admitted to nicking one and growing it for himself, do you?"

"Well, no. It was just an opportunity, that's all. Worth a try."

"When we get back home, why don't you call the fellow in San Francisco—the one who discovered the rose? You'll learn much more from him, I'd imagine."

"I plan to. My only interest is finding out how a rare English rose ended up in an American prison, that's all. It's an intriguing horticultural anomaly, not a bloody murder mystery."

"And thank the Lord for that." Andrew looked at his watch. "Why don't we just go and have an early dinner, then?"

Kingston nodded. "I know you suggested Jamie Oliver's in Oxford, but that's at least an hour away. Why don't we go back to the Rose and Thistle? The dining room looked very gastro and we can be there in five minutes."

"Sure, if that's what you want," Andrew said, looking at Kingston with a don't-try-to-fool-me grin. "Maybe you could make a discreet inquiry with the landlord or barmaid, ask what they know about Reginald Payne, tell them you were in the army together—but you'd probably thought of that already."

"I hadn't," Kingston fibbed. "But that's not a bad idea. If it's dark secrets or dirty linen you're trying to uncover about the local gentry, there's no better repository, no place where more wagging lips can be found, than an English pub. It's worked before and it can work again."

At the Rose & Thistle, they were seated right away. All thoughts of Belmaris Castle and its gardens, Jimmy Cosworth, and Reginald Payne were put aside for the moment, as they focused their attention on ordering drinks and perusing what, for a small pub, was an unexpectedly voluminous and diverse menu and wine list. Andrew seemed duly impressed.

Kingston had promised he wouldn't try chatting up the owner or locals about Payne until their meal was over and they were about to leave. As it turned out, his promise was irrelevant. Since arriving they'd seen no one who resembled a landlord or manager. And after a purposefully circuitous visit to the gents', Kingston was disappointed to conclude that no one among the drinkers or diners might be considered a regular.

An hour and a half later, finishing the remains of an excellent bottle of Côte de Nuits-Villages and waiting for their bill to arrive, Kingston noted a sudden twitch of surprise on Andrew's face. Looking up as he lowered his wineglass, he saw why. It wasn't their waiter carrying the faux-leather folder containing the bill but a smartly dressed gray-haired woman heading their way.

"I hope everything was satisfactory, gentlemen," she said with an unreserved smile, placing the folder on the table. "I'm Clare Davenport."

Kingston began to stand, but she motioned for him to remain seated.

"I must compliment you and your chef for a most enjoyable meal," he said. "I recognized your name from the licensee sign in the bar."

"Excellent wine list, too," Andrew interjected.

"I'm pleased it met with your approval. I hope you'll come back and see us again. Are you visiting the area?"

"Only briefly. We came down to see an old friend."

"Down from—?"

"Chelsea. We were at Belmaris Castle visiting Jimmy Cosworth, the head gardener."

"Ah yes, the Fitzwarrens. Charming people. They come in to see us from time to time. I've also had the pleasure of meeting Mr. Cosworth several times—the man's not only a genius at what he does, he's so generous with his time. I can't tell you how often he's bailed me out with gardening advice over the years."

"Actually, it was because of him that we found you. He told us about a local chap named Reginald Payne who grew old roses. He recommended that we try to contact him while we were here. Your barmaid was kind enough to give us directions to his house, earlier this morning. On the off chance that he might be home, we stopped by to chat with him, only to learn, sadly, that he'd passed away."

"That must have been Mary—our new girl. She wouldn't have known about Reggie." Clare Davenport's face clouded over. "Yes, it was quite a shock, I must say. The locals are still talking about it. Naturally, we've had a few reporters snooping around, too."

"What happened?" Kingston asked.

"The police haven't provided any details yet—as far as we know, that is."

"Police?"

"Yes. It seems that foul play might be involved."

Kingston glanced furtively at Andrew. "Really?" he asked.

Clare Davenport nodded. "From all accounts, it was originally thought by the police to be an unfortunate accident: that he'd tripped or had had a dizzy spell and fallen into the pond in his garden. But now the coroner has called for a full inquiry.

"No wonder the young woman at the house was so evasive," he said.

"Probably Reggie's niece. Apparently she's staying there with her mother."

"Would that be Reggie's sister?"

She shrugged. "Could be."

Kingston could not contain his curiosity. "When did this all take place?"

"About . . . a few weeks ago, a little longer, maybe. Needless to say, the entire village has been gossiping about it ever since. The police interviewed quite a few people, shopkeepers, tradesmen, and the like, including me and my husband."

"I take it that there are no suspects yet."

She shook her head. "Not that I know of."

"You said 'Reggie'—you and your husband knew Mr. Payne, then?"

"We did, yes."

"Were you friends?"

Clare Davenport frowned. "You're asking a lot of questions. You're not policemen, are you?"

Kingston chuckled. "Heavens no. We're both unemployed—retirees, you might say. I'm Lawrence Kingston, and this is my friend Andrew Duncan."

"Kingston? Your name sounds vaguely familiar. Should I know you?"

"Oh, I wouldn't think so," Kingston said, as Andrew raised his eyebrows and looked away.

"Hmmm." She nodded. "Well, anyway, getting back to your question. We didn't really know Mr. Payne that well. Everyone called him Reggie. He used to say that Reginald should be reserved for statesmen, poets, and BBC announcers. He'd pop in from time to time but never mingled or stayed long, kept pretty much to himself. I wouldn't go as far as to call him a recluse, but it was generally known in the village that he was . . . well, not what you'd call the sociable kind." She shrugged. "I don't know what else I can tell you."

"It's not really important," Andrew cut in.

Kingston nodded. "Thank you so much for your time, Mrs. Davenport. And for the information—as well as the lovely meal."

Back in the car, Kingston asked, "Well, Andrew, what do you make of all that?" as the TR's engine coughed to life.

"More than anything, I'm wondering how everything you do seems to thrust into the middle of a murder."

"How was I to know there was a murder—a still pending one—involved? A casual comment by Jimmy Cosworth, an innocent visit to see a rose collector—we simply reacted quite normally and rationally. Tell me how things could have turned out otherwise?"

"If we hadn't gone back to the pub," Andrew replied, buckling his seat belt with a snap. "Before that we didn't know Payne had been murdered, only that he'd died. We could have easily gone on to Oxford, but you wanted to go back to the Rose & Thistle. It wasn't about being closer than Oxford or the time. You figured there was a slim chance that someone there would know more about him, to satisfy your insatiable curiosity."

"Come on, Andrew. Now you're being unreasonable. It was nothing more than coincidence."

"Coincidence?"

"Yes."

"Here's a question for you," Andrew said. "On average, do you know how many people are murdered in the UK every year?"

"I've no idea."

"Well, I do, because I looked it up when you were knee-deep in that case up in Staffordshire, the bloke found murdered on the grounds of Sturminster Hall."

"And?"

"It's roughly eight hundred."

"What's that got to do with the price of eggs?"

"Since there are roughly ninety counties in the UK, that averages out to, let's say, nine homicides per county."

Kingston simply nodded, keeping his eyes on the road.

"So it would be reasonable to say that Gloucestershire, being average in size, would have nine murders per year."

"If you say so."

"What I'm getting at, Lawrence, is Bayes's rule—a mathematical theory commonly called the law of conditional probability. It's taught in computer science."

"Then you would know."

"Given today's . . . let's just say unusual series of events and coincidences, I got to thinking. What if that rule were applied to you? What would the odds be—the probability—that in the entire county, in a mere three hours, with conversation limited to fewer than a half dozen people, that you could manage, by sheer happenstance, to run across someone who is a murder victim? Even you would have to admit that the chances against that happening would be a thousand-to-one—a million-to-one, more likely."

Kingston was listening with amusement, trying to hide his smile by not looking at Andrew.

"People win the football pools and the lottery every week. Similar or worse odds, wouldn't you agree?" Kingston suggested.

"Maybe, but in your case, there's a big difference."

"There is? Why?"

"Because unlike the lucky punter, this is not a one-off. You have a track record, a recurring pattern. You operate by your own set of rules. In the eighties, the software designers and engineers at Apple came up with a name for this type of behavior; they called it a 'reality distortion field'—a condition where your reality becomes flexible, negotiable."

"Come on, Andrew, listening to you, one would think that I'm looking for trouble."

"That's exactly right. I had a strange feeling, right from the beginning, that this trip wouldn't end without something spoiling it. Something untoward. I'm not sure what I expected, but it certainly wasn't murder."

After an awkward pause, he finally turned to look at Kingston, who could no longer contain himself. A suppressed chuckle turned into full-throated laughter. For a moment Andrew looked helplessly confused, then he grinned. In a couple of seconds they were both laughing uncontrollably.

"I give up," Andrew said, brushing tears from his eyes. "You're beyond bloody redemption."

7

As if to cast an echoing pall over the events of the day, the capricious English weather did an about-face. Ten miles after crossing into Oxfordshire, a fast-moving storm system snuffed out the last of the gloaming, turning it into a drizzling gloom. Headlights went on and windscreen wipers soon followed. Further conversation was sporadic and of little consequence. Andrew appeared to be content within his own thoughts and eventually dozed off for an hour, and Kingston was obliged to put aside further speculation about the rose to focus his attention on the wretched driving conditions. What normally would have been a two-hour drive took almost double that time. He dropped Andrew off, parked the TR4 in his garage, and went directly to his flat.

Tired and exhausted by trying to make sense of all the untoward things that had happened in a single day, Kingston made straight for the living room, where he poured himself a well-earned nightcap of Macallan with a splash of water.

Ten minutes later, checking his e-mails before turning in for the night, Reginald Payne's name popped up again his mind. Before putting the computer to sleep, he decided to do a brief Google search for him, even though he knew with so little to go on, his chances of digging up anything noteworthy were highly unlikely.

The expected Facebook and Linkedin entries revealed nothing that suggested a rose fancier of that name, or anyone else whose attributes or achievements could apply to Payne. The following three pages were much the same. He tried a different spelling, Paine, but the results offered nothing new. His only conclusion was that Reggie had not made a sufficient mark in life to warrant Google's attention or—unlikely—that he'd managed somehow to avoid cyberspace scrutiny.

That night was one of the most restless he'd experienced in a long time. He tossed and turned for hours, his mind refusing to shut down. Like a hyperactive child on a pogo stick, it bounced from Andrew, to Jimmy Cosworth and the Belmaris rose, to Payne, to Clare Davenport at the pub.

Rearranging the pillow and turning on his side had no effect; his muddled thoughts drifted to Emma, and the packet of notes she'd given him, and what a stroke of luck it was that Inspector Sheffield had suggested that she participate.

As he pulled the covers over his eyes, an idea suddenly took shape. The pragmatic and reasoning voice in his head told him that the likelihood of it coming to fruition was tenuous at best. But if he could pull it off, everyone would profit—him, Andrew, and Emma.

His last coherent thought before slipping into the arms of Morpheus was the hope that he would still remember the idea when he woke in the morning.

The next morning at seven thirty, as was customary, Kingston was seated at the kitchen table, with whole wheat toast and marmalade and a second cup of tea, tackling the *Times* crossword puzzle. He was stuck on 24 Across: *Vive la difference with the beginning of renaissance brings about another renaissance (7)*

He was determined not to quit until he'd solved it. By the time the solution dawned on him, his half-finished tea was lukewarm. It was an anagram of VIVE LA (different) plus R (beginning letter of renaissance). VIVELA + R = REVIVAL (another renaissance). Pleased with himself, he put the paper aside and glanced up at the wall clock: eight o'clock. A good time to call the United States.

In his office, with the newspaper article in front of him, Kingston was surprised to reach Greg Robinson, the rosarian who had first spotted the rose, right away at his nursery in California. They had a lengthy, amiable chat about the discovery, and though Kingston learned a little more than had been reported, he came away with no information or clues to shed further light on the mystery.

His call to Andy Harris produced much the same results. The Alcatraz historian was exceptionally friendly and interested in everything that Kingston asked about the globetrotting rose. He talked at length about his experience growing up on the island as the son of a correctional officer, describing in detail the few gardens on the island at the time it was a federal penitentiary. He elaborated on the warden's garden, the few privileged inmates who were allowed to work in the gardens, as well other aspects of life inside the walls of America's most notorious prison. Yet like Greg Robinson, in the end he could offer no rational explanation of how the rose had ended up there. He did promise to let Kingston know if any further thoughts occurred to him or if new information came to light. Harris also encouraged him to call back anytime with further questions.

Little did Kingston know that he wasn't through with America. Not for today, anyway.

That afternoon, when he returned from Smith & Hunter Garage in Kensington (where the TR was being fitted with new front tires), he found another e-mail from his daughter, Julie.

Hello Dad,

The big news! Brandon and I got engaged last week, so you'll soon be getting a son-in-law. He can't wait to meet you.

Glad to know that the airline tickets arrived okay, so all you have to do is pack your bags and bring lots of English tea. We'll pick you up at the airport—if your flight plans change let me know. The attached photo was taken at the restaurant where Brandon popped the question. Don't know if I mentioned it, but he's got a nice sailboat, a Cheoy Lee ketch, so bring along some deck shoes and shorts.

I apologize for such a short letter, Dad, but I'm sure you understand. I can't wait to see you—it's been far too long.

Love and kisses,
Julie

Kingston opened the attachment and gazed fondly at the photo of the smiling happy couple, toasting with champagne glasses. *She looks more like her mother every day*, he thought, *just as beautiful and elegant.*

The planned trip, his third since Julie had left for Seattle and a job with Microsoft, had been a gift to celebrate his birthday. Julie had recently been promoted to a senior position and had told him that her new salary "had more zeros attached than she could have ever thought possible."

He made a mental note that a visit to Austin Reed was in order to purchase a couple of items of clothing—and now some deck shoes.

There was one other item that needed tending to—Emma's notes.

Comfortably settled in his worn leather wingback, Kingston spent the next half hour reading them. As he'd expected, they were well organized and written with noteworthy clarity. In chronological order she had laid out the events of each day, starting with the morning of September 12, 2003, when Fiona McGuire had left the house, dropping off Letty at Molly's, as she often did, never to return.

Interviews conducted in the days and weeks that followed were all listed, showing the date, the approximate time, the persons questioned, their calling and relationship to the McGuires—if any—and a brief summary of their statements. Every now and then, she had added a comment, an explanation, or a question to herself.

After two passes, he was satisfied that, as far as he could tell, there was nothing in the dozen or so pages that appeared even mildly unusual or inconsistent. It seemed there was no need for further conjecture on his part, that the investigation was as Emma and her superior officer had stated: unsolved as a result of lack of evidence and viable leads. He put the papers back in the envelope and placed it in a desk drawer. He couldn't think of any reason why he would want, or need, to refer to them again.

In the kitchen, he put the kettle on for tea and glanced at the crossword again. It was a particularly tough one, and he had a hunch who had composed it: an old nemesis "setter" whose clues were fiendishly clever. As he was pondering what to do for dinner, the phone rang. He went to the living room, and picked it up.

"This is Kingston," he said, a trifle more politely than normal.

"Oh, hello, Lawrence. It's Emma."

"Emma." He smiled. "Surprised to hear from you so soon."

"Yes. I just got back from Cheltenham about twenty minutes ago."

"It went well, then?"

"Exceptionally well, I'd say. I was with Letty for over two hours."

Kingston listened raptly as Emma described their conversation. When she was finished, he was convinced that their chat had more than achieved its desired result.

"She'll never forget her mum, nor should she, of course," Emma said. "But she promised me—hands on the Bible—that from now on she'd work every day on training her mind to think of herself, and her future."

"You make it sound all too easy. Though I'm sure it wasn't."

"You're right." Emma sighed. "At least not to begin with. Then I told her about an experience I'd had when I was younger—when my closest friend was killed in a car accident. To this day, I still hold myself partly responsible."

"I'm sorry." Kingston didn't know what more to say; they were both silent for a minute.

"May I ask what happened?" he said finally. "Though if you prefer not to talk about it, please say so, and we can—"

"No it's perfectly fine. We were both eighteen. We'd been to a wedding in Tewksbury, and when we left it started to drizzle. Wendy had had quite a lot to drink, but I'd taken it easy all evening because of an upset stomach. She insisted on driving, that she was okay and that it was better if she drove because I'd only just got my license a few months earlier. I knew damned well she was in no state to drive—I even tried to wrestle the keys from her. By the time she dropped me off, it was raining cats and dogs. I pleaded with her to spend the night at my place rather than drive another ten miles home, but she wouldn't hear of it. Her mother called me the next morning to say that Wendy had skidded off the road had hit a tree and was dead. My lasting memory was the radio playing as I slammed the door and she drove off. The song was 'Without You' by Badfinger. I can't listen to it anymore. It makes me want to cry. I still think of it as prophetic."

"That's terribly sad. I can see why Letty would have related to your loss."

"It's all about learning to stop fighting what's happened in the past, the unchangeable, accepting it for what was, and recognizing that there's nothing—not a single thing—you can do that will ever alter it." She paused, but Kingston didn't interrupt. "To stop worrying about the things you can't change and instead focus on those that you can—a cliché maybe, but oh so true. I think what convinced Letty more than anything else was the risk she was taking not only with her mental health but physical, too. I didn't need to press the point because she confided that the last year or so had been more stressful than she was ready to admit."

"Well, that's all good news indeed. You saw her foster parents?"

"They were both there when I arrived. Nice people. She's very lucky in that sense."

"And will you and Letty will keep in touch?"

"Yes. We talked about that at length. We're going to get together on a regular basis, see how she's progressing. On top of everything else, she showed a lot of interest in police work, asking surprisingly intelligent questions. I promised I'd take her to the Gloucester district station where I worked to give her an idea of what community police work was like and to introduce her to a few of the staff, take her out one day in a patrol car, maybe."

"Terrific idea."

"Oh—and by the way, I asked about the books, too."

Kingston frowned. "The books?"

"You know, Fiona's 'library'? You wondered if they might give any hints to Fiona's or her husband's lifestyle—remember?"

"Oh, yes, of course. Any luck?"

"Sorry to say, no smoking gun. Molly said that they chucked most of them away. I went through those they'd kept, mostly cooking and how-to books. The only one that struck me as likely to be of interest to you was a garden book. I think the author was a man named Thomas."

Kingston felt a tingle of excitement. "Graham Stuart Thomas?"

"I think so, yes. Hold on a moment and I'll get it."

He heard her set down the phone, and walk away.

Graham Stuart Thomas, Kingston thought. Twice his name had come up in recent days.

Emma was back. "Yes, it's Graham Stuart Thomas. *The Old Shrub Roses.*"

"I'm familiar with it," Kingston said. "If it's signed, it could be worth a bob or two."

"It's not signed, but there is an inscription in it. And some penciled notes on some of the pages."

"Really. Fiona was hardly the gardening sort, was she?"

"Not that I'm aware."

"What does it say?"

"Let me look again," she said, as Kingston waited.

"Here it is: 'This may give you some ideas, R.' The initial R trails off in a wiggly line, as if it were the person's casual way of signing—maybe Robert, Richard—"

"R," Kingston muttered to himself, thinking about the single initial and other names it could stand for—male and female.

"That's very interesting," he said. "I'd like to see the book, if I may?"

"Of course. I can mail it to you or, even better, I can arrange to have it hand delivered. No charge."

"You have someone coming up to London?"

"Yes. Me. Tomorrow."

Kingston smiled. "What a nice surprise, Emma. Naturally I'll take you up on the offer. And if time permits, perhaps we can squeeze in lunch or an early dinner. I'd enjoy that."

"Lunch is possible. I'm coming up by train to see a specialist at Moorfields Eye Hospital. My appointment's at eleven forty-five, and they say it should take no longer than an hour. If I cab it, I could meet you somewhere in the West End around one o'clock."

"Excellent. Let's meet at the Ivy. You'll like it. It's off of Shaftesbury Avenue. The driver will know it, it's been there close to a hundred years."

"Sounds wonderful. I look forward to it. If there are any hiccups, I'll call you."

"Please do." He hesitated a moment, wondering how to broach the idea he'd come up with the night before. Particularly in light of the book and the inscription she had just described.

"Lawrence?" Emma asked. "Was there something else?"

"There is," he replied, his mind off the book. "Among other things, I was going to tell you what happened after we left you the other day—but it's quite a long tale. There'll be plenty of time for that tomorrow. You're going to be amazed. I'm not exaggerating."

"That's not fair. Now I can't wait."

"Until tomorrow, then. Good night." he said with a satisfied smile, putting down the phone.

Graham Stuart Thomas, he thought. And then: *This may give you some ideas, R.*

He considered Andrew's law of "conditional probability" and wondered what the odds were that, somehow, all these incidents and events were in fact related.

There was, he had already decided, only one way to find out.

8

Kingston sat at a white-clothed corner table sipping a glass of Evian in the Ivy's elegantly understated dining room. Keeping a close eye on the entrance, he eagerly awaited Emma's arrival.

As a matter of habit, whenever he invited a woman to lunch or dinner, each arriving separately, he made it a point to be at the restaurant fifteen minutes before reservation time. It had nothing to do with punctuality but everything to do with manners: not wanting to risk the chance that his guest would find herself waiting alone in a restaurant. He knew that in this he was one of a dying breed: men who still obeyed their mothers' stern instructions on how to behave, and who always dressed for the occasion.

Today, it was his Burberry double-breasted navy blazer with tan gabardine slacks and French-cuffed blue poplin shirt, with red-and-silver-striped university tie. It irked him to see people dining in London's best restaurants wearing T-shirts and jeans. In addition to enjoying the Ivy's excellent food, Kingston approved of the restaurant's "dress code": Men were required to wear ties, and shorts and microskirts were not "acceptable forms of attire" for women.

At that moment, he looked up to see Emma being escorted across the room by the maître d'. She was dressed fashionably in a tailored gray-tweed jacket, silk blouse, and black, knee-length—thankfully not micro—skirt, quite a different Emma from the one he'd met in Winchcombe. He stood and took her hand in his while they exchanged greetings, and then sat down.

"It's a lovely room," she said, looking around while reaching into her shoulder bag, taking out the book, and placing it on the table next to Kingston. "Here's your special delivery, and thank you for inviting me." She smiled. "The alternative would probably have been a ham and cheese baguette on the train home."

"Not on my watch," he replied, picking up the book and opening it to the page with the inscription. He looked at it for a moment before closing it and putting it aside on the table. "I appreciate your thinking of me when you spotted the book, and please pass on my thanks to Molly when you next see her. It's one that I don't have and, as I mentioned on the phone, it holds special meaning for me, having known Graham and been a long-standing admirer of his enormous talents. Do you know most of the paintings and drawings in the book are his?"

"I didn't realize that. They're exceptionally well done."

"They are. He could have made a decent living doing just that." He glanced at the book. "Did you have any further thoughts on the inscription?"

"I didn't give it much thought, to tell the truth. Should I have?" She shrugged, as if wondering why he was bothering to ask. "It could only mean one of two things, I suppose. Either the book was given to her, or possibly to her husband, by a friend or acquaintance, whose first name started with R, or it came into their possession in the same way that books usually do: They bought it at a used-book store or a car boot sale, or it was a used book given to them by someone whose name didn't necessarily begin with R. In the case of the latter two, the inscription was already in the book. Does that help?"

"Hardly at all," he replied, smiling. "Although I hadn't thought of her husband. But from what we know about him, that would make even less sense, wouldn't it?"

"You're probably right," Emma replied.

Small talk continued over glasses of chilled Sancerre until their hors d'oeuvres plates were brought to the table. During the natural lull in the conversation, while the waiter was fussing with the silverware and topping up their wineglasses, Kingston decided this was as good a moment as any to tell her the story of the Belmaris rose and how he'd stumbled on the unsettling news about reclusive rose fancier, Reginald Payne. She would probably ask soon, anyway. If she showed more than just a passing interest—and he couldn't imagine otherwise—then he would broach the delicate question of whether she would be willing to find out more about him and why someone might have wanted to murder him. There, he knew, he would be walking on eggshells. If he was also going ask for her help in solving the Alcatraz rose mystery, he had to make very clear from the start that his interests were solely with regard to that and nothing to do with Reginald's murder.

Resting his fork for a moment while taking a sip of wine, he glanced at Emma. There was no doubt that she was enjoying herself. He appreciated her healthy appetite; her appetizer was disappearing more quickly than his.

Emma saved Kingston from having to devise a way to segue into the story of the rose. "So, Lawrence," she said, raising her wineglass to her lips and holding it there for a moment. "Tell me what happened after you and Andrew took off the other day. As I recall, you were off to Belmaris Castle to see your friend. Why so mysterious on the phone?" She smiled and took a sip of wine. "I'm waiting to be 'amazed.'"

Over their entrees—asparagus risotto for Emma and seared scallops for Kingston—he told her what had transpired that afternoon, being careful not to make it sound too dramatic, which he knew wouldn't go down well with her. As he was talking, he noticed that—though she was clearly listening to what he was saying, looking at him all the time while she was eating—she hadn't interrupted him once and furthermore had shown no signs of either surprise or curiosity. He shrugged it off it as most likely having something to do with her police training. It wasn't until he got to the part where Clare Davenport had told them about the postmortem and suspicion of foul play that she set her knife and fork aside and gave him her full attention.

What followed wasn't at all what he'd suspected, particularly since he'd taken great care to stick with the facts and treat Payne's suspicious death with the gravity it warranted. She looked at him across the table, an inscrutable smile crinkling her face.

"As I live and breathe," she said. "A firsthand account of how Dr. Kingston gets himself tangled up in other people's misfortunes. What did Andrew have to say about that?"

Kingston shrugged. "Very little," he fibbed.

"I can see why going to Payne's house to find out if he could provide you with information about the rose was a logical decision, but I have to be honest with you, Lawrence, your going back to the pub had nothing to do with the rose. It had everything to do with finding out about Payne's demise."

"I'm surprised you see it that way. It was nothing more than natural curiosity on my part. As a police officer, wouldn't you have done the same?"

"In all probability, yes. Any law enforcement officer or private investigator would have. The problem is, that you're neither—not anymore."

Realizing that he was on the losing side of the discussion, Kingston decided to retreat as graciously as he could. Trying to find the right words to save further loss of face for what was now clearly seen by both Andrew and Emma as poor judgment on his part, he was relieved to see that her "policewoman" look had been replaced by a complacent smile.

"Curiosity is admirable, but it has been known to dispose of cats from time to time, you know," she said, with a forgiving smile.

"Mea culpa," he responded, taken aback by her candor, wondering if Andrew could have whispered in her ear without telling him.

During a brief interlude while their water glasses were refilled and plates taken away, he saw fit to change the subject, remarking on the restaurant's long history and the many memorable meals he'd enjoyed there since arriving in London.

Emma caught him completely off guard with her next comment. "Why do I have a feeling that you were toying with the idea of asking me if I could find out more about Reginald Payne? About his supposed homicide?" The question was accompanied by an amused look and an enigmatic smile.

Under her inquisitive gaze, Kingston picked up his glass and, in one smooth and nonchalant motion, took a long, slow sip of his wine—a patently transparent attempt to buy a little time before replying, which he knew Emma would see through. But he had to come up with a satisfactory answer, one that was truthful and wouldn't make her think for one moment that he was taking advantage of their friendship to further his own ambitions.

He put down his wineglass—more abruptly than he intended—and began.

"Earlier, I'll confess the thought had crossed my mind. But since then I've given this whole business a lot more thought and done some soul-searching, for want of a better phrase. So let me simply say this: As a matter of courtesy and respect for your former position, I would never presume to ask that of you without first knowing where you stand personally. I also realize that there is the issue of whether it would be permissible for you to do so in the first place, given your former job." He paused. "For all I know, there could be other considerations as well."

Emma showed no intention of debating or questioning anything he'd said, so he continued, his tone a trifle more upbeat.

"What I *was* toying with was proposing that you and I become partners of a sort in trying to solve the Alcatraz rose mystery, and only that, I want to stress. From everything we know, there's nothing to suggest criminal activity—and, I'm sure you'll agree it's rather unlikely that there would be. There would be no police conflicts that I can think of, you wouldn't be breaking any rules or conditions of termination, so to speak, and it might give you something challenging to do to spice up the humdrum of retirement. Look on it as somewhat like tackling a particularly difficult brainteaser—you must admit, it is most intriguing."

Emma's attentive expression melted into the same knowing smile as earlier.

"I could be mistaken, Lawrence, but do I see an equation taking shape here?" she said with a sprinkle of good-humored sarcasm. "Rare English rose shows up thousands of miles away on Alcatraz—chances are, sent by someone who knows about and is personally familiar with such a rose. You, by sheer happenstance, learn of such a person who could have had access to said rose. Unluckily for you, the man has just died—murdered. Have you stumbled on the beginnings of an answer to the puzzle, you ask yourself? It's not out of the question, you tell yourself, even though the odds are about the same as winning the National Lottery. But in order to take it the next step, you're in a bind because, first, you've no way of getting more information on Payne's murder—the police aren't going to provide it—and, second, I get the impression—although I admit it is subtle—that your best friend would prefer that you weigh the possible consequences before getting embroiled in inquiries of this nature. Enter Emma. Am I on the right track?"

Fortunately the need for an immediate response was cut short once more by the arrival of dessert. As the plates were lowered with near reverential deliberation, Kingston told himself not to underestimate Emma's remarkable perception. It was apparent that she had been an excellent police officer. She was right and trying to explain or elaborate would make matters worse. If he wasn't careful, he could come off appearing recalcitrant, like a schoolboy caught scrumping apples.

He needn't have worried. In due course the conversation picked up and, as if by mutual consent, the dialogue drifted from the rose mystery and Reginald Payne to more sociable topics. Emma was interested in learning more about Kingston's career as a professor of botany at Edinburgh University, about his daughter's career in the States, her fiancé, and Kingston's planned trip to visit them. It soon became clear that Emma did not intend to address his request—at least not yet—and he had no intention of pressing her on it. All in good time, he supposed.

Outside the restaurant, fifteen minutes later, Emma in a cab ready to depart for Paddington Station and the journey home, she looked up at him through the half-open window.

"Thank you one more time for a delightful lunch," she said.

"My pleasure. We should do it again. I'll keep you informed of any new developments."

"Please do," she replied, glancing toward the worn rose book in his hand. "One more thing occurred to me. Is it possible that you might have asked yourself if the *R* in the book might stand for Reginald?"

The same knowing smile appeared on her face then, just as the cab pulled away, leaving Kingston standing at the curb, frowning.

"The woman," he muttered to himself, "is just too damn clever by half."

9

THAT EVENING, AFTER enjoying two of Mrs. Tripp's Cornish pasties and a pint of Guinness, Kingston took out Graham Stuart Thomas's book and studied the inscription once more, focusing on the neat handwriting, in black ink, on the otherwise blank page:

This may give you some ideas, R.

Try as he might, he couldn't come up with any other ways to interpret it, other than the obvious: R, whoever he or she was, had presented the book to someone mostly with the intent to encourage and stimulate him or her to grow roses, or had given it to a seasoned gardener who could be making a transition from hybrid tea and floribunda roses to the heady fragrance and beauty of old garden roses.

He was no handwriting expert but recalled once reading that women tended to be neater writers than men. This writing, though neat, was bold and indicated a strong and steady hand. The ink impression was consistent, with no alternating heavy and fine strokes—all the full stops decisive. After a few moments, he gave up trying to be a handwriting analyst.

How on earth, he wondered, had the book ended up in Fiona's possession when, according to Emma, no evidence had surfaced to suggest that either Fiona or her husband, Terry, had any interest in gardening? Furthermore, it hadn't been stated that the flat they'd rented had a garden. Even if it had, he doubted that either of them would have appreciated or been inspired by such a scholarly and esoteric work like *The*

Old Shrub Roses. What's more, it is somewhat unusual for a novice rose grower to start with old garden roses.

He started to leaf slowly through the pages, looking for the penciled notes Emma had mentioned.

The first appeared on the right border of page 30. Faint but legible, it read *Celsiana, damask, pre 1750.* On page 45 there was another: *Madame Plantier, hybrid Alba, 1835, to 6 feet.* Similar notes appeared on six more pages, each referring to a specific old European shrub rose, listing a date and, occasionally, growing characteristics. Kingston saw nothing unusual about them; they were probably specific roses recommended to the person who'd received the book as suitable for planting in his or her garden.

He began flipping through the pages faster, ignoring the few additional notes. At the very end of the book, as he was about to close it, he noticed a final entry on the last right-hand blank page. It was considerably longer than any of the others. His eyes narrowed as he read it.

In terms of rarity, there is one other rose worth mentioning, even though it may now be impossible to locate. It's called the Belmaris rose, a climber, easily growing to 20 feet or more. It is undated but known to have existed in the garden at Belmaris Castle* in Gloucestershire for several centuries. While its lineage is unknown, it comes with historic English provenance, striking red-black coloration, and a subtle fragrance of lily of the valley with hints of myrrh; overall a rose of indubitable grace. It would be a prize exhibit in any garden—a conversation piece—because, in addition to its other laudable qualities, I believe it has been classified as extinct. From a collectible viewpoint, I can't think of another that would serve our purposes better. You might want to initiate your inquiries at Belmaris.

*Kings Henry VIII, Charles I, and Richard III; Queens Katherine Parr and Anne Boleyn; Lady Jane Grey and Queen Elizabeth I all played parts in Belmaris's story.
  R.

Kingston's eyes were riveted on the orderly handwriting.

He read the paragraph and its footnote again. Two things struck him as worthy of note. First was the accuracy of the horticultural and historical credentials of the rose and the succinct yet informative manner in which it was described. The second—more revealing, he thought—was the language and style of writing. He pictured the writer as being if not elderly, then certainly mature. In a few words, using short sentences, he or she had painted an expressive and explicit picture of the rose that demonstrated not only an impressive feel for the language but also excellent writing ability. Few people that he knew used words like "indubitable" and "laudable" in their everyday jotting. Something about the spelling niggled at him, too, but he wasn't sure what.

Despite all that, the mention of Belmaris Castle raised implications far more thought-provoking and perplexing than simply the description of a plant and good prose. Until now, the idea he'd harbored since returning from Gloucestershire had been nothing more than a fanciful "what-if," an idle supposition he'd summarily rejected whenever it had entered his mind. Now his pie-in-the-sky theory suddenly looked as if it might not be so crazy after all. He leaned back, chin rested on the forefinger of his clasped hand, wondering how Emma would react when he told her.

He couldn't read it any other way: Unlikely as it seemed, he was now convinced that there was a connection of some kind between the Alcatraz rose and Fiona or Terry McGuire.

Perhaps with Reginald Payne's murder as well.

It took until eleven o'clock the next morning for him to catch up with Emma. She sounded breathless when she answered the phone. "Sorry, Lawrence," she huffed, "I've just lugged in three big sacks of potting soil from the car. I didn't expect to hear from you so soon. How are you? All right, I trust?"

"Couldn't be better, thanks. I'm calling about the book."

"It's important, I take it?"

"Yes. I think it could be. It concerns the handwritten notes on some of the pages. Clearly these were meant to highlight specific roses as recommendations or suggestions for the reader to consider growing."

"Makes sense," she said, sounding considerably less enthusiastic than he had hoped. "But I don't see how—"

"That's not all. There's a longer notation on the last page. One that describes a single rose in considerable detail, including its growing habit, pedigree, fragrance—and its rarity."

"And?"

Careful not to sound too carried away, he voiced his next words with more restraint. "The rose described on the last page is the Belmaris rose. And it's named as such."

He paused, curious to see how she would respond. She didn't—not for several seconds.

"What you're suggesting is that your mysterious rose is somehow associated with the McGuires. Is that it?"

"That's right. Which suggests that our friend Reginald could well be the R who signed the book."

"I'm not quite sure why you're insisting that makes him suspect. It could still have been someone else—a Roger, a Robert, or a Rita? And one of the McGuires could still have bought it at a rummage sale."

"All true—if it were any old rose. But it's not; it's the Belmaris rose. An extremely rare variety—in fact, I don't think it's mentioned in any of Graham Stuart Thomas's books, and he's the ultimate authority. Furthermore, according to Jimmy Cosworth, Belmaris's head gardener, Payne, would have known about the rose when it was growing there and had plenty of opportunity to nick some cuttings. Now we have a rose book, signed by someone whose first name begins with R, and furthermore, one that includes a full description of the Belmaris rose by name. This is more than coincidence."

"Added to which, he was murdered," Emma interjected. "Or so says Mrs. what's-her-name."

"If he'd died of old age it wouldn't change matters, would it?"

"Perhaps not," she conceded after a pause, as if still not completely persuaded.

"If I'm right, it also means that the Alcatraz rose mystery and Fiona's disappearance are connected in some way."

"You could draw that conclusion, I suppose." Another pause. "All right, Lawrence, supposing I go along with your theory. If the two events are indeed connected, how or why was Reginald Payne associated with the McGuires? And what does it have to do with Fiona going missing?"

"I've asked myself the same questions, and I'm damned if I know. But if we're right, the next question is, Where do we go from here?"

"You mean, where do *you* go? Perhaps you're forgetting I've not yet agreed to help you in this escapade."

"I hadn't forgotten, Emma. But if we could find out more about Payne, what he did these last sixty years or so, and how he died, that might be a good start."

There was another pause, and then he caught what sounded like a slight chuckle on the other end.

"Goodness," she said, "you're even more bloody-minded than I was led to believe!"

"Is it asking too much?" he asked, ignoring the accusation.

"I'm not sure. I'd have to pose that question to DI Endersby, my former boss. I haven't the foggiest idea of where I stand in a situation of this type. That brings me back to the question you asked at the Ivy, about helping you solve the riddle of the Alcatraz rose. I never gave you an answer, and for that I owe you an apology. It was rude of me."

"It's not necessary. It was probably disrespectful of me to ask in the first place."

"Well, I've given it more thought and, against my better judgment, have decided to give it a try. It'll give me something to do, and I might learn a few things about roses along the way."

"Yes," Kingston said, wishing Emma could see his smile. "Yes, and you will. That's wonderful news. I'm—"

"There's one caveat, however," she interrupted. "If the search leads to areas that are even vaguely criminal, I won't be able to continue without express guidance from those upstairs at Gloucester police."

"Of course. I understand completely. And I couldn't be more delighted. I think Andrew will be chuffed, too."

"I hope so. So, getting back to Mr. Payne and the McGuires, specifically—where *do* we go from here, Inspector? What do you think the next step should be?"

"Perhaps a return visit to Payne's house might be as good as any. With luck we might encounter someone other than that tight-lipped woman, Reggie's niece. Mrs. Davenport at the pub said she thought the niece's mother was also living there. If we could talk to her, she might be more cooperative."

"If she is Reginald's sister—which seems probable—then I'd expect her to know a lot about him."

"That's true," Kingston said, encouraged by Emma's more receptive mood.

She continued, "If we do get lucky and get to talk with her—or anyone else, for that matter—you've no doubt given thought to revealing who we are or why we want to know. We can hardly show up on the doorstep expecting her to blithely discuss her brother's life story to a couple of complete strangers, no matter how presentable and charming we might be."

"I've always found a little creative fibbing works quite well, actually. Perfectly harmless and does away with what can sometimes end up being embarrassing explanations."

"Why do I not find that surprising? I can't wait to know what our cover is going to be."

"Don't worry about it," Kingston said, "though we may have to carry false identification. I'm sure I can come up with something that will be convincing and not raise suspicion."

"Good grief!"

"Look, Emma, joking aside, I'd be happy to go alone, if you prefer. But I think it would be much better if we go together."

"If you want to keep the peace with Andrew, you really can't go alone."

"I can't argue with that."

"All right. I'll start by making a couple of phone calls to see if I can find out more about the circumstances of Payne's death."

"Excellent. Let me know when you'd like to go, and I'll run down and pick you up. Payne's place isn't far from you, just east of Cheltenham."

The conversation ended, and Kingston put down the phone with a satisfied smile on his face.

The game, he thought, was afoot.

10

About midafternoon four days later, Kingston parked on the grass-edged lane outside Beechwood, Reginald Payne's house. As arranged, he and Emma had dressed informally, Kingston in a tweed sport coat and corduroys, she in a suede jacket, blouse, and Liberty silk scarf. Unlike his first visit, with Andrew, this time there were signs of habitation. Wisps of smoke spiraled languidly from behind the house, and the accompanying smell of burning leaves filled the crisp air. From the house they could hear a small dog yapping. They also heard what sounded like an old hand-pushed lawn mower coming from somewhere behind the house. Two cars were parked on a small gravel drive alongside a row of tall yew hedges that ran along that side of the property: a newish Audi and the same mud-spattered Land Rover.

Kingston gave the familiar brass knocker on the front door two hard raps. This only served to make the dog yap with more gusto. After a minute, it became clear that if anybody were home, they were either hard of hearing, taking a shower, or in the back garden, which, given the mowing and woodsmoke, seemed the most logical explanation.

"Let's see if we can get into the back," Kingston said, walking across a small patch of lawn toward the side of the house. Emma followed reluctantly, several paces behind, until she caught up with Kingston, who had stopped and was inspecting a wooden gate abutting the hedge.

"Looks like it's locked from the other side." Kingston ran a hand across the top of the six-foot gate looking for a latch. "I may have to climb over."

"I see now how you get into trouble. That's breaking and entering."

"Only entering, my dear. I don't plan to break anything. Anyway, you needn't worry because I've found the inside latch," he said, as the gate creaked open.

They walked along a narrow stone path, flanked by thick clumps of hellebore leaves, eventually arriving at the end where it met the corner of a huge sloping lawn as smooth as a putting green. The lawn was divided down the center by a narrow rill that flowed down the long slope over shallow stone steps, spaced every ten feet or so, the bubbling water finally emptying into a large pond some fifty feet away. It was planted with white water lilies and, from where they stood, what looked like forget-me-nots and spikes of blue iris.

The mower stood unattended at the far corner of the lawn, in front of a shoulder-high holly hedge. The scene facing them was spellbinding. The quintessential English garden was Kingston's first thought. He glanced at Emma, who seemed speechless as she gazed over Reginald Payne's tour de force. If indeed it was his creation, he must have taken inspiration from a dozen of the best gardens in England and managed somehow to distill and combine the best features and plantings from all to create a veritable Eden. It was evident, by the age and size of some of the trees, shrubs, climbing roses, and vines, and by the lichen-splotched stone balustrades, walls, and York paving, that it had taken several decades to evolve and mature into its present state of sublime beauty.

Beyond the mower and the long hedge, Kingston spotted a head bobbing up and down in the vicinity of where the smoke was originating. He took off across the lawn and under a long curved arbor of espaliered apple trees underplanted with feverfew, stock, and golden marjoram. Walking around the end of the holly hedge, he spied an elderly man in work clothes and Wellingtons heaving mounds of leaves onto a bonfire with a pitchfork. Between the billows of smoke and his concentration, he hadn't noticed their arrival.

"Good morning," Kingston shouted.

The man rested his pitchfork and looked across at them. "'Ow can I 'elp you?"

"I'm a long-ago friend of Reginald Payne's and recently learned of his passing. We were told by a mutual friend that the lady who's living here now might be Reggie's sister."

"That's right. Is she expecting you?"

"She's not, but we have some information about her brother that should please her."

Kingston ignored Emma's frown. "It won't take too much of her time. We just wanted to show her this," he said, taking out his iPhone from his inside jacket pocket, sliding it open with his index finger, tapping the Photos icon. "Here," he said, holding up the phone so that the gardener could see the picture.

"Very nice. What is it?"

"It's an award that Reginald won but never got to receive."

Emma's eyes looked heavenward.

"Well, Grace will be pleased to learn that, I'm sure. If you go back through the garden and jog right along the path toward the east wall, by the long 'erbaceous border, you'll come to a conservatory. That's where she works most of the day."

"Do you know if she's home now?" Emma asked.

"She should be. She usually tells me if she's leaving." He stopped to take off his cap and wipe his forehead with the cuff of his shirt. "Was there a black Audi in the driveway when you arrived?"

Kingston nodded. "There was."

"Then she's 'ere for sure."

Kingston thanked him, and they set off toward the east wall between waist-high boxwood hedges that corralled a confection of white iceberg roses, blue hardy geraniums, and gray santolina. As they approached the glass-walled conservatory, they saw a woman inside, standing at an easel. A light rap on the glass got her attention right away.

The woman put down her brush and walked to the door, opening it halfway.

"Can I help you?" she asked, her cautious gray eyes glancing from Emma to Kingston. She was tall and thin as a wafer, her graying hair pulled tightly back and held in place by a black ribbon. This accentuated her gaunt face and pale complexion, the skin wrinkled in the hollows but stretched tight over her high cheekbones and prominent forehead. In the luminescence of the conservatory, her features resembled an alabaster sculpture. Kingston could picture her as having Pre-Raphaelite beauty in earlier years. Under a beige smock she wore a black turtleneck and slacks to match.

"Perhaps," Kingston replied. "First, let me apologize for interrupting you and for showing up on your doorstep uninvited. It's certainly not our custom. But let me explain. You are Reginald Payne's sister—Grace, I take it?"

"Yes." The woman frowned. "And who are you?"

"Lawrence Kingston—Dr. Kingston. And this is my friend Emma Dixon, formerly with the Gloucestershire police." On the word "police," Kingston raised a hand. "Please don't be alarmed, this has nothing to do with police matters or the recent death of Reginald Payne."

"You know about Reggie, then?"

Kingston nodded. "We do, yes."

"May I ask how?"

"Of course. Several days ago I stopped by with a friend, hoping to chat with him. A young woman answered the doorbell and told me that he'd passed away."

"It was you who'd stopped by, then? That was Sophie you spoke with—she told me. I must confess I didn't pay any attention at the time. It didn't seem important."

Kingston nodded. "There was no reason for her to think so."

"I see," she said, looking confused. "Why did you want to talk to Reggie?"

"I know it's going to sound odd, but it concerns a rose."

"A rose?"

"Yes. A very old rose. One we're led to believe might be still growing in this garden—perhaps planted by your brother or a previous owner, many years ago."

"Really? That's fascinating," she said, looking even more at a loss.

He nodded. "A friend of mine—coincidentally, Reginald's, too—the head gardener at Belmaris Castle, told us about it."

"Well, it all sounds very interesting, but I think you'd be far better off speaking to Thomas, the gardener. He's worked here for several years, and in any case I'm not at all familiar with the garden."

"As a matter of fact, we met him on the way in. If he could find time to give us a quick tour, even better. Speaking as one who's seen a lifetime of beautiful gardens, yours is very special."

"That's settled, then," she said, as if ready to close the door. "Tell him I said to give you all the time you want."

"Thank you," Kingston said. "But if I might—we did want to talk to you first, because it involves Reginald in another way. You see, the rose is only part of it."

"I'm still not sure that I understand what it is you want," she said, shaking her head.

"It'll only take a few minutes, that's all," Emma said.

"All right, then. But we can't stand on the doorstep all day. That smoke is making my eyes water. You'd better come in." She opened the door and stepped aside. "I still think it'll be a waste of your time. I've only been here for a short time. For the last twenty-five years I've lived abroad."

Kingston followed Emma—who was following Grace—through the conservatory, past the beginnings of a still-life canvas on a wooden easel, into a spacious, high-ceilinged sitting room furnished with overstuffed sofas and chairs, complemented by antique country furniture. A clutter of botanical watercolors and oil paintings left little room for the age-worn color of the walls to be seen. With Kingston and Emma seated on one of the sofas and Grace facing them in an easy chair, the conversation resumed.

"Outside, Dr. King—?" she said, looking embarrassed.

"Kingston."

"Yes, forgive me. Outside, you mentioned my brother's death. Are you aware of the circumstances? How he died?"

"We are. Mrs. Davenport, the landlady at the Rose & Thistle in the village informed us. And please accept our condolences."

"Thank you." There was a notable absence of emotion in the two words, as she clasped her bony hands in her lap. "So, what's so special about this rose and why does it involve Reginald? And why does it merit your making what I assume to be a special trip here to inquire about it?"

Kingston leaned forward slightly and spoke in a more measured tone than before. "Well, in the first place, the rose in question is considerably rare, having been declared extinct fifty years ago. But what has made it somewhat of a celebrity lately is that it was discovered recently to be growing in America—of all places on Alcatraz Island."

"You mean the prison?"

"The former prison, yes."

"What on earth has that got to do with Reggie?"

"We believe that your brother was not only familiar with the rose but could also have been one of the few people who'd managed to clone it—that is, to replicate it from cuttings."

"Yes, I'm familiar with the process, not having been very successful at it, I'm afraid."

Kingston was ready to steer the conversation to her relationship with her brother and ask a few questions about him, when Grace interrupted.

"What is it that you do, Dr. Kingston? I'm curious. Are you a medical doctor?"

"No. It was remiss of me. I should have told you in the first place." Out of the corner of his eye, he caught a glimpse of Emma, who was trying to get his attention—without being noticed by Grace—shaking her head almost imperceptibly. This, he knew, was a subtle signal to stick with the truth, which was his plan, anyway. So far, it had gone well, and there was really no reason for imposture, embellishment, or anything like that—as long as Grace was cooperating. He met her questioning eyes with a kindly half smile.

"In addition to being a professor of botany," Kingston said, "I have served as liaison to various law enforcement agencies, where my background and experience has been considered of help to the case. Another way of putting it would be that, in a court of law, I would be considered an expert witness."

"And what about you . . . Ms. Dixon, was it?" Grace asked, looking at Emma. "The doctor, here, said you were formerly with the police? I must say you look awfully young to be retired."

Emma smiled. "Thank you for the compliment. I was forced to step down from the force—a nasty accident."

"I'm sorry to hear that," she said, getting up and walking toward a butler's table laden with various bottles, siphons, and glasses. "Would either of you care for something to drink? Fizzy water? Aperitif? Something stronger, perhaps?"

Kingston and Emma asked for mineral water. Grace poured herself a rather generous measure of sherry, considering the time of day.

"So let's get to the point," she said, placing the last of the drinks on the table and sitting. "All this twaddle about a rose that Reggie might or might not have been familiar with. Is there something you're not telling me? What is it that you hope to find out?"

Kingston took a sip of his Perrier and cleared his throat. "If it were only about the rose, we wouldn't be here. And you're right. The fact that a rose has migrated over five thousand miles, across an ocean, without help of any kind, would eventually come to be accepted as just another of those capricious tricks of nature and soon forgotten. However, quite recently, and by chance, in totally separate circumstances, while Emma and I were trying to help a distraught teenager, Letty McGuire, find out what happened to her mother who's been missing for eight years, we stumbled upon something unexpected, puzzling." He paused briefly. "On a bookshelf at Letty's foster home we came across an old book about roses that might have belonged to her mother—or grandmother, perhaps. At first it appeared to be of no importance, but upon further examination it contained a handwritten note on the last page describing the rose in considerable detail. It's called the Belmaris rose. The writer also knew that the rose was either extinct or about to become so."

Kingston scratched his cheek, pausing, while Grace took a large sip of sherry. "But here's the interesting thing," he continued. "The inscription in the front of the book was signed with just the initial R. No name. We think that it could—and I want to emphasize the 'could'—have been written by your brother. If it was indeed Reginald's hand, then it would not only corroborate his familiarity with the rose but might also connect him to the Fiona McGuire missing persons cold case in Cheltenham. It's too early yet to say if this will have any bearing on the circumstances of Reginald's unfortunate death, but we—Emma, in particular, with her background and experience in these matters—felt the connection reasonably evidential to justify further inquiries."

"That was a charitable deed you did for the child," she said. "And I can see why you became suspicious when you saw the inscription. But good heavens, it's far from proof, isn't it?"

Kingston nodded. "That's true, but it can't be overlooked."

Emma added, "And I'm sure I don't need to tell you that proof is a rare thing in police work."

"Have you told the police about it?" Grace asked.

"Not yet. Emma will contact them in the coming days, but only if we feel that the information we have so far warrants it. That's another reason why we needed to talk to you first. I'm sure they must have contacted you by now. The police?"

"They have. Two days after I arrived."

"Did they give you an explanation of what happened? If it was an accident or not?"

"Yes, they did. It seems like a wretched dream. I still can't believe it," she said in a tired voice, shaking her head. "He was such a kind and considerate man. I know it's a cliché, but he wouldn't hurt a fly." She brushed a finger across the corner of an eyelid. "It's impossible to believe that anybody would want to kill him."

"Can you tell us what the police said?" Emma asked gently.

She nodded. "There's not much to tell. Anyway, from what I've gathered—as you know—it's no longer a secret." She took out a handkerchief that was tucked in the sleeve of her turtleneck and dabbed her nose delicately several times.

Other than the distant sound of the lawn mower chattering again, a brief silence fell over the room. After a few moments, looking more composed, Grace continued.

"The inspector I spoke to—his name escapes me right now—said that the pathologist's report from the postmortem examination determined that Reginald had been forcibly drowned, in all likelihood in the house or another location, and then his body dragged to the pond in the garden to make it appear accidental. He went on to explain briefly how they were able to determine it was a homicide—something to do with freshwater algae—but by that time, I'd heard enough." She paused, looking right into Kingston's sympathetic eyes. "His death wasn't accidental. There's no question about it."

"I wish that we could make things easier for you, Grace," Emma said. "But I know from experience that in these circumstances there are no words to make things more tolerable. The best we can promise is to find out who did this, and why."

"I hope to God that you can. And I wish that I could be of help in some way." She picked up her glass and downed the last of the sherry.

"You can," Emma said.

"How?"

"Tell us about Reginald. What it was like when you were children growing up together, in school, where you lived, what happened in later years, what hobbies Reggie had, his jobs, who his friends were, if he married, if he had problems of any kind like money, business failures, large debts, gambling—anything you can think of, no matter how trivial it seems to you."

"That's quite a tall order. But that's all right, because most of the things you mentioned about his past I can't answer," Grace said. "I told you I've been abroad for many years."

"That's fine," Emma said with a quick nod. "Just tell us what you can."

"I'll do my best," she replied doubtfully, dabbing her nose again with her hanky. "I've lived in Canada for the last twenty five years. During all those years I had very little contact with Reggie. In the beginning we exchanged Christmas cards and sent a few birthday cards, but all that ceased after three or four years, and I doubt there were more than a half dozen phone calls over the years. We were never what you would call a close family in the first place. You see"—Grace sighed—"Reggie is not my true brother."

Kingston and Emma glanced at each other in surprise. "Really?" Kingston said. "That may or may not have bearing. But we'd like to—"

"We share the same mother, but his father died at quite a young age and four years later she remarried—and that man was my father. That's why we have different surnames. Mine is Williams—it's never been Payne. We grew up together in a typical semidetached house in North Harrow. We went to the same primary school. When we reached our midteens we ended up in different schools, though."

"Ah." Kingston nodded.

"Yes. So you see, Doctor, when you ask me to remember things about his youth—hobbies and all that—there's not much to tell." She paused, glancing aside for a moment. "The only thing that comes to mind is his playing the drums. When he was about sixteen, he played in a band for a while. I used to go to the Red Lion, our pub, to see them. His group was quite popular, back in the day." She paused for a moment, thinking, then continued. "It was when Reggie got his first job that we began to drift apart. He started to spend less and less time at home, staying out with his friends, yobs, mostly. By that time there were the usual cars and girlfriends, too."

"Do you recall what the job was?" Emma asked.

Grace smiled for the first time since they'd arrived. "I do, as a matter of fact, because we teased him mercilessly. He worked in a women's shoe shop." She looked up to the ceiling. "I can even remember the name of the store—Dolcis. It didn't last long, though."

"What did he do after that?"

"I'm not sure. Drifted along. I know he was out of work for some time. I don't think he was looking that hard, though. For a while we phoned each other regularly, then all of a sudden he stopped calling and wouldn't return any of my calls. Soon after that his phone was disconnected. I remember being very hurt and angry at the time, but I got over it fairly quickly. You know how it is when you're young, working six days a week and having a good time on the weekends. My mother was more upset about his behavior than I was. Come to think of it, that might have been the last we heard of him for quite a few years. By that time I was bent on a career and had pretty much given up on him."

"What years were those?" Kingston asked.

Grace looked down briefly, then back at Kingston. "Let's see. Gosh, I don't know—1953, '54, thereabouts."

"You said that was the last you heard of him for several years. So you did hear from him, eventually, then?"

"We did have one get-together. I stopped in London one year, on a layover to Paris. I was curating a Postimpressionist exhibition that was going to tour several Canadian cities."

"What year was that, approximately?" Emma asked.

She gazed at the ceiling for a moment. "Probably 1999, 2000, thereabouts. He'd read about it in the newspaper—my name was mentioned. We had lunch in the West End. I was surprised to discover that he was fairly well-off, or appeared to be. As I recall, I did most of the talking, which was really foolish of me and I later regretted it, because I went away still knowing very little about what he'd been up to all those years, other than he'd done well with investments and was part owner in a company that had something to with the financial markets and international trade. As a result, he often traveled abroad. It all sounded awfully complicated at the time. He'd never married and owned a house in Buckinghamshire—the Chalfonts, I believe."

"Nice area," Kingston said.

She gave a curt nod. "So I'm told."

"Anything else?" Emma asked, after an awkward pause.

"Not that I can think of. It was a long time ago," she said, shaking her head.

Kingston looked quizzical. "Is Sophie your niece?"

She smiled. "No, Sophie's my daughter."

"Sorry, we weren't quite sure."

"I got married a year after arriving in Canada. My husband passed away eight years ago. When I told Sophie about Reggie—that he'd died and I was going back to England for a while to sort things out—she insisted on coming with me. I was cool to the idea at first because we've had our ups and downs these last few years, but it's turning out to be a good decision. As you can imagine there's so much to deal with: solicitors, Inland Revenue, local matters, this tax, that tax, it's never ending. So much more than I'd anticipated."

"Well," Emma said, giving Kingston a subtle eye-over-the-shoulder glance signaling that they should be on their way, "you've been more than cooperative, and I hope we haven't been too intrusive with our questions."

"Not at all," Grace replied, taking a long pause, a distant look in her eyes, as if she'd been reminded of something. "There was one thing that really upset me. It may not mean much for your purposes, but in 1975 our mother passed away, and I tried to locate Reggie to tell him about the funeral arrangements. He'd said earlier that he might be moving, so I called the few friends and people we both knew, but nobody had any idea where he was. In the end, I concluded that he must have moved out of the country."

"Without telling anyone?" Emma said.

"It certainly looked that way at the time."

As if impelled by some invisible force, they all stood at the same time, apparently in agreement that nothing more was left to be said, on either side, and that the meeting was over. The only courtesy remaining was for Kingston and Emma to thank Grace for her time and make a respectable exit. As they were making tentative steps toward the door, Emma stopped and turned to Grace. "There is one last question, if I may? It's personal in nature, and if you feel uncomfortable answering it, please say so."

"That's all right, go ahead, Emma."

"Are you heir to your brother's estate?"

"I don't see that it's any of your business, but yes, I am. Soon after Reggie died, I received a call from his solicitor to that effect. That's the main reason why I'm here."

"Thanks again for allowing us to steal so much of your time. We appreciate it very much," Kingston said. "If we learn anything that sheds further light on Reginald's death, we will certainly let you know."

"I would appreciate that," Grace said as they reached the front door.

"And if you think of anything else in the coming days that might be helpful, please do let us know," Kingston said, handing her his card.

"I will."

Kingston raised a hand momentarily. "One last thing. We'd like to chat with Thomas before leaving, if it's still all right with you. It's doubtful, but he may have some information on the rose in question. One never knows."

"Yes, of course. You might still catch him. Unfortunately, he suffers from severe arthritis and usually quits about this time. The black gate by the corner of the house, over there," she said, pointing.

Kingston and Emma had taken no more than a half dozen steps down the front path when they heard her call out.

"Just tell him you're old friends. That's all."

11

As Kingston and Emma entered the rear garden, Kingston said, "Thomas certainly looks old enough to know if the Belmaris rose was growing here at one time, or perhaps still is. Depends on how long he's worked here, I suppose."

"We'll soon find out."

The smoke had abated and there was no sign of Thomas.

"Damn," Kingston muttered.

"Looks like we missed him after all." Emma looked at her watch. "It's four thirty. We could check out the pubs."

"A possibility. Never mind, we'll just take a little tour of our own. Grace won't mind, I'm sure."

Emma smiled gamely. "Lead on, Macduff."

Walking along the perimeter path, past a fifteen-foot-deep perennial border, Kingston remained mostly silent, his eyes roaming with practiced concentration, punctuated now and then by his muttering about a certain plant or pointing out something that he thought might interest Emma.

Walking under the shade of a meticulously spaced avenue of pleached lime trees, Emma spoke for the first time. "This rose, is there any way you could recognize it if it's not blooming?"

"Never having seen it and not knowing if it had any unusual leaf characteristics, I'd say no. If it were a thornless rose, like *Rosa banksiae*—Lady Banks' rose—it would certainly narrow the field, but there's still a good chance it could be in bloom at this time of year. As you can see, there are still a lot of roses out, like that white climbing one on the brick wall over there. That could be Madame Alfred Carrière."

"It's lovely," Emma murmured, smiling at Kingston's inability to give a simple yes or no answer when it involved roses.

A half hour later, they'd walked every inch of the roughly four-acre garden with no signs of the small red-black Belmaris rose.

"Too bad," Emma said, as they headed for the car. "I'd like to have seen what it looked like."

Kingston nodded. He would have liked seeing it, too—though not finding it didn't prove it hadn't been growing here at some time in the past. After all, it had died out at Belmaris Castle as well. Gone extinct.

Or so it was believed.

"Well, Emma, the rose aside, what do you make of all that?" Kingston asked, looking in the Triumph's rearview mirror at what was now Grace Williams's house.

"It all seemed tickety-boo. Nothing obviously contradictory, but why should there be? I'd like to have been able to take notes, though, particularly with regard to all the dates—but I'm not sure that it really matters anymore."

"Why do you say that?"

"Well, we've learned nothing whatsoever to advance the hypothesis that Payne is connected to the Fiona McGuire case, or who might have wanted to kill him, or why. Everything the woman said seems perfectly plausible, and her absence abroad for so long explains why she wasn't able to provide much that might interest to us. Frankly, I heard nothing that warrants our further involvement. Maybe you picked up on something that I missed?"

"Not really." Kingston shook his head.

They'd reached the end of the lane from the house when a red VW convertible zipped by, within inches, in the opposite direction, headed to Beechwood. The driver was a young woman.

"Whoa," Kingston hollered, swerving. "Idiot!"

Emma smiled. "Sophie, no doubt."

Kingston righted the TR4, then looked over at Emma, who was gazing silently out the window at the bucolic scenery.

"You don't mean to tell me that you're giving up already? What about the book? The inscription? I know she said it's not proof, but you and I know that's nothing more than a platitude. The odds are at the least fifty percent that Reginald Payne wrote the notes and that the R stands for Reggie."

"All right. Then where do we go from here? Whom do you suggest we talk to next about the elusive Mr. Payne?"

"I have to give it more thought," he replied, eyes on the road ahead.

A minute of silence passed, then Emma looked at Kingston again. "By the way, that award thing with your mobile was a bit dodgy. What if Thomas asks Grace about it?"

"I knew you would frown on something like that—and rightfully so— but I thought it was a quick way to gain the gardener's confidence. He could easily have sent us packing. We just have to hope he doesn't ask."

"If he does, I'd love to see you explain your way out of that."

"I'd have to buy the trophy and have it engraved, that's all. As it was, they allowed me to photograph it in the shop as a precondition of purchase. In any case, it seems highly doubtful that we'll be going back there."

"You're something else," she said, with sigh and a shake of the head.

Small talk followed until they were about a mile past Bourton-on-the-Water. Stopped at a traffic light, Kingston turned to Emma, who was doing a quick makeup check in the rearview mirror. She'd adjusted it while they were stationary.

"I have an idea," he said.

"About Payne?"

"Yes. It's hardly brilliant, but at least it's worth a try. You remember Grace's mentioning that Reggie played in a band when he was a teenager?"

"Some pub, right?"

"The Red Lion," Kingston said. "In North Harrow, I believe. And apparently they were—as she said—'quite popular.'"

"So?"

"Well, there's an outside chance we could track down some of the other musicians in the band. Ask them about Reggie."

"Wow!" Out of the corner of his eye, he saw Emma shaking her head. "That is a really long shot. If it was a small band—which it probably was—you're talking about four or five men, now all in their mid- to late seventies, surely half of them would be dead by now." She paused, brushing her cheeks lightly, as Kingston readjusted the mirror. "So, Lawrence, tell me how you're going to find two or three men who played in a nameless amateur band, in a London suburb, over sixty years ago? Where would you even start, for heaven's sake?"

"It could be friend or a fan who remembers them."

"You're kidding, right? That would be even harder."

Kingston sighed. "I suppose so. It was a good idea while it lasted."

Ten minutes later Kingston stood by the car outside Emma's house after having said goodbye to her with a promise to keep in touch. He'd reluctantly declined her offer of tea. It was getting late and he had a long drive ahead. As she opened the red front door, she stopped and turned to face him.

"Don't get me wrong, Lawrence," she called out. "I didn't mean to be a wet blanket. I think you should follow up on your band idea. You've nothing to lose. In any case"—she smiled saucily—"you're not going to be doing much else in the coming days, by the looks of it."

"That's true, but I was hoping that we—you and I—could continue to, well, work as a team."

"Oh, I think you can manage this one perfectly well without my help." She smiled. "I doubt Andrew will object to your tracking down a group of octogenarian musicians."

Kingston had to smile back at that.

He gave her a goodbye wave, got in the car, and drove off.

12

K<small>INGSTON WOKE LATE</small> the next morning. It had been a wrinkled-sheet night of successive dreams—none memorable—punctuated by lingering thoughts of the day's exploits. The opportunity to see Reginald Payne's extraordinary garden had been a high point and, of course, working with Emma. Considering it was their first excursion together, he couldn't have been more pleased. Their chemistry surpassed anything that he'd anticipated or hoped for. He could not recall any awkward moments, unease, or ticklish differences of opinion. If anything, the outing had left him with a growing respect for her abilities, a greater appreciation of her quick-witted humor, and an awareness of how comfortable he now felt in her company.

Despite her lukewarm reaction to his band idea, he planned on pursuing it anyway. In fact, the next time they met or talked, he was going to tell her about a hero of his, Scotland Yard's celebrated Victorian-era Detective Inspector Jonathan Whicher, who had once said—an observation Kingston had long ago committed to memory—"The detective's job is to reconstruct history from tiny indicators, clues, fossils. These traces are both pathways and remnants: trails back to a tangible event in the past and tiny scraps of that event, souvenirs."

Whicher's pronouncement certainly applied to a number of cases that Kingston had worked on over the years. If not for a tiny porcelain Meissen figurine, sitting on a mantelpiece in a stranger's house, Kingston wouldn't have solved the mystery of his missing colleague and two murders. Were it not for a wire coat hanger that the police had overlooked but he'd bothered to study in detail, he could not have followed the trail to a London dry-cleaning establishment, where he would eventually solve the crime, putting another murderer behind bars.

The problem that now faced him was that with no clues or "souvenirs," he didn't know how to go about a search, where to start. The Internet was the obvious place, but unless the pubescent members of the band had gone on to make some kind of mark for themselves in the musical world, a Google search would be unlikely to reveal anything. At best, it would simply provide names and a brief résumé of the group. After that, where could he go, whom could he talk to? Why was so little known about a man who, according to his sister, had been very successful in his chosen career and appeared to have accumulated sufficient wealth to enjoy a life that few people could afford? Beechwood would have cost plenty.

He wandered into the kitchen, surprised to find Mrs. Tripp already there and making tea. They wished each other good morning, and she put a plate on the table. "My Arthur asked for apple scones, and I made extra for you and for Mr. Andrew."

Kingston offered enthusiastic thanks which, as usual, embarrassed her.

Mrs. Tripp had been organizing Kingston's life for more than six years, and he couldn't imagine functioning without her. He had told her about his trip to see Julie, and it occurred to him now that there was no need for her to come to the house during that time. Andrew could check in once a week to make sure nothing catastrophic had happened.

"Mrs. Tripp, you know that I'll be leaving for the States soon," he said.

"Ooh, that's right. Tell me the dates again."

"Don't worry, I'll write it all down, like I always do. Anyway, I don't see any reason for you to work while I'm on vacation. So I am giving you a vacation, also—paid, of course—"

"Oh, Doctor, that's hardly necessary—"

"Yes, it is, no arguing."

"Oh, Doctor . . . well . . . thank you." She stopped there, before she lost her composure.

Minutes later, a cup of Earl Grey tea with a slice of lemon and scone crumbs and the *Times* on the table in front of him, he was starting to feel part of the world again. Rarely did his early-morning routine change. He would read the newspaper front to back, often tearing out pages containing articles that he would read later. That done, he would go to the cryptic crossword puzzle.

He was on the last page of the second section, when a photograph caught his eye. It was the front of a shop, and it looked familiar. He took a closer look, and a smile crossed his face.

Exhibition planned to honour historic record shop, Dobells

The British Record Shop Archive plans to recapture the halcyon days of the classic Charing Cross Road record shop.

By Alistair Crawford, Entertainment Editor

The exhibition will commemorate one of Britain's greatest record shops, Dobells, that closed its doors in 1989. The exhibit, currently in the funding stage, is planned for the the Chelsea Space, London, and will feature the original shop fittings in situ that have been held in storage for the past 23 years.

Dobells was started in 1946 by Doug Dobell from his father's bookshop in Charing Cross Road. It became one of the premier independent jazz record shops of the time and one of the few record shops outside the USA to stock blues, jazz and folk music.

The organizers are seeking relevant exhibit materials, stories, anecdotes, comments, photographs, videos, posters, etc. Please submit your contributions to their website.

For a moment he was transported back several decades, reflecting on the many occasions when he had visited London for seminars and conferences and long weekends with Megan. Over the years on those trips he'd bought many records and, later, CDs, at Dobells. The store was a Mecca for anyone with a love of jazz, a place to hang out, where you could find records that were available nowhere else, and where occasionally you might run into a famous musician or two. Memories of those long-gone days and the music of that era were powerful, and they rekindled warm feelings of nostalgia and happy times.

If anybody would have knowledge of an obscure band that played around the London suburbs in the early fifties, it would be people who had been associated in one way or another with Dobells: the people organizing the exhibition, musicians, former staff, frequent visitors to the shop. What's more, the call was out already to track down contributors to the exhibit, the very kind of people who might remember a band that played sixty years ago at the Red Lion in North Harrow and, with luck, their young drummer.

Spotting a telephone number at the foot of the page, he picked up the phone. His call was answered in a flash, by a man who introduced himself as "Matt Robbins, Dobells Exhibit."

Kingston told Robbins why he was calling, using a cock-and-bull story about Payne's expatriate sister in Canada trying to determine if he was still alive, after their having lost contact in the fifties. Robbins said that he'd be happy to put word out about Kingston's search via the rapidly growing e-mail database they'd established since going online with the exhibit. Kingston left his contact numbers and thanked Robbins.

No sooner had he put down the phone than it started ringing.

"Lawrence Kingston," he said, thinking it might be Robbins, with a forgotten question.

"There you are. So what have you been up to these past few days? I stopped by and phoned, but your mobile was off."

Kingston smiled. "Andrew, good to hear your voice. Sorry about that. I was only gone for one day. I went down to Gloucestershire again."

"To see Emma, no doubt?"

"Yes. We went back to Payne's house and talked to his sister. And before you get your knickers in a twist, it was all aboveboard, and Grace, Payne's sister, was very cooperative. We even did a walk about the garden."

"This all had to do with the rose, I take it?"

"Of course. As a matter of fact, Emma was all for it. I also had lunch with her the day before—at the Ivy."

"The Ivy? This is getting serious, by the sound of it."

"It's not at all like what you're thinking. She called me saying that she'd come across something unusual that had a bearing on the Alcatraz rose mystery and was coming up to London that day for an eye exam. What would you have done?"

"So what was the 'something unusual'?"

"She'd found a book at Letty's foster parents' house with an inscription inside that could link the dear departed Reggie Payne with the Alcatraz rose."

"Really? I was right, then?"

"About what?"

"When I said that your—quote—innocent investigation into the mystery rose would end up being far from innocent." He laughed. "Lawrence, your plots don't thicken, they coagulate."

Kingston described the inscription, speculating on its possible significance, opining, for Andrew's sake only, that in the end it would probably turn out to be nothing more than a coincidence. The phone call ended amicably, with their agreeing to get together for dinner at the Antelope, three nights hence.

The day before that dinner, Kingston received a call back from Matt Robbins. He said that although the response to his request had been disappointing, he had received an e-mail from one Harry Walters, living in Pinner, who had been a regular at the Red Lion pub in North Harrow back then. He claimed his sister was going out with the trombone player of one particularly popular band at the time. Robbins gave Kingston the man's phone number and wished him good luck.

The phone was answered not with a hello or even the person's name, but with the number called, which Kingston always found off-putting.

"Is this Harry Walters?"

"One and the same."

"My name's Lawrence Kingston. I was just talking to Matt Robbins, the fellow who's organizing the Dobells exhibit. You'd answered his inquiry about a band in North Harrow."

"Oh, right. The lads who used to play at that pub near the train station. The Red Lion."

"They're the ones."

"What would you like to know?"

"Anything and everything you can recall."

"Well, back in the early fifties, me and me mates used to go see them on Saturday nights. They played there regularly, what must 'ave been for quite a few months. Now and then we'd sit and 'ave drinks with 'em when they'd finished playin'. Considering that they were a bunch of youngsters, they were bloody good. Trad jazz, we used to call it in those days—New Orleans revival."

For a second, Kingston flashed back to the crossword puzzle answer a few days ago: REVIVAL. It must have been an omen.

"I remember it well," Kingston said, smiling. "Whenever I got the chance, I used to knock around Soho in those days. I saw most of the bands that were playing at the time: Chris Barber, Ken Colyer, Cy Laurie. I've still got a lot of their records."

"So you're an old geezer, too, then?"

Kingston chuckled. "You could say that. Tell me what you remember about the band members. How many were there?"

"Six, usually."

"How old were they?"

"I wouldn't know. Late teens, I suppose—a couple a little older, maybe. They were a snazzy-looking group, wore white shirts and black ties, not like a lot of today's long-'aired, rock 'n' roll soap dodgers. The trumpet player was Jeremy Lock, of course. And Keith Sheldon played the clarinet. Trombone was a ginger-haired lad called Johnny Daniels. As a matter of fact, my kid sister was knocking around with 'im for a while."

"And the others?"

"Let's see—Billy Wells, banjo. Desmond Scott on double bass, and the drummer, Brian . . . umm . . . Jennings. That's right, Brian Jennings."

Kingston frowned. "Brian Jennings? Not Reggie Payne?"

"Nah. It were Jennings."

"You're sure?"

"Positive."

"Did they ever have another drummer sit in? A substitute?"

"Nah. Not that I'm aware of. And I would 'ave known."

Yes, Kingston thought. *It sounds like he would have.*

"What happened to the band?" he asked. "Did they go on to play elsewhere?"

"I don't think so. I think they just broke up. If they 'ad played somewhere else, I would 'ave found out through me sister."

"Well, Harry, you've been very helpful. I can't thank you enough."

"Your name again?"

"Lawrence Kingston. Maybe we'll see each other at the exhibition. I'd enjoy that."

"Me, too. Don't 'esitate to call me if you 'ave any more questions, Mr. Kingston."

"Don't worry, I will. Thanks."

Kingston put down the phone, muttering "Brian Jennings. That can't be." Was it possible that Walters's memory was faulty? Grace Williams had been so sure—and why not? But what other explanation could there be?

One came to mind immediately. He decided to call Emma and run it by her.

"Let me get this straight, Lawrence," she said, after they'd exchanged greetings. "What you're saying is that Reginald Payne started off life as Brian Jennings?"

"Unless Mr. Walters is mistaken, which, as I said, I doubt very much. I distinctly remember Grace Williams saying that, with different fathers, she and her brother had different surnames. I assumed all along that she meant Williams and Payne."

"That's how I understood it, too."

"Which may mean that she was lying."

"Certainly looks that way. I wonder why?"

"The only answer is that she knows something about her brother that she wants kept secret."

"Right. And the usual reasons people have for changing their names is either vanity—they can no longer live with the surname Crapper—or to hide something unsavory from their past. Occasionally, that something is criminal in nature."

"Grace also said that he owned a company that dealt with the financial markets and that he'd made a lot of money investing. Maybe he'd been indicted for fraud or something like that and decided to start over with a new name. Every time you open a newspaper these days, another executive is off to jail for financial malfeasance of one kind or another."

"If she lied about his name, she could have made all that up, too. Anything's possible, I suppose. For that matter, he could have done time, for all we know."

"If he had, could you find out?"

"When I was on the force I could. Now, I'm not so sure."

"What do you suggest we do next, then?"

"Let's think about it a bit. Another chat with Grace might be in order. I'll see if I can't pull a few strings to find out if there's a sheet on Brian Jennings. If there is, it might clear up a lot of things."

"An arrest record?"

"Yes, sorry."

"Would you like me to talk to Grace Williams?"

"Why not. You're good with the ladies. And I'll work on Jennings."

It wasn't until the following morning that Kingston was able to reach Grace Williams. At first, she seemed pleased that he called again, but her tone of voice changed markedly when he started to ask about Reggie having played in the band. He hadn't told her that he now believed Reggie's real name was Jennings and soon realized that not only wasn't she prepared to discuss the matter further, she was also determined to end the call as quickly as she could.

Her last words were, "Thank you for calling, Dr. Kingston, but the matter is now closed, and I wish to hear no further from you or your companion. It was obviously a mistake to allow you into my home, asking personal questions that are none of your concern. I hope you solve your rose riddle—but I seriously doubt that was the real reason why you came to Beechwood in the first place. Goodbye," she said curtly.

Kingston was disappointed but, in retrospect, he'd doubted that she'd have admitted to lying and would have tried to find a way to cover up or explain why she'd mentioned the band in the first place.

The thought crossed his mind then that her antagonism could have something to do with the inheritance: She didn't want suspicions of any sort becoming public that could affect the outcome of Reggie's last will and testament. And if it were to surface that Reggie had made his money fraudulently . . .

Well. There was a lot of money at stake.

People did a lot worse than lying when it came to those sorts of things.

13

FRIDAY EVENING IN the upstairs dining room at the Antelope, it was almost seven thirty, and still no Andrew. Kingston had arrived promptly at seven—the time they'd agreed on—and his first pint of London Pride ale was no more than a half-inch of froth circling the bottom of the glass. Kingston had a simple rule when it came to punctuality: Fifteen minutes late, with a plausible excuse, was acceptable; anything over thirty minutes, without an explanatory phone call, was either rude or suggested something out of the ordinary, or a mishap of some kind. Andrew was always on time and by now would certainly have called Kingston's mobile or left a message with the landlady or bartender. Now anxious, he was about to call Andrew when his phone rang. It was Andrew.

"Lawrence, I'm sorry about the no-show. Have you eaten yet?"

"No. I was thinking about it, though. Are you all right? I mean, it's unlike you to be this late and I'd figured that there was good reason—something important."

"There is a good reason. A bad reason, more like it. I'm at home. I'll explain when you get here."

"You want me to come now?"

"If you don't mind. And if it doesn't take too long, could you have Zoe fix a quick takeaway for both us. I probably won't eat much, though. I'll leave the front door open."

"Are you sick?"

"In a manner of speaking. I'm more pissed-off than sick. I'll tell you all about it when you get here."

"I'm on my way."

Twenty-five minutes later, Kingston entered Andrew's living room, not knowing what to expect. The room was softly lit and Andrew was stretched out on his leather Corbusier sofa with a blanket over his legs. On the glass-topped coffee table was a half-filled glass of whisky along-side the bottle it came from. He raised a hand when he saw Kingston and let it flop lethargically to his side. "Thanks for buying dinner," he said, with a wincing half smile.

"Not a problem." Kingston placed the paper bag with the food on the table, and sat down to face Andrew. It was only now, in the light from the nearby floor lamp, that he was able to see why Andrew hadn't made it to the Antelope. There was a nasty abrasion on his nearside cheek and a livid bruise on the opposite cheekbone. His lower lip was red and grotesquely swollen.

"Good God, Andrew. What an earth happened?"

"I was mugged."

"You what?"

"Well, not mugged in the regular sense. Done over, I guess."

"Did you report this? Get medical attention?"

Andrew nodded. "The works. A bloke walking a dog saw the whole thing and called the cops, who arrived with an ambulance in tow."

"They didn't take you in to be checked out?"

"They were going to at first, but after a thorough going over by the paramedics, they decided that I was none the worse for wear and let me go home. It's painful, all right, but it looks worse than it is."

"You weren't robbed?"

Andrew sighed. "No. I simply asked the wrong question, obviously to the wrong guy—a mistake on my part. Could have been a lot worse, I guess."

"What an earth did you ask him? I'm confused."

"Pour yourself a drink, Lawrence, and get a couple of plates and some cutlery and I'll tell you while we have supper. What is it, by the way? Nothing too chewy, I hope?"

"Two mini steak-and-ale pies and peach crumble with crème fraîche. Will that do?"

"Good choice. And get a bottle of whatever you want from the wine case."

A few minutes later with the pies and mashed potatoes on the coffee table alongside two glasses of Côtes du Rhône, Andrew elaborated on his misfortune.

"I was just leaving to meet you when I saw this chap ringing your doorbell. He was wearing a suit and tie and was empty-handed—not as if he were peddling anything. I asked him who he was looking for. He turned round and looked down at me—he was on the porch, and I was at the bottom of the steps. 'None of your bloody business,' he said, starting to come down the steps toward me. He didn't look threatening, or anything like that, but I decided not to say anything more, just in case. He was about my size, but I could tell by his tight-fitting suit that he was very muscular. Anyway, by this time he was on the bottom step and I was about move aside to let him go on his way, when he jabbed me on the side of my face. I was so taken by surprise that I couldn't defend myself quickly enough. He was very fast. I tried to dodge his next punch but couldn't and ended up on the pavement, twisting my ankle." Andrew paused to take a sip of wine and forced a smile. "I hope I'm not boring you."

Kingston shook his head. "From the way you describe it, he could quite easily have inflicted serious damage if he'd wanted to."

Andrew put the glass down. "I was coming to that. While I was seeing stars, curled up on the pavement, my face hurting like hell and praying he wasn't about to give me a farewell boot, he looked down at me and said, 'Tell your friend to mind his own business, too. He'll know what I mean.'"

For what seemed a long time, Kingston stared at Andrew in disbelief. "I don't know what to say," he muttered, at last. "It doesn't make any sense. Why?"

"It makes perfect sense. It doesn't take a genius to figure it out. You, of all people . . ." He paused, as if waiting for a response. Kingston said nothing, still shocked by what he'd just heard.

"Someone—or some people—is starting to get nervous about this new investigation of yours," Andrew continued. "This was a shot across the bow. These kinds of people know damned well that threatening to harm friends and loved ones can be far more effective than going after you. It's one of the oldest methods of persuasion in the book."

"Yes, I know all that. But it can't possibly have anything to do with what Emma and I have been doing these last couple of weeks. All of our efforts have been directed solely toward helping Letty, and a harmless search for a damned rose." He shook his head. "There's been nobody to intimidate or threaten."

Andrew rested his fork and looked up at Kingston. Perhaps it was the swollen lip, but Kingston thought he caught a wincing smile when Andrew spoke.

"That's what you think. But they—whoever 'they' are—obviously think differently. You've unwittingly struck a nerve somewhere."

"It would appear so."

"I'm not blaming you, Lawrence, if that's what you're thinking. In a couple of weeks I'll be none the worse for wear and let's hope that'll be the end of it. It's you that worries me."

"I don't think—"

"Let me finish, because there's one more thing worth mentioning."

"What's that?"

"Lately, I've noticed a car that's been cruising or parked in our neighborhood. A silver Volvo XC90, newish. At first, I thought nothing of it—a new resident, probably. But now I'm wondering if I should have been more suspicious—made note of the license plate. I'm thinking that I might have been right."

"Meaning that they were watching us?"

"You, more likely. This means that they could've followed you and Emma down to Gloucestershire, to Payne's house, for whatever that's worth."

Kingston reached for the Côtes du Rhône and topped up their wineglasses. He knew that Andrew was closer to the truth than he wanted to admit and had decided that further discussion along these lines would serve no purpose.

"I must tell Emma right away," he said. "She has to know."

Andrew nodded.

"You'll be okay, for tonight?"

"Sure. I can move around slowly. I'll take some more codeine before I hit the sack."

"Would you like me to have Mrs. Tripp come in tomorrow? She could fix you lunch and dinner."

"No, thanks. She's a wonderful woman, but all her fussing will give me the collywobbles. Don't worry, I'll be fine. I'll give you a call in the morning. Let me know what Emma says. I'd like to see her again one of these days."

Kingston nodded. "I'll work on that."

"Oh, and by the way, do please thank Mrs. Tripp for the scones."

Ten minutes later, in his office, he had Emma on the phone.

"Hello, Lawrence. Didn't expect to hear from you so soon. What's up?"

"Sorry to call so late. Something nasty happened tonight that you should know about."

He told her about Andrew getting roughed up, and the threat by the man who'd attacked him. She listened without interrupting, a characteristic that he had come to appreciate.

"Is this the point when we turn the whole thing over to your people?" he asked, when finished.

Emma hesitated before answering. "From what you just told me, the Met is already involved. But chances are that unless they start asking more questions about the veiled threat and your indirect involvement, it will be shelved as just another altercation in a city that has thousands a week. On the more serious side, the fact that someone has a tail on you—and me, too, probably—moves things up a notch or two. Someone's obviously getting a little more than fidgety about our sniffing around and wants to put a stop to it."

"What do you suggest we do, then? Call the whole thing off?"

"If we ignore the threat and keep digging, we run a real risk of getting the same or worse treatment. If the information that this person, or persons, is trying to protect is such that it could destroy his reputation or his life, then he's not going to stop now. You may be right, Lawrence. We may have reached the point where we have to tell my former boss or your friend Inspector Sheffield what's going on."

"Do you want to do that? I mean, make the call?"

"Let's sleep on it. I'm expecting the results of the Brian Jennings search any day now. It'd be nice to know who he really is and what he's done."

"If anything."

"That's always a possibility."

Kingston smiled. "You could always try Facebook."

"Oh, sure. Here's a bloke who's spent most of his life as a recluse with a phony name, and he's going to post his life story on the Internet looking for 'friends' and 'likes'?"

"It was a bad joke."

"I know. But when it comes to that stuff, I'm old-fashioned, too. Fifteen minutes of fame for anyone living and breathing who has a computer or smartphone."

"Couldn't agree more. We're reaching a point where we love our phones more than we love each other."

"By the way, on a cheerier note, I'm coming up to London again next week, on Tuesday. It's a little short notice, but I'd like to return the favor and treat you to lunch before you take off for the States. You're still leaving on Thursday, I take it?"

"Yes, Thursday's the day—and I'd enjoy that very much."

"I've heard that the Tate Gallery restaurant is very nice, and I haven't been there since I was in my teens."

"It's closed for refurbishments, I'm afraid. But we can find somewhere nearby. Shepherd's is good."

"Whatever. I leave it up to you to decide. You'd better not trust me when it comes to restaurants." She chuckled.

"I just remembered something. When I saw Andrew tonight, he asked about you."

"Is he going to be okay?"

"Yes, he's fine, though I doubt very much that he'll be up for lunch. But time permitting, we could stop by afterward, just to say hello. Cheer him up a bit."

"I'd enjoy that. I'm free after eleven thirty. Let me know where and when we should meet."

14

WHEN ANDREW OPENED his front door on Tuesday afternoon, his face revealed in full daylight, Kingston could see that his cheek bruise was still purplish, while the abrasion on the other side of his face had improved measurably, and his lip was no longer swollen.

Lunch with Emma at Shepherd's had not disappointed, even though most of their conversation had been devoted to Andrew's misadventure and to speculation as to the future of their nascent investigation of the Alcatraz rose.

After a few words of welcome, Andrew ushered Kingston and Emma into his contemporary-furnished living room, where they sat and exchanged pleasantries for a minute or so.

"So how was lunch?" Andrew asked. "I've never been to Shepherd's."

"It was very nice, I must say," Emma replied. "For me, one of the treats in coming up to London is the restaurants. Lawrence tells me that you've wined and dined your way through a good deal of them and that you're a regular Gordon Ramsay in the kitchen. I don't mean that in an expletive sense, of course," she smiled.

Andrew shrugged modestly. "I wouldn't go that far. And talking of wine, could I offer you something to drink?"

"Thanks, but no, Andrew. We just polished of a bottle of Châteauneuf-du-Pape."

"Lawrence?"

"No, thanks. I'm fine."

"So what do you make of my being duffed up, Emma?" Andrew asked. "I imagine you've seen a lot of this type of thing in your day."

"I have. After pub closing, it's commonplace, usually over something trivial and nearly always resolved on the spot. Yours is different. Perpetrated as some kind of threat of further action takes it into a more serious category of misdemeanor. But in your case, with the assailant gone, and no vehicle identification, it's hard, if not impossible, to follow up. You were right, though. I think we can agree on one thing: There's no question that your being assaulted was meant to be a not-so-subtle warning for us—Lawrence and me—to cease all further activity where Reginald Payne is concerned."

Andrew sighed, shaking his head. "It's about bloody time. He won't listen to me, but maybe you can knock some sense into him."

Emma nodded and glanced at Kingston. "I've been working on it."

Kingston listened silently; it was futile to protest or raise any pleas of defense, even signs of resentment.

"So what do you plan to do now?" Andrew asked Emma.

She looked at Kingston.

"We're pulling the plug," he replied. "We talked about it at lunch. There's really no choice."

"That makes me happy," Andrew said, looking anything but. "Which doesn't mean I wouldn't like to find the bastard, and whoever he's working for."

"It's frustrating for both of us," Emma said, "because we were starting to make progress."

Kingston was pulling on his earlobe. "With our dropping out, I doubt we'll ever find him. The only person who might have been able to help is Grace Williams, and there's no welcome mat there anymore, not unless she has a divine manifestation of some kind."

"I don't think she's the sort," Emma said.

On the word "sort," a phone started ringing. It took a couple of seconds for Kingston to recognize the musical ringtone: the first bars of "Without You." Emma's phone, he realized. She got up, taking it from her blazer pocket as she walked across the room to the window, where she stood with her back to them, though still within earshot.

"This is Emma . . . Oh, hello Paul."

Kingston and Andrew watched for a moment, as she moved to the other side of the window, lightly holding the curtain, looking out. As much as Kingston would have liked to eavesdrop on the conversation, he knew that Andrew would—and rightly so—find it inexcusable manners. Instead, he attempted to make small talk with Andrew in a voice not loud enough to distract Emma yet low enough to catch the drift of her one-sided conversation.

"You did—that's great," she said, starting to pace slowly across the end of the room, now oblivious of Kingston and Andrew. She stopped suddenly.

"Good grief. I should say . . . Jackpot is right . . . Are you sure about this?"

She looked down at the carpet for a second. "It changes everything . . . Thanks for doing this for me, Paul . . . and please keep me posted on how it develops."

By now Kingston and Andrew had given up trying to talk and were exchanging quizzical looks.

"Yes, I will for sure," she said. "Thanks again."

She turned off the phone, put it back in her pocket, and stood for a moment staring into middle space before turning and coming back to join them.

"You won't believe this," she said, her expression ambiguous.

"Good news, I hope," Kingston said, trying, but not succeeding, to mask his curiosity.

"Putting it mildly. That was Paul Anderson. He's an old friend on the Gloucester force. He put a trace on Brian Jennings, and guess what?"

Kingston shook his head. "What?"

"You've heard of the Great Highway Robbery?" Emma asked.

"Of course," Andrew said. "Who hasn't?"

"Well, our mysterious Mr. Jennings, it turns out, was one of the ringleaders."

Kingston was speechless.

"I needn't remind you, I'm sure," she continued, "that they never found him—or any of the money."

15

OCTOGENARIAN ROSE FANCIER, reclusive gardener, and one of Britain's most wanted. It was like a bad movie script, Kingston thought.

"The Great Highway Robbery." Andrew shook his head. "I can't believe it."

"It's true," Emma said. "Moneywise, it was the second-largest heist in British history: sixteen million pounds in today's money. The Great Train Robbery, several years later, was the biggest."

Kingston frowned. "But it was when? Back in the fifties? Surely—"

"There's no mistake, Lawrence. Paul said that Jennings was twenty-two at the time, which would make him close to eighty right now—about the same age as Reggie is—Reggie *was*, I should say. It all fits. The years he was missing, where his money really came from, why the anonymity, Beechwood—all of it."

"Look, I can understand the significance of this," Andrew interjected, "but will someone tell me what led up to this? What have you two been up to behind my back?"

"Very little," Kingston replied. "All we did was interview Payne's sister, and found out that in his late teens he played in a band in Harrow. I got lucky and found an old jazz groupie who knew the band at the time. He said the lad's name wasn't Payne—it was Jennings, Brian Jennings. Emma persuaded a former colleague to put a trace on him, and Bob's your uncle!"

From his befuddled expression, it was clear that Andrew was not buying Kingston's glib explanation. "This is becoming like a riddle wrapped in a mystery inside an enigma. Wouldn't this Grace woman have known this all along? She was his sister, for God's sake."

"Seems clear now that she did. And who knows what else she's covering up."

"It could explain why she skipped off to Canada for twenty five odd years, too," Kingston added. "But none of this is going to help us much now. She refuses to have anything more to do with us."

Emma was wearing her policewoman expression. "Now that it involves a much more serious criminal matter, all that could change. There's still Payne's murder, though; we can't lose sight of that. Now that we know who he really was, we can't overlook the possibility that whoever did him in might have been connected to the robbery. Paul said that there were six or seven in the gang, two never apprehended, and that there were other shadowy characters who played behind-the-scenes roles in the crime, too. None of them was ever identified or caught either."

Andrew leaned forward. "This is getting *very* complicated."

"And it's going to get even more so. I think we've only scratched the surface," Emma said, looking at her watch. "I think I should call a cab, Lawrence. I don't want to miss the four o'clock train."

"But—"

"I know," Emma said, her patience clearly exhausted. "There's a lot to talk about. But the next one's not until six. And we won't solve any of this tonight, of that you can be certain."

Ten minutes later, with Emma gone, Kingston and Andrew sat with glasses of Bass Pale Ale trying to weigh the ramifications of her bolt from the blue. Kingston remembered sketchy details of the Great Highway Robbery, but Andrew, being younger, was only vaguely familiar with it. Kingston related his hazy recollection of that rainy afternoon in Berkshire, nearly sixty years ago, when £800,000 was hijacked from an armored security van.

"Well, it looks as if your Alcatraz rose will remain a mystery—for now, anyway," Andrew said, when Kingston was finished.

"You're right. The damned rose." Kingston sighed. He had almost forgotten about it, what with everything else that was suddenly happening. "One thing's for sure. I'm convinced more than ever that Brian

Jennings, alias Reggie Payne, wrote the notes in that book. That he's a link between the rose and the robbery."

"Why don't you have the handwriting analyzed? Compare it with Reggie's."

"Good idea," Kingston said, then frowned. "Though I seriously doubt that Grace Williams is going to part with samples of his handwriting. By now it would be difficult to find his writing elsewhere, I would imagine."

Andrew wasn't finished. "But why would he give the book to Letty's mother?"

"We don't know for sure that he did. Just because it was found on her bookshelf doesn't mean it was hers. As Emma insists, it could have been given to her husband, or bought at a boot sale, for that matter."

"Have you considered that Letty's mother could be tangled up in this somehow? She did disappear, after all."

Kingston frowned. "You mean that she was mixed up in the robbery? Fiona?"

"Yes." Andrew nodded.

"That's not possible. The robbery took place in the late fifties. I don't think she'd even been born then. If she had, she was a toddler."

Andrew looked exasperated as he stood and picked up his empty glass. "I meant later on, but just forget it. I don't know why we're even discussing it anymore. Isn't it case closed now, as far you and Emma are concerned?"

"It rather looks that way, I'm afraid," Kingston replied, adding silently to himself: *For the moment.*

Back in his flat, the hum of the vacuum cleaner reminded Kingston that Mrs. Tripp was there. With his brain still whirring like a Cuisinart, the last thing he was in the mood for was a detailed report on her cat Tinker's health issues. He would be polite, yet forceful, make a pot of tea, and disappear as quickly as possible into his office, where he would scour the Internet, searching out every website he could find that had information about the Great Highway Robbery.

Fortunately, he didn't have to visit many sites. He quickly found that Wikipedia had devoted more than a dozen pages to the subject, covering just about every aspect of the crime. Skipping pages and data irrelevant to his purposes, he printed out ten pages and started to read them carefully, discarding insignificant passages, charts, and graphics as he went. Ten minutes later, he'd culled and edited them down to seven pages. These, he condensed further, ending up with a clear picture of the crime itself—and Brian Jennings's role in it.

He took a long sip of tea and started to read once again:

Summary

The Great Highway Robbery is the name given to the £800,000 (evaluation of £16 million in today's money) armored van robbery committed in April 1957, in Berkshire, England. The bulk of the money was never recovered. Although members of the gang and one of the guards inside the van were armed with handguns, no serious injuries resulted. It is listed as the second-largest robbery by value in British history. The Great Train Robbery, approximately ten years later, ranks first. Much of the information provided here was obtained from transcripts of the trial, individuals connected with the case, various law enforcement press releases, and newspaper articles, letters, biographies, and books written by both investigators and three of the robbers.

The armed robbery

The robbery took place at 3:15 on April 15, 1957, on a quiet stretch of road near the village of Ruscombe, situated between Swindon and Reading. On that day it was raining heavily. The armored van, transporting thirty canvas bags, containing £800,000 in English banknotes of varying denominations, collected that day from eight regional Berkshire and Wiltshire banks, was on its way to a central reserve bank in London. Three uniformed guards were assigned to the small van. A driver and his assistant occupied the front cabin, and a third guard, carrying a sidearm, sat in the rear with the sacks of money.

The first of two cars, occupied by gang members wearing black balaclavas over their heads, took the van driver by surprise, forcing the van off the road, where it was partially hidden among bracken and small trees. Immediately, the van was surrounded by three of the gang members, one of them armed with a pistol, the others with sledgehammers. Quickly, the two guards in the front were overpowered, without a shot being fired. By that time, a second car, containing more gang members, had pulled up in the rear of the van. Three of the assailants jumped out of the car and hooked up chains to the van's rear door handles and through the car's front axle. The driver reversed, tearing the doors off the van, revealing the armed guard and the sacks of money. The guard got off one shot, which missed the closest gang member, and he was quickly disabled with a blow from a pickaxe handle. With the car driver now helping, the sacks of money were hustled into the car. Simultaneously, all three guards were bound with rope to their seats and their mouths taped. The keys were taken from the van's ignition, and within seconds, both cars took off. It was later reported that not a single word was spoken among the robbers during the entire operation, which took less than ten minutes, and that neither car bore a number plate. The van and its trussed-up but unharmed guards were spotted approximately a half hour later by a passing truck driver, who had stopped to investigate.

The robbers, and their associates

The gang was led by Ronnie Butler and abetted by Brian Jennings, Sean Kennedy, Charlie Gilbert, and Michael Jones. The driver was Richard Ball and the lookout man, Pete Heatherton. The organizers, planners, and behind-the-scenes participants were never identified or caught, despite the fact that all but two of the robbers were subsequently arrested, underwent rigorous interrogations, and served lengthy jail sentences.

The two-page section went on to link each robber to his specific role in the crime and to describe them in some length—including age, background, occupation, and previous criminal record. It also described the extensive organization and planning of the meticulous operation, proposing that it was masterminded by one or more influential, shadowy individuals and possibly crime syndicates. Kingston focused first on the section that discussed Jennings, for obvious reasons, and second, on Butler, the ringleader:

Brian Edward Jennings was born in 1935 (22 years of age at the time of the robbery) to Thomas and Doris Jennings in Battersea, London. Among his childhood friends were Charlie Gilbert, who, as a teenager had been up before the magistrates several times on petty crimes, and Geoffrey Miller, who spent his juvenile years in Borstal, a youth detention center. Jennings never married and had little to do with women, either in his adolescence or years to follow. In his late teens he met Michael Jones and Richard Ball, two young car mechanics–turned–car thieves, who eventually introduced him to Ronald Butler, a full-time criminal who had spent a succession of short spells in jails for minor offenses. Up to that point, it appeared that Jennings had managed to either steer clear of involvement in any of his friends' criminal activities or he'd been lucky escaping the long arm of the law. Jennings was never apprehended.

Kingston took a break, heading into the kitchen to add hot water to the teapot, then returned to his office and continued reading where he'd left off.

Ronald James Butler, who was 35 years of age at the time of the robbery, had turned to crime for fun and profit at an early age. As a youth, he and his mates stole merchandise from lorries, stole cars, and sold various goods on the postwar black market. Butler was the unofficial leader of the gang and was believed to have conceived the idea to rob the van. A year or so before the robbery, it is purported that he was introduced to a man known only as the "Manager," a shadowy figure who had no contact of any kind with the other robbers. It was the scuttlebutt that in addition to his having close ties to London's major crime syndicates, that this "Manager" had connections in law enforcement and even ties with prominent political figures. It remains unknown if Butler shared his idea first with Brian Jennings, and it was unclear if they had worked together on previous crimes. They were the only two robbers who were never apprehended, each walking away with close to £80,000. Today's valuation, approximately £1.6 million or more.

Butler wasn't married, but when questioned by the police his girlfriend at the time denied having any knowledge of the robbery or Butler's criminal activities, and was never called as a witness at any of the trials. As with Brian Jennings, it is assumed that Butler had managed to flee the country immediately after the crime, and has spent the subsequent years living with a new identity in a foreign country.

Kingston stopped reading, his mind bucking the implausible sixty-year leap back to 1957. He would read all the pages again, but with so much ground to cover and so much information to digest, any sort of review would have to wait for later. The most important information he'd gleaned from this first pass, though—other than the "Manager" and those who participated in the behind-the-scenes operation of the robbery—was that only two of the men were never apprehended and both could still be alive: Butler and Jennings.

Kingston did a mental calculation: Jennings would be in his late seventies and Butler in his late eighties by now—a little old to be running around intimidating and murdering people or, possibly, now dead. The same could be true of the organizers. Just how many of them were still living was a big question mark but he knew the answer was probably few.

Perhaps Emma could find out more about them. As he thought on it, he realized that he was deluding himself thinking she would still have access to police information on the case. By now, that door would surely have been closed. With an unsolved murder and the cobwebs being dusted off the files of one of Britain's most sensational crimes, the case would be back in the hands of the top law enforcement agencies in the country. Emma might prefer it that way. Everything considered, perhaps it was best for both of them.

He had to begin thinking seriously about the new life stretching ahead of him, though it was still just a tad early to start down that road. He had his visit to the States to finalize first. That would give him plenty to occupy his mind, not the least of which was making sure that his relationship with Emma didn't die slowly on the vine. He liked and respected her too much to let that happen.

He put the papers in a desk drawer, put the iMac to sleep, and went to the kitchen to make a list of things to buy from Partridges and Sainsbury's; not much, since he was going to be gone for a while. Staring into the half-empty fridge and making mental note of what he needed, an intriguing idea struck him. Distracted for a moment, he dismissed it as being frivolous and went to the table to jot down a shopping list. Putting pen to paper, he looked up at the ceiling: The idea was back. This time, he let it take shape, weighing its viability and the chances of its producing tangible or useful results. He knew exactly what Andrew would say about it and how Emma would feel. *Forget it,* he decided. Putting the idea out of his mind, he finished his list.

Minutes later he stepped out onto the square, keeping his eyes open for a cab. He started walking; he would easily find one on Sloane Street in less than a minute. Crossing the road at the corner of the square, he saw the familiar redbrick Charles Hotel and the row of international flags angled over the covered entrance. In the center, waving lazily in the light breeze, was the Union Jack—and next to it, the Stars and Stripes.

The idea had returned, and now he gave it full rein. He made up his mind: He was going to San Francisco. And why not? It was, without question, his favorite city in the United States. It was geographically breathtaking: multicultural, with world-class museums and art galleries, internationally acclaimed symphony and opera. It had more restaurants by far than any other U.S. city, hands down the best food—mostly from surrounding farms, dairies, and the Pacific Ocean, and—a mere forty-five minutes away—the magical blue-skied Sonoma and Napa wine valleys. It wasn't entirely coincidental that Andy Harris, the Alcatraz historian, lived there, too. It all made perfect sense.

And not to mention, that by the time Andrew and Emma found out, it would be too late for them to protest.

A black cab pulled up to the curb and Kingston got in and slammed the door closed.

"Where to, guv?" the cabbie asked.

"San Francisco," he said.

"'Wot?" The cabbie turned around and looked at him strangely.

"Sorry." Kingston smiled. "Duke of York Square, Partridges," he said. And then, more quietly, "That'll do for now."

That evening, he called British Airways and changed his itinerary to include a four-day stay in San Francisco.

16

San Francisco, two weeks later.

WITH EARL GREY tea in a china cup and saucer, Kingston sat reading a Bay Area restaurant guide in the Union Street Inn's garden. The small, congenial, and unexpectedly luxurious bed-and-breakfast, a ten-minute cab ride from downtown, had been recommended by an acquaintance who worked at Kew Gardens, a young woman who had stayed there on her honeymoon. The British couple that owned it knew every nook and cranny of the city and its nontourist restaurants, and was equally familiar with the Sonoma and Napa Valleys. It suited him to a T. The fact that he had his choice of the Wild Rose Room or the English Garden Room—he chose the former—further persuaded him of the rightness of his side trip to San Francisco.

Kingston couldn't have been in better spirits. His holiday with Julie and Brandon had exceeded his most ambitious expectations, and from the very beginning, when he arrived bleary-eyed at Sea-Tac airport, it was apparent that they were as close to a perfect match as could be wished for. Julie was the same lovable Julie: vivacious, full of life, and with her mother's ever-present winsome smile. Brandon impressed him from the start. By central casting standards he was leading man caliber: a couple of inches shorter than Kingston, straw-colored hair, and a tennis player's physique. The even tan, Kingston guessed, came from sailing, according to Julie his favorite pastime. When he wasn't working long hours running his small but highly successful accounting business that catered mostly to clients from Seattle's ubiquitous technology companies, he was out on Puget Sound.

Their two-bedroom waterfront house on Lake Washington was contemporary in décor, with accents of more traditional furnishings: Oriental rugs, and several pieces of antique Japanese furniture, including some very fine country Tansu chests. On the second day, Kingston was pleasantly surprised when Julie announced that Brandon was going to be the chef de cuisine that evening. When he learned that Brandon was also savvy about and had a keen appreciation for wines, their friendship was sealed.

His days were spent mostly with Julie, who had taken time off to play tourist with her father. They wandered leisurely through the old part of the city, the waterfront and its famous markets, several museums, taking in the architecture, sights, and smells. One day they sailed the island-dotted waters off Seattle on Brandon's ketch, a new and exhilarating experience for Kingston. Another day they took a ferry trip to Bainbridge Island for lunch, shopping, and to visit galleries. Of particular interest to Kingston, one afternoon was spent exploring Washington Park Arboretum. They dined at Seattle's better restaurants, attended the symphony, and there was Brandon's well-kept surprise: a night baseball game at Safeco Field. Alone one afternoon, Kingston had taken a guided tour, roaming the spooky underground passages and alleys beneath the streets of old downtown Seattle. He was genuinely sorry when the time came to say goodbye. He couldn't have wished for a better time and, most important of all, there was no doubt in his mind that Julie had picked the right man.

It had been a wonderful vacation. But now . . .

He put down the restaurant guide and stood. It was time to get back to work.

He and Andy Harris had agreed to meet at Sam's Grill, one of San Francisco's oldest and most iconic restaurants. When Kingston stepped inside, he was met by a wall of chattering men and women squeezed into a small reception area, alongside a long mahogany bar. Most of the men—many holding drinks—were wearing suits, and the few women were also dressed for business. Kingston edged his way in, looking for someone resembling a maître d'. With his height, he had a slight advantage and was about to elbow his way to the other side of the room, glimpsing white-clothed tables, when he saw an equally tall man with military-cropped gray hair wearing a navy blazer and open-necked shirt, waving to him from several feet away.

Kingston waved back.

"Dr. Kingston, I presume?" The man smiled. "Andy Harris."

The two shook hands. "A pleasure to meet you," Kingston said.

"And you. Your timing's impeccable, Doctor."

"Lawrence, please."

He nodded. "Okay, Lawrence. It appears our table is ready."

He gestured toward a black-coated waiter, who was motioning to them, and within a couple of minutes they were seated at the far end of the main dining room, well away from the hubbub. As if out of nowhere, another waiter appeared and took their order for a bottle of Chateau St. Jean Fumé Blanc, placed two menus on the table, and disappeared with a gravelly, "Thank you, gentlemen."

"So how was Seattle?" Harris asked. "Your future son-in-law?"

"It was truly wonderful, couldn't have been better," Kingston replied, with a gleam of pride in his eyes. "He's a really nice chap. We got on famously together. As for the two of them, the cliché 'made for each other' is the best way I can put it. I wish I could have spent more time with both of them, but you know how that goes."

Harris nodded. "Plenty of time for that in the years to come."

"Right. They're planning to come over to England next year."

Further conversation about Julie and Brandon and Kingston's reacquainting himself with Seattle ended with their studying and exchanging thoughts on the menu, moving on to a round of small talk, mostly about San Francisco and London.

As if divining the suitable moment, the waiter returned with the wine, pouring it and taking their orders with an atypical economy of words, which Kingston appreciated.

"So, the plot thickens, eh?" Harris said, sipping his wine. "Quite a hornets' nest you've stepped on, Lawrence. You start off looking for a rose and end up getting bloodied by thorns."

"Not literally, but as I mentioned in my letter, my friend Andrew did."

"Yeah, that was tough. How is he?"

"Oh, he's fine."

"That's good."

"By the way, I hope I didn't saddle you with too much information." Kingston had e-mailed Andy, telling him about the recent developments, along with a copy of the abbreviated history of the Great Highway Robbery, as well some notes he had made concerning the rose. "It was difficult to know what to leave out."

"No, not at all," Harris said. "You did an excellent job, and I can see where your reputation comes from. A while ago, I took the liberty of reading your life story on Google. I hope you don't mind."

"Not at all. Most of it's reasonably accurate, I suppose."

"Having read the material several times, I have to agree with you that it's possible—even though a bit remote—there could be a connection between the Belmaris rose growing on Alcatraz and one or more of the people involved in the robbery. Incidentally, your summary of the heist and everything that followed was unbelievable. Like a British movie."

Kingston nodded. "It wasn't difficult, most of it was easy to find online. So much has been written about it: books, hundreds of serialized newspaper and magazine stories, and the Internet, of course."

"I know what you mean. It's reminiscent of our Great Brink's Robbery in Boston. Oddly enough, that was in the fifties, too. I believe three or four movies were based on it."

"The name's familiar. I'll have to read up on it."

"So tell me what's your plan now. You're touring the island, you said?"

"Yes. The last tour this afternoon, so I have to keep an eye on the clock."

"Don't worry, I'll get you out of here in plenty of time. Cabs are easy and it's only a ten-minute journey this time of day."

"It's going to be interesting to revisit the scene of the crime, as it were."

"The crime." Harris smiled. "With the police taking over, what is it, exactly, you hope to achieve?"

"As far as the murder and anything to do with the robbery—nothing. But I still want to know how that damned rose crossed three thousand miles of ocean and almost another three thousand overland, to end up where it did."

"Well—" Harris frowned. "The warden would have been the only one with the authority to order plants and such, unless he delegated that responsibility—but even then it would only be up to his secretary. And that begs the question: How the hell would he have learned about such a rarified rose? Not only that, but from everything you've told me, it would be damned near impossible to obtain one—even at a price. Would he have known all that?"

"To be honest, I rather doubt it. Not unless he was an avid collector. Frankly, if I wanted to lay my hands on one, I wouldn't even know where to start, and I've been involved in plants and roses most of my life."

"If it wasn't the warden, then you've got me."

Kingston downed the last of his wine and placed the glass on the table.

"In one of our earlier conversations, I remember your saying that, in addition to the warden's garden, there were a couple of others that good-conduct prisoners were permitted to work in."

"That's right. Over the near-thirty years that Alcatraz was a federal penitentiary, there were a few places on the island where there were what you would call gardens. One, as you said, was the garden surrounding the warden's house. There was another, larger one near the old NCO cottages, with a greenhouse that was used for propagation and whatever else they do in greenhouses—you would know all that, of course. A third, I remember, was above the roadside wall, planted over some old foundations that were never removed. I'm not sure if any prisoners worked in the warden's garden, but a few privileged inmates were allowed to work regularly in the other gardens. In fact, there was one whose name escapes me—a convicted counterfeiter—who built a garden shed that still stands."

"A counterfeiter and a gardener." Kingston smiled. "A rare combination."

"He was a gifted man, all right. But that's about all I can tell you." Andy paused, shaking his head. "You know, Lawrence, over the years I've been asked the damnedest questions but very few about plants."

Kingston smiled back. "I beg to differ with Kipling when it comes to the world's oldest profession. I believe that gardening came first."

Harris chuckled. "It would certainly make more sense. But not as much fun, maybe?"

"I can't argue against that," Kingston said.

Harris snapped his fingers. "Ryan Matthews, that was the gardener's name, the counterfeiter. As kids, we were forbidden to talk to the prisoners, but I chatted with him briefly now and then. He was an exceptionally intelligent man and genuinely friendly."

"How many wardens were there over the years?"

"Four, with very different and progressively more lenient management styles. The last two, Madigan and Blackwell, were the least strict—more humanitarian might be a better way to put it. Naturally they were the more popular, too. I think it would be fair to say that under their stewardship, more inmates were permitted to work on various tasks outside the prison walls. You, of all people, can appreciate that working in the gardens was one of the most sought-after jobs."

"What years were they running the prison?"

Harris had to think for a moment. "From 1955 to 1963."

"Which happen to be the years following the robbery," Kingston noted, sipping his wine. "Is there any evidence—records and such—to suggest that either of them was personally involved in gardening—a hands-on sort?"

Harris smiled and shook his head. "Lawrence, give up on the warden idea. It's not going to wash, take my word for it."

"I suppose you're right. It's too convenient an answer."

"Although—" Harris paused, frowning. "I just remembered something. Thinking of the two wardens reminded me. The secretary who served through both their terms was Elliot Hofmann. I'd have to check, but I'm pretty sure he had a hand in developing the gardens when he first came on board. I seem to recall that he was the one who influenced the warden to increase the number of privileged inmates allowed to work outside."

"Really?"

"Yeah. So if it helps any, it's possible he could've received permission from the warden to go ahead and purchase seeds and plants. But why would he have wanted to get his hands on a rare rose from another continent?"

"You'd be amazed, Andy. Gardeners are among the most obsessive collectors in the world and sometimes go to extremes or pay huge sums for a rare plant. Not long ago, a Chinese orchid was sold at auction for £160,000—that's nearly a quarter million dollars. You might not believe it but there are serious collectors out there who'll pay up to $50,000 for a cycad."

"A cycad?"

"It's the oldest living plant on the planet, over 250 million years old. It's sort of a cult plant. There are stories about collectors traipsing all over the world to find mature ones. I read about one man risking his life going into a guerrilla-held jungle area in Colombia to get a specimen. Needless to say, like arms and drugs, there's an illegal trade in cycads, which, as we all know leads to smuggling and host of other crimes."

"Jeez, all for a damned plant? That's hard to imagine. So, what you're suggesting is that if Hofmann was fanatical about roses, he might have gone to similar extremes to get his hands on the world's rarest rose?"

"Maybe not quite that far. It could've been quite a trophy, though."

Harris was slow to answer, his expression muddled and mildly incredulous.

"I just don't think that's the case, here," he said. "We have an expression for it, you're 'whistling Dixie.' These men—the wardens, the secretary, and the correctional officers—had far too much on their minds, huge responsibilities to deal with each day. I just can't buy it."

"Perhaps you're right," Kingston replied. "I'm probably overreaching. But bear with me for a moment, and let's stay with Hofmann. Assuming that he had set his mind on getting the rose, where could he have learned of its existence? Books, garden magazines, nursery catalogs, other members of the staff—there would have been plenty of sources. And what about all the civilian employees?"

"As for civilians, I'm rusty when it comes to the numbers, but I believe that, at any given time, there were sixty families living on the island, about a hundred children. The number of guards hovered around a hundred, too."

"So any of those people could have learned of the rose and told Hofmann," Kingston said, breaking off as the waiter appeared with two bowls of steaming clam chowder. Once placed in front of them, he checked the table to make sure everything was as it should be, then retreated with a polite, "Enjoy."

For a few minutes, all thoughts of Alcatraz and the robbery were cast aside as they enjoyed their soup. It wasn't until the main courses arrived—boned Rex sole for Kingston and sautéed shellfish for Harris—that they picked up where they'd left off.

"Going back to what you were saying, Lawrence—even discounting the fact that the rose was the best-kept horticultural secret of its day—I don't think we will ever know how Hofmann or the warden would have learned about it—or if they even did."

Kingston detected a subtle change in Harris's tone. Was he starting to lose interest? he wondered.

He rested his fork and looked at Andy with a shamefaced smile. "I hope I'm not boring you to tears. Sometimes I get carried away without realizing it. Perhaps we should change the subject for a while?"

"Not at all, Lawrence. I'm just as curious as you to get to the bottom of the mystery. Ninety percent of all the questions I ever get asked are about the prisoners and the escapes—Al Capone and the Birdman, the sensational stuff. So it's actually a pleasant change for me to discuss other aspects of life on the island. Though, from what you've told me, I can now see that gardening can sometimes be a hazardous occupation."

"I haven't told you about the plant hunters yet, Andy. Some of those stories would make Indiana Jones's hair stand on end."

Kingston was wondering how to keep conversation on the subject alive. For the moment, he seemed to have run out of questions. Harris saved him from having to concoct one.

"Well, maybe we've been going about this the wrong way—backward," Harris said, knife and fork suspended. "Perhaps we should be looking at it from the perspective of those on your side of the pond. Who acquired the rose and arranged for its shipment to Alcatraz? What difficulties would they have encountered and who would they be sending it to?"

"Unfortunately, there's not much to go on there, either. I doubt that export licenses for plant products were as stringent then as they are now. Even if it was sent by legitimate means, the chance of finding any records or documentation sixty years later is wishful thinking."

"I notice that when you talk about the rose, you refer to it as a plant. Why wouldn't they ship seeds? Wouldn't it be a lot easier?"

"Generally, you're right. But in our case, if someone wanted to be certain that the rose he was sending was identical to its parent, the Belmaris rose, the most reliable method of propagation at the time would have been by stem cuttings, which, incidentally is quite simple and can be done by a novice, if the right steps are followed."

Harris nodded. "I've heard about it."

"It's done with many plants. Seeds are much trickier to deal with and often produce a plant and flower that differ from the rose the seeds came from. It's complicated, all about pollination. Anyway, it can take a long time to germinate seeds, and you've got to know what your doing. It requires controlled conditions, and I doubt anyone would've wanted to go to all that trouble."

"What about shipping the cuttings?"

"Not a problem. It's been common practice for well over a hundred years, believe it or not. With the advent of the Internet, millions of newly propagated plants are shipped worldwide every year. It's so simple that almost anyone can do it." He paused, placed his knife and fork neatly side by side across the empty plate, and leaned back with a satisfied sigh.

Harris smiled. "Good, eh?"

"I should say. Best sole I've had in a long time."

Not thirty seconds later, the attentive waiter returned to take their plates and orders for coffee. Both declined dessert.

"Talking of the plant hunters," Kingston said, chagrined to realize he was about to lapse into his professorial mode but unable to stop himself, "in Queen Victoria's day, the botanists used what were called Wardian cases to transport and ship young plants back to Britain from all over the globe. The wood-and-glass case was named after its inventor, Dr. Nathaniel Bagshaw Ward."

"Quite a handle."

Kingston smiled. "Very Dickensian. It was nothing more than a tightly sealed container of condensed moisture, that looked like a small greenhouse, the forerunner of today's terrarium. He couldn't have chosen a more demanding voyage to try them out, though. He shipped two cases filled with ferns and grasses to Australia, a journey that took several months. The plants arrived in perfectly good condition."

"You're teaching me new respect for horticultural history."

"You'll have to forgive me." Kingston smiled and shook his head. "It's been fifteen years now and I still forget I'm not in the classroom."

"Dealing with the history of Alcatraz every day, I know the feeling."

"I believe it was Samuel Butler who said, 'God cannot alter the past, but historians can,'" Kingston said, smiling.

"Amen."

Kingston's smile faded as something suddenly occurred to him. "Andy, you raised the idea that we may have been going about all this backward, and should be looking at it from our viewpoint, from England."

Harris nodded. "It was just a thought, that's all."

"But think about it. We've been assuming—or I have—that Jennings, aka Reginald Payne, wrote the notes in the book for a friend, or friend of a friend, who was interested in rare roses. But what if he did it not for anything as prosaic as an English garden, or for the warden of Alcatraz, but for one of the inmates?"

Andy's eyebrows shot up. "An inmate? What would a murderer or a bank robber want with a rose? It makes no sense."

Kingston held up a hand. "Perhaps not, but hear me out. What if one of the inmates approached the warden or his secretary—who happened to be obsessed with roses, as many people are—and said that he could lay his hands on the rarest rose on the planet? What do you think the response would be?"

"I have no idea. Fiction is the first word that comes to mind. The men we're talking about were America's most notorious, hard-core prisoners: murderers, rapists, kidnappers, and high-profile gang bosses. They spent most of their time figuring out how to escape, not planning how to import roses."

Coffee arrived, giving Kingston a short breather before having to respond to Harris's unequivocal reaction. "You're right, of course," he said, stirring cream and sugar in his cup. "But what if—and this may be an even greater stretch—what if it was an inmate already known to Jennings?"

Harris's expression was ambiguous, and he seemed hesitant to answer right away. Either a sign of self-reproach, after his being so defensive, thought Kingston, or he was tiring of what he thought were harebrained questions.

"Highly unlikely," Harris said, "considering that Jennings is English and all the Alcatraz inmates were American."

Kingston took a careful sip of hot coffee, looking at the historian over the steam from his cup. "That doesn't necessarily mean that Jennings couldn't have had some kind of previous criminal relationship with one of the prisoners. I don't have any evidence that Jennings went to the States, but it's conceivable that one of the inmates might have crossed paths with Jennings in London."

"Even if that were the case, where does it get you? I can't see that it changes anything."

While Harris was taking a long sip of his coffee, Kingston was pulling on his earlobe, his eyes wandering vacantly around the room. "I have a question, Andy," he said, shrugging off his lapse of attention.

"Shoot."

"The robbery in England took place in 1957, and Alcatraz closed in 1963. How many prisoners were on the island during those six years? A reasonable guess."

"Over twenty-nine years, the highest number of prisoners was around three hundred and the lowest about two hundred twenty. If I were to guess for the last six years, it would be the lower number."

"I assume there's a list, a record of those incarcerated in those years?"

"I'm sure there is."

"Would it provide a history, a background of each inmate?"

"I can see where you're going, but I still think it's an exercise in futility. By combing through the lives of two-hundred-plus inmates, you hope to find evidence pointing to one prisoner who could have known Jennings?"

Kingston shrugged. "It's worth a try. We've exhausted everything else."

"You're a stubborn son of a gun, I'll say that much. I'll see what I can come up with. All I can say is that you'll have a lot of reading and crystal ball gazing to do."

At Sam's front door, they shook hands and exchanged cards, with Harris promising to get to work right away pulling together the list of prisoners.

Fifteen minutes later, Kingston stood on the deck of the *Hornblower*, the Alcatraz ferry, as it sliced through the whitecapped chop of San Francisco Bay, seagulls circling and squealing over the throb of its engines. On such a cheerful though breezy afternoon, the fast-approaching island, its gray rocks daubed with wildflower color and patches of untold shades of green, wasn't quite so forbidding as he'd remembered from a previous visit twenty-some years ago when he was merely a curious tourist with no agenda.

He was looking forward to the tour, particularly the restored gardens that Greg Robinson and Andy Harris had told him about and, of course, he was excited at the possibility of seeing the Belmaris rose, if it was still blooming.

17

CLANG! CLANG! CLANG! The resounding metallic din echoed around the steel and concrete walls, stone floors, and three-story ceilings of Cell Block D. For effect, the park ranger conducting the tour had just slammed shut a steel-barred door to a nine-by-five-foot cell, the only fixtures a narrow bed, a toilet, a tiny wall-mounted sink, and a metal table, all affixed to the concrete walls.

Kingston was among a group of two dozen visitors. Already knowing most of the facts and figures, he remained in back of the group, often moving away, more intent upon observing than listening, trying to imagine what it must have been like being an inmate in what was once the most formidable maximum-security prison of all time.

"That's a sound that no prisoner ever forgot, even if he was lucky enough to get out of here," the ranger said, facing the unsmiling visitors. "Within these walls lived the country's toughest and most dangerous and most famous prisoners." He waved a circling hand.

"When they arrived here, prisoners had a decision to make: whether to obey the rules or not. That decision affected their lives dramatically. Prisoners who chose not to behave ended up in a harsher place, here in the prison's treatment unit."

"There are four blocks like this, A to D, and each of the corridors had a name. There was Michigan Avenue, Broadway, Sunset Boulevard—and this one, between Blocks C and D, was aptly nicknamed Seedy Street."

This is Block D," he said, voice echoing. "Thirty six of the least popular cells in Alcatraz, where the unruly and violent inmates were housed.

Inmates here stayed in their cells twenty-four hours a day. Typically they were only allowed out once a week for a shower and exercise.

"Down there at the end," he said, pointing, "are the solitary confinement cells, numbers nine through fourteen. The notorious 'hole,' as they were called. The cell doors there don't have bars; they're solid steel. Those isolation cells had no toilet or running water, no mattress, no light fixture, and they were colder than the other cells. Treatment in these cells sometimes included total darkness, sleeping on the floor with only a blanket, and a restricted diet. Confinement usually lasted several days, but no longer than nineteen. By the way, at night the wind used to howl through those windows up there. They face San Francisco and the setting sun."

Kingston looked up at the gun galleries at each end of the block, visualizing the armed guards watching the inmates round the clock. He closed his eyes, imagining the yelling and swearing, the whistles, the bells and incessant hubbub from the cells, the clatter of boots on the iron walkways and stairs, the guards shouting orders. It was grim and depressing. He walked back to his group.

The ranger, standing next to the bars of one of the standard cells, was still talking. "Cells like this one had to be kept tidy and in good shape. Any articles found in the cells or on prisoners, such as drugs, alcohol, money, tools that could be used to inflict injury or employed in escape attempts, were considered contraband and subjected the inmate to disciplinary action. Toilet paper, matches, soap, and toiletries were issued to the cells twice a week, and inmates could request hot water and a mop to clean their cells. The bars, windows, and floors of the prison were cleaned daily. Talking was permitted in the cell block and in the dining hall as long as conversations were quiet and there was no shouting, loud talking, or singing. Any questions?"

A young boy raised his hand. He wanted to know what the prisoners did all day.

"A good question, young man." The tall ranger smiled. "Prisoners were woken at six thirty and breakfast was served in the dining hall at seven. After returning, they had to tidy their cell and put their wastebasket outside. At seven thirty, those inmates who were allowed to work started their shifts. They were assigned jobs in the laundry, tailor shop, electrical shop, model shop, where they made furniture, and so on, all overseen by guards and civilian shop foremen. They returned for lunch at eleven thirty and afterward could rest in their cell for a half hour, then resume their work until four thirty. At nighttime, in later years, starting at six thirty they had what was called music hour—usually harmonicas, guitars, small instruments. Dinner was a half hour later and lights-out at nine thirty . . ."

The tour continued to the library, then into the prisoners' mess hall and kitchen. Still lagging behind, Kingston was content to simply look around and take in the grim, characterless surroundings.

Finally, they emerged into the cheering sunshine of the recreation yard. Again, Kingston attempted to transport himself back over fifty years, imagining what the "yard" meant to prisoners. One of the few times they were not locked up in their cells or elsewhere within the pitiless walls of the prison. Today was sunny, with a stiff breeze coming off the treacherous waters of the bay, but he knew that many days it was bitterly cold and cloudy or fogbound. He gazed around the large rectangle with its concrete floor tufted with weeds, the high stone walls topped with cyclone fencing and barbed wire, the guard cage and walk high in the corner. He pictured the impromptu handball and softball games and prisoners huddled in groups on the wide terraced steps—the "bleachers," as they were called—leading to the cell blocks, some sitting against the wall, out of the wind, playing chess and checkers.

"Sir! Sir." Kingston looked over his shoulder. He'd lagged a little too far behind; his group was waiting on the steps. The ranger was calling him. "Don't want to leave you here," he said. "We're going to the museum next."

The tour of the prison finally over, Kingston spent the next forty minutes visiting the gardens. There were seven in all, including the Warden's Garden and the Prisoner Gardens. This was where one of the privileged inmate gardeners, Ryan Matthews—whom Andy had mentioned—had used salvaged materials to build garden terraces, a greenhouse, and even a birdbath. Although these gardens had been replanted and now were cared for by the Garden Conservancy, Kingston marveled at the creation these inmates had wrought, the visual pleasure and cheer they had provided for all the inmates to enjoy. Starting with little or no knowledge, with limited seeds, plant material, and other resources, it was testimony to their fortitude, determination, and perseverance in striving to somehow improve and beautify the surroundings and miserable existence under the most severe and hopeless of conditions.

"Gardening is the purest of human pleasures," Kingston muttered Sir Francis Bacon's quotation to himself.

Fifteen minutes later, he stood on the deck of the Alcatraz ferry, hair windblown, gripping the cold iron railing, watching the fog roll in. In the near distance, but always appearing deceptively close, loomed the gray-white silhouette of the city, its skyscraper windows shimmering with the reflected light of the sun setting over the Golden Gate. Civilization and its discontents crossed Kingston's mind.

He had a few discontents of his own at that moment, chief among them what had happened at the very end of the tour, when he had inquired about the Belmaris rose. The docent had taken him to an uncultivated section on the west side of the island to show him the rambling specimen.

The rose had finished its once-a-year flush and was no longer in bloom.

Examining the canes and leaves only, the rare and elusive Belmaris rose could have been any of hundreds. He was beginning to believe that he'd come all this way for nothing.

And that was a disconcerting thought indeed.

18

WHEN KINGSTON RETURNED to the inn that evening, after an excellent dinner at Fisherman's Wharf, a message from Andy Harris awaited him at the desk requesting that Kingston call him any time up to eleven P.M. or, failing that, in the morning. In his room, he took Harris's card from his wallet and made the call. Harris answered after two rings.

"It's Lawrence, Andy. I just received your message."

"Good. How was the tour?"

"Outstanding. A huge improvement on the one I took back in the eighties. The landscaping is very impressive. I bought a book, *Gardens of Alcatraz*, which shows a lot of the old and the new. I'm sure you've seen it."

"Indeed, I have a copy. I recommend it whenever I get the chance. They've done a great job over the years, sprucing the place up." Harris cleared his throat. "Anyway, Lawrence, I wanted to get to you as soon as possible because driving home this afternoon, I started thinking about our conversation, and a thought occurred to me. I don't know if it's of interest, but one of the surviving Alcatraz prisoners lives right here in the Bay Area."

"An inmate?" Kingston's ears pricked up.

"Yes. I met him once at a reunion—"

Kingston couldn't help interrupting. "Reunion? I find it hard to imagine these . . . what shall I call them, alumni? . . . getting together to reminisce about the 'good old days.'"

Andy chuckled. "Actually, it *was* called the Alcatraz Alumni Gathering. It was in 2003, the seventieth anniversary of the prison, and all ex-inmates and guards were invited. A surprising number attended. Anyway, this chap, Darrell Kaminski, and I got on quite well, despite his knowing that my father was an officer. He's probably in his eighties by now. If you can squeeze in the time, and he's agreeable, I may be able to set you up with an interview."

Kingston didn't hesitate. "That's extraordinary. I wouldn't turn down an opportunity like that. What would you tell him, though? The reason?"

"I'd just tell him the truth—that you're a respected doctor and botanist from England, here on a very short trip, trying to find out why and how the rose showed up at Alcatraz, and if he can give you thoughts about life on the island from an inmate's viewpoint. From what I recall, he's not the most talkative type, but with your accent and charm I'm sure you'll be able to get him to open up."

"I'll do my best."

The two men talked details, including Kingston's schedule—he was leaving in two days—and Harris's own availability. Andy agreed to call Kaminski first thing in the morning and see if they could arrange to meet.

"I'll get back to you the minute I have word."

"I can't thank you enough for doing this. If he does agree to a meeting and nothing comes of it as far as the rose is concerned, at least it will give me something to tell the grandkids: that I once interviewed a prisoner of Alcatraz."

Harris chuckled. "You'll be the only living person in England to have done so."

Two days later, on Thursday afternoon, Harris and Kingston, in Harris's Ford Explorer, emerged from the connector tunnel from Oakland into Alameda, a laid-back mostly residential community on the Bay, and arrived at their destination: Magnolia House, a cluster of single-level apartment units. Andy parked under the shade of a giant magnolia, and they followed the signs along a path that crossed a lawn, still damp from the morning's sprinklers, leading to Kaminski's apartment.

Harris rang the bell and the door opened almost immediately. Facing them, with what could barely pass as a smile, was a tall man in his eighties, who seemed in remarkably good shape for his age.

"Come in," Kaminski said in a gravelly voice, opening the door into a short hallway. As they entered the living room, Kaminski moved purposefully, with no telltale signs of age whatsoever. A few wrinkles here and there and thinning white hair, but other than that he showed none of the physical legacies expected of a man who had spent more than half his adult life behind bars.

After introductions, they sat in a sparsely furnished but near-obsessively clean and tidy room with a picture window that looked out onto dapple-shaded lawns and sandy pathways. In the car, Kingston and Harris had laid out basic ground rules for the interview, agreeing to limit the scope of their questions, focus the conversation on the Alcatraz rose, at least until Kaminski seemed comfortable, and not complicate matters by mentioning Brian Jennings or the security van robbery in England.

Both men declined Kaminski's offer of coffee or a soda. Kingston crossed his legs on the lumpy sofa, looked into Kaminski's unblinking eyes, and got down to business.

"First, Darrell, let me say that I truly appreciate your allowing us into your home for a brief talk. As Andy told you, my interest in your time spent on Alcatraz is limited only to a rare rose—nothing more, nothing less. It may all sound frivolous and trivial to you, but we—a couple of botanists and a historian back in England and myself, who have been working on this puzzle for months now—are still at a dead end."

Kaminski glanced at Harris before speaking. "Yeah, Andy told me your problem. But I still don't know why you'd think I'd know anything about roses."

"I understand. It must have sounded like a strange request."

"I gave up doing interviews years ago. It took only two or three before I realized that all the reporters really wanted to know about was the sensational stuff, what it was like locked up in America's toughest prison: the escapes, the brutality, riots, killings, all that kind of crap. You're lucky. Andy is pretty persuasive."

"And it's much appreciated. So can you tell me what you remember about the gardens on the island? How many there were?"

Kingston's question was met with a grudging smile. "Depends what you mean by garden. Some were not much more than a few plants stuck in the rock walls along the roadside. One like that was planted in the foundations of some old houses that had been demolished. That was nice. Then there was the warden's garden, but none of us ever saw that. The others were mostly on the west hillside—a couple, maybe. The only one familiar to us was near the Road Guard Tower below the yard—the recreation yard. We could see it on our way to work at the New Industries building. That was what I'd call a real garden. It was on a slope, each level was different, always lots of flowers in the summer, even a greenhouse built from scrap lumber by one of the guys assigned to the garden." He paused and rubbed his chin in thought. "Ryan Matthews, that was his name. We talked a couple of times. He worked on it for years."

"Matthews." Kingston nodded. The same man Andy had mentioned. "An inmate, I take it?"

Kaminski nodded. "Yeah. And I can tell you, getting to work in the gardens didn't come easy. Work assignments had to be earned. If you gave the staff no trouble, minded your own business, they'd give you some kind of grunt work first. If you stuck it out and did a good job and kept your nose clean, you could be awarded what was called 'good time.' That could eventually lead to a paid job in the industries building, where all the workshops were—the laundry, paint shop, carpentry, maintenance, that sort of stuff."

"Did you know any other men who worked in the gardens?"

"Yep, a few—Curtis Sullivan and Vince Wellman were two. I didn't know them that good, though. Sullivan was obsessed with plants and growing stuff. He could drive you crazy. He never talked about much else. Wellman was the opposite, quiet as a mouse. It was hard to believe he'd murdered someone."

"How were they chosen to work in the gardens? Who decided that?"

"Hmm. I remember someone—Sullivan, probably—once mentioning that an assistant to one of the wardens took it on himself to start taking care of the gardens—that required labor, of course."

"Eliott Hofmann," Harris said. "He was the secretary."

Kaminski shook his head. "I wouldn't know. All I do know is we appreciated what he did. It was a god-awful depressing place and he, or whoever was responsible, made it a bit more cheerful."

"This Ryan Matthews that you mentioned. He must have gained a lot of trust and respect to be allowed to have the run of the garden."

"He did. He was one of the most intelligent guys on the island, as far as I was concerned. Some prisoners didn't like his getting special treatment. I think it was because of the key."

"Key?"

"Yeah. It happened before I arrived, but it was common knowledge. Not much went on in that place that remained a secret for very long." For the first time, Kingston noticed a distant look in Kaminski's deep-set eyes. "Sometimes information and knowledge could be like currency. And other times that sort of thing could be like a curse—could be dangerous. Something you wished you'd never known."

"I can imagine," Kingston said, having a good idea what the man was alluding to.

"No one can, really, Doctor, but that's okay," Kaminski replied. "Anyway, so the story goes, one day in the yard Matthews found a key a guard had dropped. Most of us might have been tempted to keep it, but he returned it."

"No wonder he landed the garden job."

"It was not only good for him, but in a way, good for us too, I guess. We got to enjoy the fruits of his labor, as it were."

"Do you know if Matthews or any of the other men who worked in the gardens were involved in any of the plant purchasing?"

Kaminski shook his head. "That I wouldn't know."

"What about you, Darrell?" Andy Harris asked. "You worked in the Industries Building, right?"

"Yeah. I started in a workshop where they made concrete blocks used for building retaining walls around the island. After that, I worked in the laundry and then the carpentry shop." He stopped, that same enigmatic smile again. "That's what I did for a living outside, before I convinced myself that I could make a better living holding up banks."

Harris nodded, smiling. "What about conversation?"

"Conversation? I'm not sure I know what you mean."

"Well, with over two hundred men confined in such close quarters, with a monotonous routine and a controlled existence around the clock, with little or no news of the outside world, what did you talk about in the yard and the dining room, in the few times that you had the chance?" Harris asked.

Kingston was surprised. This was far from a gardening question. He wondered why Harris had asked it. To keep the man talking, he supposed, to keep him comfortable. Not a bad idea, Kingston thought. A tactic he'd used on more than one occasion himself.

Kaminski was shaking his head. "I dunno—about anything that happened that day, news from outside. Meaningless stuff mostly. Sports was always big, mostly baseball for some reason, though we never got to watch any. No TV, only books and magazines." He scratched his broad forehead and glanced around momentarily. "What did we talk about?" he murmured to himself. "Friends, families, places we'd been, jobs we'd had, cars . . ." He paused and shrugged. "Anything at all that happened, I guess. It didn't matter, really. It could be something stupid, like the food we'd had that day, or more exciting, like arguments among the prisoners, fights, protests . . . escaping, of course. That was always on everyone's mind."

"Escape." Kingston, despite himself, was curious. "When an escape was being planned or actually taking place, how was it kept a secret, not so much from the guards but from the other prisoners?"

Kaminski glanced briefly at Andy Harris. "I'll answer your question in a roundabout way. Andy knows how this all works as well as anybody. In Alcatraz, more than most prisons, there was an unwritten set of rules you learned starting from day one. These were not rules laid down by the warden or the screws but by the prisoners. Call it an inmate culture if you wanna be fancy. The shrinks called it the convict code. It's an understanding of the 'them' and 'us' state of coexistence: them being the guards and us being the prisoners.

"Some of this you learned early on from other prisoners, a lot by seeing what went on around you every day, like how other inmates handle given situations, right or wrong. It was all about putting up a united front against the guards and authority. Standing up for each other, never ratting on another con, not getting into arguments or fights with other inmates, not being nosy, keeping stuff to yourself, never lying or stealing—the goal for all of us was to serve the least possible time on the Rock and get to enjoy what little pleasure and privileges there were, until we got our walking papers." Kaminski paused, looking at Kingston with an awkward expression. "I don't think I answered your question too well, Doctor, did I?"

"After a fashion. It was about how you kept things secret from one another. If an escape attempt was in the planning, how was it kept secret in such a tight-knit community? I assume there was a sort of prisoners' grapevine."

"Most things, you kept to yourself. But once in a while some prisoners got to know—like it or not—about things like escape attempts because it often involved their help or cooperation, particularly those in the workshops who could lay their hands on materials and tools and machinery, what have you. But nobody would ever tip off a guard if he knew something was going down. *Never*."

Kingston couldn't help noticing that Kaminski had that same faraway look in his eyes as before—when he'd talked about information as something that could be dangerous to possess.

"I'm wondering, Darrell," he continued, knowing he was straying from the game plan. "Did you ever hear anything that you wished later you hadn't?"

A longer pause followed. Kingston wondered if Kaminski was going to answer the question, or dodge it altogether.

"Only once," Kaminski said at last. "I never told anybody about it. At the time, it gave me a few sleepless nights, though. I haven't given it too much thought since. No reason to, really."

Kingston and Harris exchanged a glance.

"Go on," Andy urged.

"It happened about a year before Alcatraz was shut down, and I was moved to McNeil Island. One weekend I got lucky and was assigned to collect the softballs and handballs that landed outside the recreation yard walls. Usually there were only a few, so most of the time you could just sit and look at the view or just walk around the scrubby area outside the wall."

"Presumably in view of the guard," Kingston said.

Kaminski smiled cynically. "Are you kidding? From the minute you got up at six thirty, a guard was watching what you were doing—even when you were asleep." He paused, rubbing his chin in thought. "Yeah, there was always a guard on the catwalk around the yard, watching for trouble down below, another in the guardhouse. Anyway, that day, a couple of minutes before the bell went off at four o'clock, the guard waved for me to go back into the yard, so I picked up the few balls I'd gathered, headed back in, and put them in the small storage room in a corner of the yard. Nearby were a few small tables where the guys played dominoes and checkers. As I was putting the balls back in the baskets, I could hear some men at the table near the door talking. Three men. And they weren't talking about dominoes, or checkers, or chess. No." Kaminski shook his head. "They were talking about diamonds."

"Diamonds?" Kingston's eyes widened.

"Yeah. Some diamonds that had been hidden by one of the inmates before he went to prison, probably from some robbery, I guess. They didn't mention how much they were worth, but it wasn't chicken feed, it was big. They had some kind of plan going—something that involved one of the guards."

Harris frowned. "A guard?"

"That was my reaction. I realized right away that I'd gotten myself into a tight spot. If I walked out right then, they'd know that I'd overheard what they were talking about. Not a healthy situation. So I decided to stay, praying that the bell would go off and I could come out after they left. Course, the danger in doing that . . . either of the two guards might wonder why I was taking so long and decide to investigate."

"So what happened?" Kingston asked.

"After what seemed like forever, the bell finally went off. They packed up and I managed to slip out unnoticed. But in those last few seconds— or however long it was—I heard more of what they were planning. Only snatches here and there, but I knew it was for real, not some movie they were talking about."

"Was it part of an escape plan?" Kingston asked.

Kaminski shook his head. "No. From what I could make out, the one who'd hidden the stones wanted one of the other two—whoever got out first—to find the diamonds and deliver them to a third party. He'd get a sizable cut if he pulled it off."

"And where did the guard come in?" Andy asked.

"As a last resort. If it turned out that neither of the other two could carry out the mission—you know, not everybody left Alcatraz alive—then it would have to be left to someone else. That's probably why one of them suggested a guard as the only possibility."

"No names were mentioned, I take it," Andy said.

"No. But it was as if they had a particular screw in mind because they discussed the likelihood of his going for it." Kaminski looked off to the side for a few seconds. "There was one other thing. I'm pretty sure the stash was hidden in another country."

"What made you think that?" Kingston asked.

"One of them talked about the money already having been converted into diamonds and not having to get involved with foreign currency."

"I see." Kingston pulled reflectively on his earlobe and gazed absently out the big window, where two squirrels were chasing each other on the lawn. *A cache of stolen diamonds. A decades-old plan to bribe a guard. They were a long way off from the Alcatraz rose*, he thought.

He turned back to Kaminski, who showed no signs of being troubled by the shift in questioning. "Men like yourself, sent to Alcatraz from other prisons, were all serving fairly long sentences, I presume."

Kaminski nodded. "Yeah."

"So, based on what you'd overheard, it would be reasonable to think that the prisoner who'd hidden the diamonds knew that he was either likely to spend his remaining years in prison, or perhaps, if he were in poor health, knew he wouldn't outlive his sentence. That could explain why he wanted to line up surrogates who would give him a degree of assurance that this relative or friend would receive the inheritance, even though it was stolen goods. If the next in line were to be killed or die before being released, the next would take on the task."

"I guess so," Kaminski said.

"Anything more you can remember about their conversation?" Kingston asked.

Kaminski thought hard for a few seconds, then leaned back. "I think they talked of having help at the other end. That's all, though."

"Did they say what kind of help?"

"No."

"And no mention of what country?"

Kaminski shook his head. "Negative."

They were interrupted by the sound of key turning in a lock and someone entering the house.

"That's my wife, Paula," Kaminski said, looking over his shoulder. "We're almost through, dear," he called out.

They were, in fact, entirely through, Kingston realized. He'd run out of questions regarding the rose and cache of diamonds—questions that Darrell Kaminski might be able to answer, that is. Was there a connection between Belmaris's peripatetic plant and the diamonds? Between Brian Jennings and the three men plotting in the Alcatraz yard?

Damned if he knew.

Kingston stood and thanked Kaminski sincerely for his time, promising a follow-up letter or call if he managed to solve the Alcatraz rose mystery.

Minutes later, he and Andy were in the Explorer, heading back to Oakland and the Fruitvale BART station.

"What did you think about that last bit?" Kingston asked. "The hidden stash of diamonds?"

"Sounds too much like a movie, if you ask me," Harris replied, his eyes on the road.

"That was my first impression, too, but I doubt he'd make it up. What would be the point?"

"You've got me."

Waiting at a red light a minute later, Harris glanced at Kingston, an amused smile on his face. "Maybe the diamonds are hidden somewhere in England. That would give you yet another mystery to solve. Or maybe the two mysteries are one."

Kingston smiled back. "You must be reading my mind."

19

Chelsea, England

IT WAS FOUR A.M., and a jet-lagged Kingston was wide awake, sitting at the kitchen table, wearing an Irish wool sweater and pajama bottoms. On his second cup of tea, he had just finished rereading the Wikipedia pages on the security van robbery, checking dates, details, and writing notes. Next he would do the same with Emma's notes.

This repeat task was the direct result of something that he'd stumbled on during the night, in the dark of the British Airways cabin, while other passengers were sleeping or watching movies. Unable to do either, he had spent these hours rehashing the details of his talk with Darrell Kaminski, particularly his recollection of the cloak-and-dagger conversation he'd overheard all those years ago. He couldn't shake it from his overactive mind. Was it meaningless—nothing more than a fantasy dreamed up by inmates with nothing else to discuss and little to live for? Or was it real and connected in some way to the robbery that had taken place five thousand miles away, six years before Alcatraz was closed? For a while he tried reading the book he'd brought for the trip, but he couldn't concentrate on it, and soon his mind was back on the robbery. He focused on Jennings and then on the rose, and all the speculation it had engendered. Soon his thoughts drifted to Letty, leading to him to wonder how she was getting along with Emma. By association, his mind then turned to Fiona and the photos that Letty had provided. She had looked quite young. That led him to wonder how old she was when they were taken. Must have been quite some time before she went missing.

It was then that something odd had struck him. What had happened to Fiona after her mother had died? As far as he could recall, that had never been discussed. How had she ended up in Cheltenham, for that matter? He started jotting dates and ages on the edge of the dinner menu that was still on the empty seat next to him. He was fairly sure that the mother had died in 1968, at which time Fiona would have been about twelve. He stared up at the amorphous shadows of the overhead compartments. When had Fiona married? he wondered. He couldn't recall a date ever being mentioned, but it was reasonable to assume that it was at age eighteen at the earliest, which meant there was a gap of six years or more in her life that was unaccounted for. That was when he had decided to comb through Emma's notes the minute he got home.

It was four thirty when he'd finished reading her notes, and he had found no mention of the missing years in Fiona's life. She was a minor and must have been placed in someone's care. But whose? It would be at least five hours before he could call Emma, so he decided to cook a full breakfast—eggs, bacon, grilled tomatoes, and toast—and read the *Times* which, mercifully, was delivered early.

At nine o'clock he had Emma on the line.

"I didn't expect to hear from you quite so soon. Didn't you just get home?"

"I did, yesterday."

"Well, welcome home," she said heartily.

The next several minutes were taken up with his describing the highlights of his visit with Julie and Brandon, and how enjoyable it had all been. She listened without interrupting until he brought up his side trip to San Francisco.

"San Francisco," she said, surprise in her voice. Isn't that where Alcatraz is?"

He suppressed a chuckle. "It is indeed, and I took the tour again. Even better than the first time. Just as depressing, though."

Emma's only reaction was a sigh.

Undaunted, Kingston continued. "I also met with the Alcatraz historian I mentioned, Andy Harris."

"I've got to hand it to you, Lawrence—"

"Wait, it gets better. I had an interview with a former Alcatraz inmate named Darrell Kaminksi."

"You're serious, aren't you?"

Kingston felt a little deflated; he'd expected a little more interest, more curiosity.

"I was very glad I did. In an odd way, I felt privileged that someone who'd lived through that experience and had survived with such a remarkable degree of stoicism and equanimity would agree to sit down for more than an hour and talk with a complete stranger. Not only that, it resulted in an interesting revelation, a *very* interesting incident that could have a bearing on a lot of the questions that have stumped us about these damned mysteries."

"What did he say?" Emma's tone had lost its edge of cynicism. "I'd like to know."

Kingston told her Kaminski's story.

Emma didn't respond immediately. For a moment, he wondered if the line had gone dead. Finally she spoke.

"I agree that it could be connected, Lawrence, that he could have been describing a scheme that was related to our robbery—even one of the robbers. But as your friend pointed out, all the inmates in Alcatraz were American. So it all comes down to whether it's fact or fiction."

"I guess it's like a lot of other questions with these mysteries—maybe we'll never know."

"Looks that way."

"There was something else I wanted to ask you," he said. Two things, actually."

"Okay."

"In your notes there was a gap in Fiona's early years—the period immediately following the death of her mother, when she was about twelve. I don't know when she got married, either. Do you recall where she went? Whom she lived with?"

"Let's see . . . When her mother died, in London—Bethnal Green, I believe—Fiona went to live with a single aunt in Cheltenham."

"Which explains how she eventually befriended the Collinses."

"Correct."

"The second question concerns the stolen £800,000."

"Follow the money, eh?"

"In this case, let's think diamonds."

"I thought we'd already discussed that."

"I know, but in order to make some reasonable deductions, I'm going to assume that Kaminski's story was factual."

"Go on, then."

"So, a sick or dying Alcatraz inmate, who's committed a robbery, wants to retrieve a cache of diamonds that he's hidden in England—"

"We don't know it was England."

"I'm aware of that, Emma. This is fact *and* supposition. For now, let's at least agree that it's Great Britain."

"Sorry, I'll try not to interrupt again."

"We also know that the plan involved a 'third party' in England to whom diamonds were to be delivered.

"We know that Jennings and Butler were close friends and that they were the only two robbers to escape. We now know a lot about Jennings but far less about Butler, only what's been reported. Okay, so far?"

"It's a little long-winded. Can you chivvy it along a bit?"

Kingston chose to ignore that admonition and continued, "In your notes, it's stated that Fiona's father died soon after she was born. Who or what was the source of that information?"

"I'm sure it was one of the Collinses," she replied after a pause. "Probably Molly, she was very close to Fiona and knew more about her."

"Do you recall if his death was ever confirmed? If your people followed up to check death certificates?"

A longer pause followed. "Golly. I can't imagine them not doing so. This was about ten years ago, Lawrence. I do remember her mother died much later than he did."

"So both parents died at relatively young ages, him in particular."

"I believe that's correct, yes."

"And before marrying Terry McGuire, Fiona's surname was Doyle. Is that right?"

"You're starting to sound like a copper. Yes. Molly stated that Fiona's mother's name was Caitlin Doyle. I see where you might be going with this. But by all means, do continue."

"According to the Wiki report, Butler had a girlfriend, whose name wasn't mentioned."

"Right."

"So—what if Caitlin Doyle's boyfriend was Butler?"

"Butler, Fiona's father?"

"It's quite possible and, if so, it would start to explain a lot of questions—"

"Excepting Butler, a U.K. citizen, ending up in America's most notorious prison."

"As I recall, it was assumed by the authorities that Butler had fled the country after the robbery and was believed to be living in another country, with a new identity. The U.S. would be a logical one, wouldn't you think? And he would doubtless have had an American passport and certainly another name."

Emma let out a long sigh.

"You've got to admit, Emma, it all fits. Not only that, but it gives us the link between Jennings and Fiona that we've been at odds about. Jennings would have known that Butler had a small child, a daughter."

"Okay, there are a lot of 'ifs' but let me give it more thought."

"Could you look into the two deaths, Emma? As a start, maybe check the transcripts?"

"I will. I'll say one thing, though. If you're right, this could certainly stir the pot."

20

THE FOLLOWING MORNING, Kingston rose much later than usual. It didn't happen often, but it was the sun streaming through a gap in the curtains that woke him, reminding him that he still hadn't fully recovered from jet lag.

At ten, he had an appointment with Clifford Attenborough at Kew Gardens to attend a meeting and a luncheon with some of the government mucky-mucks who were presiding over the upcoming conference that Kingston had committed to. He also planned to spend part of the day wandering the gardens, which he hadn't done for a long time.

Before leaving, he also wanted to chat with Andrew, whom he'd tried to reach yesterday but with no success. He planned to invite him over for drinks, to tell him about the trip and his recent conversation with Emma, and test his new theory on his friend.

When Kingston returned to his flat at four thirty, the phone was ringing. He hastened to the living room, picking it up just in time.

"Kingston," he said, fully expecting it to be Andrew.

A woman's voice, one he didn't recognize. "Hello, Doctor—this is Sophie Williams."

"Oh, yes," he replied, trying to conceal his surprise, "Grace Williams's daughter."

"I'm glad I've finally managed to reach you."

"I was out of the country for a couple of weeks."

"Sorry I missed you when you were at Beechwood to see my mom."

"You very nearly didn't. Wasn't that you in the red VW?"

"Oh!" He could almost see the wincing expression on her face. "It was. Sorry about that."

"I'm curious. How did you get my number?"

"I found your card in our address book. I thought that with you being a doctor and all . . . there's no one else who I can call. I don't know anyone in this country."

"So how can I help you?"

"It's about my mom. I'm getting worried about her. Scared."

"Why's that?"

"I'm convinced that there's more to her brother's murder than she's letting on to."

"Really?" Kingston was instantly alert, his jet lag a thing of the past. "What gives you that idea?"

"I shouldn't admit it, but I've listened in on a couple of her phone conversations, and whoever she's talking to is obviously trying to intimidate her, frighten her. Reggie's name was mentioned. Once I noticed her trembling afterward. She's up late at night, too. Something she never did before."

"Do you think it's just the one person, or more?"

"It's the same person, I'm sure."

"No other names mentioned?"

"No. When I ask her what's bothering her, she just clams up, tells me not to worry, that she can handle it."

Kingston thought for a moment. "Has anybody else come to the house recently?"

"Other than you, no. My mom told me you'd stopped by some time ago, asking about one of the roses Reggie might have planted here. She said the lady with you used to be a policewoman."

"That's right. But what you've just described is very disturbing. Don't you think you should call the police?"

"That's the problem. My mom told me point-blank that it's her business, she can deal with it, and under no circumstances whatsoever am I to interfere." She hesitated. "She really means it, Doctor. If she finds out I've called the police, I'm afraid she'll take off, and that could make matters even worse."

"But what makes you think I can help?"

"You could ask your friend, the policewoman. Mum would never know."

Kingston was trying to decide how to best advise Sophie what to do next, when she spoke up again.

"There's something else that scares me. She has a gun."

"Really?"

"I came down to the kitchen late one night last week to get a glass of water, and she was sitting there going through the phone book. The gun was lying on the table next to her. She looked startled for a moment and quickly covered it with a kitchen towel.

A gun—some kind of threats being made, related to her brother?

There was little doubt in Kingston's mind now. Grace Williams knew exactly what Brian Jennings had done—knew all about the past he had strived to keep secret for fifty years.

"How else has your mother been spending her time? Other than obvious errands, does she go out for long periods, without explanation?"

"Only once. She was gone for the best part of the day. When she got back, she said she'd gone into Cheltenham shopping and had met an old friend there. I can't say why, but somehow I didn't believe her."

He had to call Emma as soon as he got off the phone with Sophie. This was already a bad situation, which could quickly develop into something much more serious, and he had no idea how to advise the woman more than he had already. He wondered if she knew about her uncle being involved in an armed robbery—if Grace had told her. Until Sophie mentioned the gun, Grace's behavior hadn't struck him as out of the ordinary or worrisome; there could be many reasonable explanations for her conduct. Arguing on the phone, with someone she doubtless knew, and keeping it to herself was hardly cause for alarm. But the gun changed everything. Off the top of his head, he could think of only two reasons why Grace Williams would want a gun: for protection, or she planned to use it for some unknown purpose. If the former, the question was from whom? The latter, he hoped, was far-fetched.

"Here's what I would urge you to do, Sophie," he said, trying to sound comforting. "When we hang up, call the police and tell them exactly what you've told me. You shouldn't wait any longer."

She didn't reply.

"Will you do that?"

"If I do and she finds out—which she would, anyway—I'm afraid I may be putting her in even more danger. I'm not so sure it's a good idea—not yet, anyway."

"All right. After we hang up, I'll call Emma Dixon—she's the ex-policewoman. I'll have her call you direct. That way you two can work it out together. Until then the only advice I can offer—which is not much, I admit—is to keep a close eye on your mother, eavesdropping, if you can, on any future calls, and in particular listening for names. If she starts behaving irrationally, if it looks as if she might try to harm herself—or others, for that matter—call the police right away. You might also want to have another go at persuading her to tell you what's going on. If things start to worsen, she may come round to realizing that would be in her best interest."

Sophie thanked him, gave him her mobile number, and the conversation ended.

Five minutes later, Kingston had Emma on the line.

"It's Lawrence."

"I know who it is. You sound anxious."

"I am. There's been a new development and it could spell trouble."

"What's happened?"

"I just received a call from Sophie, Grace Williams's daughter. Her mother's been acting strangely lately, and Sophie's scared that she's going to do something irrational. Among other things, Grace has been receiving what Sophie is convinced are threatening phone calls. She also said Grace has a gun that she's been concealing."

"That's serious. Serious enough to call the police right away."

"That's what I advised, but she's reluctant to do that. Grace has warned her, in no uncertain terms, not to."

"No way can we get involved, Lawrence, if that's what you're thinking. If it happens to turn nasty, we would have a big problem on our hands with nondisclosure of a potentially dangerous situation. This is something that Gloucester PD or the Met should look into, immediately. It could be directly connected to Jennings's murder."

"You're right."

"I am. Nevertheless, I'll call Sophie to try to stop her from doing something stupid, to see what I can do to defuse the situation until the police get on it. There could be reasons why Grace wouldn't want the police to know. Besides, people are permitted to have guns. As long as they possess a certificate and satisfy all the rules and regulations required of the owner."

"Grace Williams could be a Canadian citizen. She might feel differently about gun regulations."

"That may be true, but on British soil, she's subject to our laws."

"What do you make of it, though?"

"Obviously someone is threatening her and she's reached a point where she has concluded that she should be prepared to defend herself—with force, if necessary. Either that or—heaven forbid—she plans to harm or eliminate the person or persons who are threatening her. There is, of course, the possibility that it's neither of the above, and there's a far simpler and more innocent explanation. Who knows?"

"I'll leave it with you, then?"

"Don't worry. I'll call Sophie the minute we hang up."

21

At five that evening, with a near-empty glass of pinot grigio on his desktop, Kingston pushed aside the notes and scribbles he'd accumulated over the last few days and sat back in his chair. Letting his mind wander willy-nilly, he gazed idly out the window, through the daylong drizzle, at his small gray-misted garden.

For the time being, he'd managed to put thoughts of Sophie Williams out of his mind, knowing that Emma would doubtlessly succeed in applying her professional negotiating skills to convince Sophie to call the police, or would do so on her behalf. As he was wondering, once more, why he hadn't heard from Andrew, the phone rang.

It was Andrew.

"Where have you been? I've been trying to reach you," Kingston said. "I've been back for three days now."

"I know. And I apologize. I went away for a couple of days. To Provence."

"Provence?"

"Right. Avignon. It was a last-minute thing—a wine-appreciation tour."

"Lucky you. Where are you now?"

"On your doorstep, actually—holding a bottle of 1985 Châteauneuf-du-Pape."

By six o'clock, the bottle was empty and Andrew knew everything there was to know about Julie, Brandon, Seattle, Kingston's side trip to San Francisco, his lunch with Andy Harris, and his tour of Alcatraz. At the point where Kingston was about to tell him about Kaminski's story and his recent conversation with Emma and postulating his theory that Butler might be Fiona's father, they both announced that they were starving and should continue the conversation over steak frites and a vin ordinaire at the Antelope.

An hour and a half later, back at his flat, Kingston was feeling the effects of the wine and the fatigue that had dogged him since his return. He was debating whether to watch the news on TV or simply go to bed and read until he dropped off. He'd chosen the latter and was tidying up the kitchen, washing the wineglasses and a couple of plates, when the phone rang. He dried his hands quickly and went to the phone in the living room.

"Dr. Kingston?" The woman's voice was faint.

Emma, was his first thought. No—she wouldn't call him 'Doctor.'

"This is he."

"It's Sophie Williams again. I'm sorry to bother you so late. I just left the police station and need someone to talk to. I don't know what to do."

"Why? What's happened, Sophie?"

Her words came quickly. "It's what I was afraid of. It's mum—she's disappeared."

"Are you at home?"

"No. I'm in London, in a café." Her voice was trembling.

"London? Tell me what happened."

"I followed her up here this morning—to this big house in a fancy neighborhood. I watched from across the street. A man let her in, but she never came out. I tried calling her mobile several times and there was no answer. That really scared me. After waiting for ten minutes, I decided to find out what was going on, so I went over and rang the doorbell. A man answered—I couldn't tell if it was the same one or not. Anyway, I told him I needed to talk with my mother, that I'd seen her go in and it was important. He insisted that no one had entered the house all morning and that she'd never been there."

"Did you call the police?"

"Yes. They came twenty minutes later and talked to someone on the staff—the owner was away, apparently. Whoever that person was assured the police that no one had entered the house that morning. He or she did admit that earlier that morning a distraught woman—meaning me—had rung the doorbell, insisting that her mother was there. The infuriating thing was that the police seemed to believe the explanation that it could have been a mistaken address. I insisted to the officers that the people were lying and that I'd seen my mother enter the house with my own eyes. No mistake. The red door, the two planters on either side—everything. They were polite but wouldn't believe me. I finally gave up and went with them to the police station and filed a report. That's where it stands right now."

"Do you remember the name of the street?"

"Er, Chiltern Terrace."

"In Primrose Hill. I know where it is. Here's what I want you to do. Get a cab and come to my flat. Do you have enough money?"

"Yes."

"All right. One last question: Does your mobile have a camera?"

"Yes."

"Then have the cabbie drive by the house on the way here, take a picture of it, and note the street number."

"I will."

Kingston gave her his address and put down the phone. His first instinct was to call Emma immediately—she had obviously not reached Sophie in time. He stared into space. What Sophie had just told him could either represent a seismic shift in their investigation, or could simply be a misunderstanding, a miscalculation on Sophie's part, suspicious circumstances that could be readily explained. He decided to wait until he'd heard her full account. Meanwhile, he thought more about Sophie, how little he knew about her. It hadn't occurred to him before, there'd been no good reason to check on her. But now it seemed clear her mother had never told her about what happened way back in the fifties, long before Sophie was born—that her uncle was one of the country's most infamous robbers who'd lived in hiding all these years under a false name.

Twenty minutes later his doorbell rang, and he ushered Sophie in.

"Thanks, Doctor," she said, feigning an apologetic smile, as they went into the living room.

"I made tea, if you'd like some," Kingston offered.

"That would be nice."

"Make yourself comfortable." A few minutes later he returned, carrying a tray with the tea and a plate of digestive biscuits. He placed it on the coffee table and lowered himself into his leather wingback, facing Sophie, gesturing with an open hand for her to help herself. He waited until she had poured the tea and stirred in the milk and sugar.

"So," he said in calming voice, as he leaned back and crossed his legs, "tell me, from the beginning, exactly what happened today."

Sophie took a sip of tea and began.

"This morning I sensed something was going on because when I came down to the kitchen, Mom was all dressed up and checking her makeup. I asked her where she was going, and she said, 'Shopping in Cheltenham.' Right from the get-go, I knew she was lying."

"Why? What is strange about her going shopping?"

"She rarely wears makeup, and certainly not to go shopping."

"Did it occur to you that she might have the gun with her?"

"I was coming to that. Yes. Normally, she's very casual about her purse, bags, keys, and so on, leaving them all over the house. But this morning she was keeping a close eye on her shoulder bag, picking it up when she went into the living room. At that point, I got kinda scared. Bells were going off in my head telling me that she could be about to do something seriously dangerous, both for her and perhaps to somebody else. I had to stop her somehow, but I didn't know how. So I asked her, point-blank, did she have the gun in her bag and where was she really going."

"How did she react?"

"She was very cool. Not the least bit surprised or upset. She said it was really none of my business; that it was her house, that I was essentially a guest, and that she could come and go as she pleased. When I pressed her about the gun, she accused me of being paranoid—but she didn't deny it." Sophie picked up her cup and took a longer sip of tea, her eyes still on Kingston's. "I considered trying to wrestle it from her, but I don't know anything about guns I didn't want to risk it going off."

"You did the right thing."

"Perhaps."

"So she left. What happened then?" he asked.

"Well, rather than call the police then and there—which I probably should have done—I decided to follow her. It was stupid, I know, but at the time it seemed like a reasonable option. Anyway, she's not a fast driver and I am—as you know—and it didn't take me long to catch up. I stayed a couple of cars behind and soon realized that we might be headed for Cheltenham after all and I could be totally wrong. Ten minutes later, we arrived at Cheltenham Spa train station. She parked the car in the lot. Now I had another problem. Should I keep going and possibly end up with egg on my face? Or should I give up? I had to move fast, so I parked my car and hurried into the station. By that time, the commuters were all gone and I could easily spot her on a seat, waiting on the eastbound platform."

"Did you know it was the one in the direction to London?"

She nodded. "I did. So I went to the ticket office and bought an open return ticket using my credit card. I'd done it once before, so I knew the drill."

Kingston placed his cup on the saucer, watching as she toyed nervously with the linen napkin. "So you ended up where?"

"Paddington. It was crowded but easy to follow her, and outside there was a row of cabs waiting. She took the first in line and I waited until it moved off before I grabbed the next one. I asked the driver to follow it. As we drove off, I mentioned that it was my mum we were following, but not why. I also told him that when she arrived at her destination, to drive past and let me off fifty feet or so beyond, so she wouldn't spot me. All he said was, 'Don't you worry, luv, easy-peasy.'"

Kingston smiled. "London cab drivers never ask questions. Only if they concern the journey."

"You're right. It was as if he did this kind of thing every other day." She gave a little sigh. "That's about it. I told you the rest, what happened when we got there. Oh, wait—" She reached in her jacket pocket and took out her mobile. "Here's a picture of the house," she said, fingers tapping the screen before handing it to Kingston.

"Very nice," he said, studying the photo. "Chiltern Terrace, you said?"

"Right."

"Number 236. Early Victorian stucco, I'd guess. 1850, thereabouts—exceptional wrought-ironwork—quite roomy by the looks of it. Must be at least a half dozen bedrooms. You don't need me to tell you that it's a very desirable area."

"Nicer than Paddington, that's for sure."

"When I first moved to London, I looked naïvely at a couple of properties in that area. Nowadays, I would guess that a house like this in Primrose Hill would sell in the neighborhood of five million." He handed her back the phone.

"The man I spoke to must have been one of the staff because he didn't look like a wealthy banker or diplomat. Far from it."

Kingston nodded. "Probably. Many families in that part of London have live-in staff. I believe there're a couple of consulates in the area, too; certainly a lot of high-profile personalities, corporate bigwigs, celebrities, and the like live there."

Sophie leaned back in the sofa and folded her hands in her lap. "I've gone over this a dozen times and I keep coming back to the same conclusion: Whoever is living in that house knows my mother and is holding her hostage. What other explanation can there be?"

"It certainly looks that way. But don't forget, she has the gun, so she's not completely at their mercy."

"But if they did know her they could've been expecting that she'd come to make trouble, then they could have easily taken her bag by force. Where would she be then?"

Kingston nodded. "Anything's possible. There's a lot we don't know, too."

An awkward pause followed, Sophie's eyes downcast. When she finally looked up, he could see that all vestiges of hope—if there had been any before—were gone. He stood, placing their cups and saucers on the tray, thinking hard, as he tidied up the table. Further discussion of Grace's alleged abduction would serve no purpose. The pressing question was what to do about Sophie.

"You'll be going back to Beechwood, I take it," he said.

"I suppose so," she replied with a defeated sigh.

"You're more than welcome to stay here overnight—I have a very comfortable guest room—though I doubt that the police will have further news by morning. I'd be more than happy to communicate with them on your behalf, if you think that's a good idea?"

"No, I'd best go back."

"Would you like something to eat before you leave? I can easily make you an omelet."

"No, I should be on my way," she said, standing. "But thanks for your kind offer. It's a two-hour journey, and I'd prefer not getting back too late. I seem to have lost my appetite, anyway."

"I'll call for a cab, then," Kingston said. "But before I do, I'd like you to answer a simple question. Because what happened today is, I think, related to events that took place many years ago, before you were born."

She looked puzzled. "What's the question?"

"It's about your mother—what she did before she moved to Canada, when she was living in England, in the fifties. Has she ever told you about her life then?"

Sophie shrugged. "Yes, of course. It was nothing that special, though. Why are you asking?"

"I'm going to level with you. I've been trying to find out more about her brother. What he did back then. That was the reason Emma and I went to see your mum at Beechwood."

"Her brother? Reggie?"

"Yes." Kingston nodded. Should he tell her or not, that Reggie was really Brian Jennings? That the money that bought Beechwood had been stolen?

No, he decided. The less she knew right now, the better.

"What about Reggie?" she asked.

"Have you any idea who would have wanted to kill him?"

She frowned, looking perplexed. "Why on earth would I?"

"I don't know. I was just wondering, perhaps, if your mum knew something and didn't want you to know, that's all."

"I wouldn't put it past her one bit. I told you how secretive she is."

Kingston gave a little smile of encouragement. "I thought that might be the case. I hope you didn't mind my asking."

"No." she shrugged. "Why don't you ask her, again?"

"When we find her I will," he said, walking to the phone to call for a cab.

22

At the front door, Kingston wished Sophie a safe journey home, telling her to call him immediately if she received any news of her mother. In turn, he promised to get back to her if he came across more information on the house and its owners. This was a white lie—he already knew how to obtain this information: an online resource that had helped him solve a case about a missing colleague, several years ago. He purposely hadn't mentioned it. In her present state of mind, Sophie could easily take it upon herself to find out who owned the house and, on impulse, do something foolhardy that could endanger both herself and her mother. That could slam the door on what appeared to a viable line of inquiry, the chance of a break of some sort. As she went down the steps to the waiting cab, he gave a long sigh of relief.

In his office, Kingston turned on his iMac and typed landregistry. gov.uk in the search bar. Land Registry, created in 1862, was a government agency that maintained records of more than twenty-three million titles and evidence of ownership of land and property in England and Wales. The world's largest property database, it processes £1 million of property every minute. He was pleased to see that his membership was still active and he could submit his search request right away.

He typed in 236 Chiltern Terrace, London NW1 in the space provided and followed the onscreen instructions. In less than two minutes, he had the information he was seeking:

Title Number: WS8765990
Date: June 19, 1995

Address of Property:	236 Chiltern Terrace, London NW1 8LD
Price Paid:	£3,600,000
Registered Owners:	St. Giles Partners LLC Greyshill Lodge, Coleshill, Buckinghamshire HP7
Lender:	Worthington Building Society

Kingston studied the information, disappointed that no personal names were listed. "St. Giles Partners," he murmured. Grace Williams had said that her brother had once owned a house in the Chalfonts, Buckinghamshire. Problem was, the Chalfonts comprised the villages of Chalfont St. Giles, Chalfont St. Peter, and Little Chalfont, not to mention the hamlet of Chalfont Common. Grace hadn't said which.

Rubbing his eyes, Kingston decided that it was too late and too confusing, and that he was trying to make something out of nothing. While waiting for the page to print, he got to thinking. If, by chance, it were Chalfont St. Giles where Reginald Payne aka Brian Jennings had once lived, then there could be some kind of connection between him and St. Giles Partners. The village was tiny. It was speculative leap, but if it proved right, it also meant Jennings could have known the people who owned the house in Primrose Hill and the one in Coleshill, a hamlet that just happened to be right next door to Chalfont St. Giles. What all this implied, he wasn't sure. "Forget it," told himself, knowing he was probably chasing rabbits anyway. He put the computer to sleep and went to the bedroom.

At breakfast that morning, he'd solved barely half the *Times* cryptic crossword clues; attempting to finish it would help take his mind off things during supper and beyond. At times like these, the puzzles were the perfect palliative, helping him escape, if for only a while, from pressing problems, like the crucial one facing him now. For the first time—and he couldn't say why—he had an uncanny feeling that he was getting a little closer to seeing a glimmer of light through the labyrinth of unsolved incidents and crimes. Were only one or two of them connected? Perhaps more? Or were they all inextricably tied together in some way? A chain of events spanning more than half century had always seemed unlikely, but if the house in Primrose Hill was a link in that chain, he was determined to find out where it led. And he had a plan.

Meantime he found himself struggling to solve the next clue: *Honestly? No, otherwise (2,3,3)*—two letters in the first word, three each in the following two. Staring at it, trying to decipher its meaning, he started to wonder if he might not be better off reading a book rather than putting his already taxed brain through more intellectual gymnastics. Then, just as he was about to put the puzzle aside, he focused on the word *otherwise*, muttering, "another way to put it." That could be it, he realized: another way to put *Honestly*—an anagram. A few seconds later, after shuffling the eight letters, he'd solved it: *On the sly*.

It seemed, somehow, very appropriate.

"For the last time, no. I'm not going to lend you the Land Rover." Andrew was calm yet adamant. They were on their second glass of London Pride ale, sitting across from each other in Andrew's art moderne living room.

Kingston had called Andrew earlier and told him about Sophie's phone call and visit, purposely playing down the seriousness of Grace's disappearance, knowing that if he were to tell Andrew the full story, he would instantly see it as yet another tempting-fate situation that Kingston had no business getting involved with.

After the first glass of ale, he'd told Andrew more about Sophie's visit—not mentioning the gun and stressing the fact that the police were already involved—and then, his nascent plan of action. The underlying motive for doing so was to borrow Andrew's old Land Rover.

The plan that he'd formulated overnight was simple and involved little or no risk. As soon as possible, he would camp in a car, out of sight, across from 236 Chiltern Terrace and observe vehicles coming and going from the house. His theory was equally straightforward: If the London house and the house in Coleshill were indeed owned by the same person or entity, there was a strong likelihood that the owner or owners would spend their weekends in the country, a time-worn English custom. If so, it would only be a matter of judgment as to which car to follow. He hoped that this would become evident if and when it happened.

The object of the exercise was twofold: first, to find out where the house in Coleshill was located, and second, to get a good look at the passengers. If Sophie was right—and he now believed she was—that her mother was being held hostage, then it stood to reason that her captors would want to move her to another location as quickly as possible. They would be smart enough to know that the police could return at any time with a search warrant. Grace Williams showing up on their doorstep must have been an unwelcome surprise. And then there was Sophie's intrusion to complicate matters. They had to move quickly. Getting her out of the house would be their top priority. If Kingston's hunch was correct, there was a good chance that they would transfer her to the house at Coleshill.

The only hitch in his plan was that to conduct such a surveillance, he required an anonymous vehicle that wouldn't draw attention or be remembered easily. His mint TR4 was out of the question, and so was Andrew's pillar-box-red Mini Cooper. But Andrew's old Land Rover was ideal. Andrew kept it at his house on the river and used it exclusively for hauling construction and garden stuff. It was drab green and showed every day of its fifteen years of use and abuse. But Andrew was being recalcitrant, even though Kingston knew that in the end he would agree.

"I'm really surprised you could come up with something so daft. It's asking for trouble, and didn't we all agree it was a closed case? And you even said that Emma was of the same opinion—that it was now a matter for the police."

"You're right. I did. But surely that doesn't preclude my carrying out something as simple as trailing a car to find out where it ends up. As long as all the right precautions are taken, what on earth could possibly go wrong? Even if they spotted me—which is most unlikely—what's the very worst that could happen?"

"Hello? Remember what happened to this face?" Andrew pointed to his cheek. "Come on, Lawrence. Let the police deal with it, for God's sake."

"Sophie's already been to the police station and filed a missing-persons report. I forgot to tell you that. The police won't take any immediate action—you know that—and by the time they do, it'll be too late. The house will be clean."

Andrew sighed.

"All right, as you wish," Kingston said, getting up awkwardly from the Corbusier chair. "I need to move quickly because they're not going to wait around. It's now or never. For all I know, they have moved her already."

"So what are you planning to do?"

"I'll just have to risk it in the TR."

"You could paint a Union Jack on the door."

"Not funny."

Andrew got up and disappeared into the kitchen. In no time he was back, dangling two keys on a fob between his thumb and forefinger.

"I'm doing this for only one reason, Lawrence, and that is to give you the least possible chance of getting into trouble—to protect you from yourself. If I don't, I know damned well you'll go anyway. You might also want to let Emma know what you're up to. I doubt very much that she'll approve."

Kingston nodded, his expression as earnest as Andrew's. He put the keys in his pocket. "Thank you. I won't mess up. And I will tell Emma, of course. You can rest assured, too, that if things start to get even the least bit dodgy, I'll chuck it in and head for home. That's a promise."

"All right, then," Andrew said, still looking disillusioned.

"If it's okay with you, I'll drive down to Bourne End this evening and make the swap. I'll take good care of her, don't worry."

"You know where the garage key is, right?"

"I do."

"Call me if you run into any problems. At Bourne End, I mean."

"I will."

"You might want to lock it if you park it anywhere. There're some tools and other gear in the back that I wouldn't want to lose."

"Don't worry, I'll take good care."

"See that you do," Andrew replied. "Of the car—and yourself."

Kingston nodded.

He left, feeling much better about his doing the right thing.

23

Twenty yards up from 236 Chiltern Terrace, Kingston parked the old Land Rover on the opposite side of the street, under convenient shadows, between the wide-spaced streetlights. He glanced at his watch: nine P.M. It was getting darker. As luck would have it, the house was well lighted from a lamppost some twenty feet away. His sheltered vantage point gave him a clear view of the residence and, unless he dozed off, no vehicles could come or go without his spotting them. As he'd expected, there was little traffic and few pedestrians. Those that there were would think little of a gray-haired man sitting in his car with the newspaper propped up on the steering wheel.

Once clear of London's suburbs, Kingston had made good time to Bourne End, where everything had gone according to plan. The Land Rover had started instantly—Andrew was obsessive about his cars—and Kingston had left his Triumph in the locked and alarmed double garage. In the roughly two-hour round-trip journey, he'd had plenty of time to think about the various scenarios that could soon confront him and how he would deal with them. Though it was prudent to anticipate everything that could go wrong, he knew that trying to second-guess what might happen and how he should react was a wasted exercise. He would have to make snap judgments if and when circumstances demanded it. He must also call Emma, but not until he had something worth reporting. If she knew that he was in a car spying on a house in a wealthy London enclave, where an armed Grace Williams might be held captive, she would call the police immediately.

He put the thought out of his mind.

Opening the flask he had brought with him, he poured a stainless-steel cup of hot coffee. Also to help stay awake, he had the radio on, at a low level, listening to music, trying to imagine being in "their" place—meaning Grace's captors, whoever they were—and what time they would choose to move her. All of this, of course, depended entirely on if she was captive there—and if so, whether that was their plan.

Night came and both street and pedestrian traffic dwindled from sporadic to virtually none for long periods. There was little or no activity at any of the houses within his angle of sight, let alone number 236. Primrose Hill was now as quiet and ostensibly as peaceful as any village in the Cotswolds. By two thirty he'd eaten the sandwich he'd brought along, as well as an apple, half a Cadbury fruit & nut chocolate bar, and had finished the coffee.

Around four o'clock he had his first scare, when a car approached slowly. It wasn't until it was almost within forty feet or so that he saw it was a police car. He slumped as low as he could in the seat, praying that they hadn't spotted him. It passed without slowing, and he let out a sigh and a mute blessing for the dark shadows.

He awoke with a jump and an ache in his lower back. It was still dark, but on the tiny scrap of horizon between the trees he could see the sky beginning to lighten. He looked at his watch: four forty-five. His first thought was that in the forty minutes or so that he'd dozed off, he might have missed something.

Five minutes later, the porch light went on at number 236. Kingston picked up his small Luger binoculars from the passenger seat and held them ready in his lap. For five minutes, no activity. It then occurred to him that the light might be on a timer. But that made no sense—why set it to go on at daybreak? He raised the binoculars.

His question was answered when a heavyset man with shaved head, wearing a suit and tie, emerged from the house. He closed the front door behind him and walked down the gravel drive. A minute later, Kingston saw headlights, and a dark-colored late-model Mercedes Estate pulled up alongside the porch. The man got out of the car and went back into the house. Kingston lowered the binoculars, reminding himself to be extremely careful at this point. The neighborhood would be soon stirring, and there was a chance of his being noticed by one of the residents of Primrose Hill, a stockbroker or type A personality who wanted to be in his City office at first light.

Almost fifteen minutes passed and Kingston was getting impatient, beginning to wonder yet again if he had been too hasty in supposing that something sinister was going on in the house. He had no hard evidence, and everything he knew was based solely on Sophie's account of the incident. What was equally worrisome was that the police didn't think the situation warranted immediate investigation, and they'd interviewed both Sophie and the people in the house. According to her, they'd even conducted a cursory search.

His funk evaporated when the door opened again. The same man he'd seen earlier was now pushing a wheelchair, easing it down the shallow single step from the house to the driveway. There, he opened the rear door of the car. Kingston grabbed the binoculars.

"Sod it," he muttered. Whoever was in the chair was only partially visible, blocked by the open door. Was it Grace Williams? He wanted it to be, praying for a clearer look.

At that moment, a second man emerged from the house. He was tall and wore a dark overcoat. Alongside him holding his hand was a well-dressed woman wearing a floppy hat. After some hesitation and a few words with the man, she got in the car through the rear door. Kingston figured that when the invalid was helped upright, prior to being eased into the car, there was good chance that he would be able to see the face. He gripped his binoculars tighter. The man behind the wheelchair helped the invalid to a wobbly standing position and then partially lifted her or him into the rear car seat, next to the woman.

At that instant, Kingston got a clear view of the invalid's face.

It was not Grace Williams. It was an elderly man.

In quick succession, the wheelchair was stowed in the boot, the heavyset man got in the driver's seat, the man in the overcoat slipped into the passenger seat, the car doors slammed silently shut, and the Mercedes eased out of the driveway onto Chiltern Terrace.

Kingston put aside the binoculars and the newspaper, turned the key in the ignition, and waited. He wanted to see which way the Mercedes turned at the end of the road before pulling out behind it.

Shadowing the car at this time of day shouldn't be too difficult. And if he lost sight of it, he would just head to Coleshill as fast as possible, with the hope of beating them there. He still had no way of knowing if Coleshill was their destination, but as the journey unfolded he had a gut feeling that he would be proved right.

The Mercedes's turn signal was blinking.

Kingston pulled out, ready to start on the next phase of his surveillance.

24

MAINTAINING A COMFORTABLY safe distance behind the Mercedes, Kingston saw the Chalfont St. Peter exit sign and knew that it was only a matter of minutes before they arrived at what was now, without question, their destination: Coleshill.

About a half mile on the west side of the village, the Mercedes began to slow, the left-hand turn signal flashing. From where he was, some twenty yards behind, he couldn't see a road on the left, guessing that it was likely a private drive. This was convenient because Kingston could take his time passing, to determine if his supposition was right. The Mercedes made its turn, and a few seconds later Kingston slowed as he passed a narrow paved driveway, flanked by stubby white pillars. Each bore the name GREYSHILL LODGE on a bronze plaque. He could see his quarry disappearing at the far end of the straight drive, but no house was visible.

Knowing that villages like Coleshill and the Chalfonts would still be fast asleep at this time of morning—it was only just past six thirty—Kingston decided to press on to Amersham, a larger town about five miles away. With luck he'd find a café or service station open and a much-needed bathroom, where he could get a cup of tea and something to eat while he decided what to do next. High on that list was a call to Emma. By nature decisive, one to tackle situations head on, he was starting to feel the need to talk to someone about what was unfolding. Despite this, he resisted the urge, knowing full well that he would get no sympathy whatsoever; she would tell him, in no polite terms, to return home immediately and report everything to the police. Until now he hadn't had a confrontation with her, but were that to happen, he suspected he would find himself on the losing end.

At seven forty-five, in Seasons Café-Deli on Amersham High Street, Kingston had just finished a full English breakfast. Now on his third cup of Darjeeling tea, he'd spent most of the last forty-five minutes dwelling on the morning's escapade. One side of his brain was telling him to just give up and go home; the other was egging him on to find out more about the house and who lived there. It was too early in the day to employ his favorite ploy of visiting the local pub to ferret out information about people and places in the vicinity. The only other possibility was to spin some cock-and-bull story to a local estate agent, claiming that he was researching properties for sale in the area, but he'd tried this once before with disastrous results. In any case, it would be at least two hours before the agents opened up.

Picking up his check, he looked up to see a woman enter the café. She was tall, notably skinny, with angular features, a pale complexion, and gray hair. In a dark turtleneck, with a hat that cast a shadow over her eyes, she reminded him of Grace Williams.

As the woman walked across the room to sit down, he realized he was frowning. It took him a moment to figure out why. It was the hat.

He thought back to the scene in Primrose Hill: the foursome waiting to get in the car. He closed his eyes and tried to recapture it in detail.

He had missed something, Kingston realized. Had been so preoccupied trying to get a good look at the person in the wheelchair, convinced that it was Grace Williams, when all the time . . .

He tried to picture the woman and man, her standing beside the chair, him holding her hand. It was odd. That gesture of affection was out of character with what was happening at the time. Then it dawned on him that there was another explanation for what he'd seen. The two weren't holding hands; the man was gripping her wrist. Or worse, the woman had been handcuffed.

He was now convinced that it had been Grace Williams. He should have taken a closer look at her face. That was probably the reason for the hat, too.

Leaving the café, he walked back to the Land Rover, parked a few doors down the street. He knew it was still speculation, but it felt right—sufficiently so to justify his staying in the area, killing a couple of hours, then visiting an estate agent's office he'd spotted coming in. Even if he found out who owned or lived at Greyshill, he had no idea of its significance or how it might change anything. But while he was on the doorstep, he could think of no good reasons not to make the effort.

Sitting in the car, he decided to call Andrew. He at least deserved to know that everything was going well and no harm had befallen his car, or Kingston, for that matter.

He took out his mobile and thumbed in Andrew's number. Barely three rings and he answered.

"It's Lawrence. Thought I'd check in and let you know what's going on."

"I appreciate that. I was going to give you until noon before I called Scotland Yard."

"No need to worry. Everything went according to Hoyle, as far as my guess about the Primrose Hill house and their going to Bucks for the weekend. I had to sit in the Rover twiddling my thumbs until dawn this morning before anything happened, though. Three men and a woman took off in a big Mercedes."

"Was the woman Grace Williams?"

"Can't say for sure, but I believe so. I followed them to Coleshill, where I gave up when they turned into the driveway of Greyshill Lodge, the house listed on the Land Registry site. It's a bit complicated. I'll tell you all about it before the day's over. Right now I'm in Amersham. I just had breakfast and I'm headed back there."

"Why? Aren't you running the risk of someone recognizing the car?"

"The risk is about zero. The house is at the end of a long drive, about a mile outside the village, and I plan to be there for ten minutes at the outside."

"To do what?"

"Try to find out who these people are. To get names. The eldest man was in a wheelchair."

"Whatever that means. I'm not going to ask you how you plan to get that information, but for God's sake, Lawrence, be bloody careful, that's all."

"I will, don't worry. All being well, I should be back after lunch, to give you a full report. I'll call you when I leave Coleshill."

"Take care."

"Oh, could you do me a favor? In about an hour, could you call Emma for me? She should know what's going on. Tell her I'll call the minute I return, when I have more information. Whatever you say, don't make it sound risky—you know what I mean."

"You're a little late. She already called a half hour ago. I told her what you were doing, and while she didn't come right out and say so, there was no question that she took a dim view. Exasperated might be the right word."

"I'm not surprised. Don't worry, I'll call you when I'm heading back."

Kingston turned the phone off, thinking. Just maybe, before the day was over, he might have some news that would cheer her up a little, change her exasperation to something resembling approval. Gratitude would be even better.

25

Two hours later, Kingston backed into a parking space on a quiet side street about a half mile north of Coleshill. Greyshill Lodge was a mile away on the other side of the village, but he wasn't taking any chances.

Sanderson's Estate Agents, a five-minute walk on the main road, was situated in a Victorian brick building, amid a short row of shops, a café, and a beauty shop. He'd spotted the sign earlier, on his way to Amersham.

Before leaving the café, he'd spent five minutes in the gents', washing and tidying up to put on a reasonably presentable appearance. Even with a five o'clock shadow, nobody would ever guess that he'd spent the night in a car with little or no sleep. The odds of his being able to pry personal information out of an estate agent were long, but worn cliché as it was, there was nothing to be lost and everything to be gained.

As he opened Sanderson's glass-paneled front door, he heard the faint dingdong of a bell somewhere in the back. With no one in sight, he waited and looked around, not that there was anything special to look at, only a tidy office with a dozen or so framed photos of Bucks scenery on the walls, a couple of passable Oriental carpets, and four modern-style desks. He heard the clip-clop of heels on hardwood flooring, and a woman appeared through a rear door.

"Good morning," she said chirpily as she crossed the office. She was fashionably dressed, slender, and looked as if she'd just spent several hours in a beauty salon.

"Please sit down," she said, pulling out a chair for Kingston and going around to the other side of the desk. "I'm Zandra Olson, estate marketing associate. How may I help you?"

Kingston detected a vestigial trace of a foreign accent, as she extended a hand with rings on three fingers.

"Lawrence Kingston," he said, shaking her silky hand.

"So what brings you here so early today, Mr. Kingston? Are you looking for property in the area?"

"I'm not, but a close friend is. He's retired and he's set his mind on this part of Bucks. I'm beginning to see why," he said, glancing around at the photos. "He spent a lot of time here as a child, at the home of friends of his parents. Quite a lovely old, rambling house, from what he remembers. As we get older, I suppose those memories take on more meaning. Anyway, he wanted to come with me today but couldn't make it. He's been out of sorts these last couple of weeks. So I promised him that while I was here for the day, I'd try to contact a local agent to set the ball rolling, as it were. He's been doing a lot of research on the Internet, but he's smart enough to know that working with an agent in or near the Chalfonts is far better—the only way to go."

"I couldn't agree more. May I ask where he lives now?"

"We both live in London, in Chelsea. We've known each other for about a dozen years."

"Will he be selling or looking for a second home?"

"Probably selling—not necessarily right away, though."

"What sort of property is he looking for?"

"Nothing too large, three or four bedrooms at the most."

"Is he thinking of country property or a house situated in one of the villages?"

"Country, one or two acres, perhaps. An established garden isn't a prerequisite but could be a big plus. He's an excellent gardener." He smiled. "At our age we don't have time to sit and watch trees grow."

She returned the smile and nodded. "What kind of price range does he have in mind?"

"He's researched the market thoroughly and tells me that somewhere in the neighborhood of one to one and a half million should buy a suitable property. I can't speak for him, of course, but if he found just the right place he might be willing to inch it up a little."

"Good." She opened a drawer, pulled out a folder, and handed him a couple of sheets of paper. "Let's do this. Why don't you have your friend fill out this form and mail or e-mail it back to me? It's quite straightforward. In the meantime, I can start looking at inventory and pull together a list of available properties for him to view. You can assure him that, at the price range you mentioned, there's no question that we can find him the right property. As a matter of fact, I can already think of two or three that he might like. Here's my card and a brochure on our company," she added, sliding them across the desktop.

Kingston picked them up and stood. "Thank you very much," he said. "You've been a great help. I'll see that my friend, Alex, gets the form back to you ASAP, and when you're both ready I hope to come up with him. Nothing I enjoy more than looking at country houses. Who knows, maybe I'll do the same one day."

"Excellent," she said, rising and coming around the desk to see him out.

Near the front door, Kingston stopped. "I almost forgot. That house I mentioned, the one that Alex visited as a child. He asked me, if I had the time, to drive by and see what it looks like today. I wonder if you might know of it."

"It's quite possible. Where is it?"

"I don't know, for sure, but it's called Greyshill."

"Greyshill."

From the deliberate way she'd said the name, Kingston knew that the house was more than familiar to her.

After a long pause, she said, "Yes, I know it. It's about a mile from here, but you won't be able to see it from the road, I'm afraid."

"That's too bad. He was also wondering if the same family owned it. Would you know by chance who owns Greyshill now?"

Her smile was enigmatic. "I do, Mr. Kingston, but as a professional courtesy we're not permitted to provide information of a personal nature concerning local residents. I'm sure you understand."

"Of course," he replied.

They shook hands and Kingston left, disappointed at coming away empty-handed. While he'd been careful not to reveal Andrew's identity, he was now wondering if he had been wise to give his real name

Back behind the wheel of the Rover, he snapped the seat-belt buckle closed and stared out the windscreen, weighing his options. Three came to mind. The first was to return to Greyshill, park somewhere out of sight and wait, hoping that a delivery person or the postman would show up, then try to get him to part with the name of the owner or the people living there. The more he thought about the idea, the more unrealistic it became. He couldn't even come up with a question or plausible reason for inquiring that wouldn't risk raising suspicion. Regardless, the response would doubtless be much the same as Zandra Olson's. And what would happen if he were chatting up the postman and someone from the house emerged from the driveway wanting to know what was going on?

The second option was the pub, but it relied on luck to a great extent. This time, though, it would carry an added element of risk, inasmuch that he'd already made one inquiry in a very small village. News traveled fast in these tight-knit, Midsomer-like communities. He'd also have to wait until the pubs opened, usually eleven o'clock at the earliest.

The third option was simply to go home. Something in him rebelled at the idea, but all things considered—his assurances to Andrew, his agreement with Emma—perhaps that was the best choice.

He started the Land Rover, then hesitated. He remembered his promise to call Andrew when he was heading back. He took out his mobile and punched in Andrew's number. The answerphone intercepted.

"It's Lawrence." Kingston glanced at his watch. "It's almost ten thirty and I'm leaving Coleshill and heading home. There's nothing more I can do here, and you'll be pleased to know that I'm still in one piece, likewise your car. See you in an hour or thereabouts. Cheers."

26

KINGSTON DROVE OFF mulling over what had happened in the last nine hours or so, disappointed more than anything that he'd been unable to identify any of the people who had sneaked out of the house at Primrose Hill at the crack of dawn. That alone suggested they had something to hide. What was it about the driver, and the man in the overcoat, too? They hardly looked like domestic staff. On the plus side, he was now more convinced than ever that the woman in the hat was indeed Grace Williams and that he was right about the hand-holding masquerade.

There were few cars on the road, and the weather was pleasant. All around, puffy domes of "Constable" clouds dawdled across the mostly blue sky, imbuing a feeling of contentment, even through the windscreen of a car. Following the gentle curves of the country road at a leisurely pace—there would come time to ratchet up the speed when he joined the A413 in a couple of miles—he was relaxed and feeling better about things, generally.

Then he glanced in his rearview mirror. What he saw spelled trouble: A large SUV was closing in at breakneck speed for such a narrow and winding road. Any moment he expected the impatient blast of a horn, forcing him to speed up or pull aside so the lunatic could pass. Kingston eased over to the left as far as the grassy verge would allow. Another glance in his mirror and he could see the SUV alongside, about to pass. He couldn't resist taking a quick look out his half-open window to see who the driver was.

It was a man, whose expression and demeanor signaled serious trouble. The instant their eyes met, the SUV swerved hard left. There would have been a nasty collision if not for Kingston's swift reaction, accelerating and lurching off the road onto the lumpy grass.

This was more than just a road rage incident in the making, he realized, struggling to keep the Rover under control as the SUV maintained its position alongside, inching ever closer. Ahead, the road took a shallow curve, and Kingston was alarmed to see that the verge ended, replaced by a low drystone wall.

There was no escape. Now all he could think of was self-preservation. He kept tapping the brakes, praying that he could coax the Rover to rest on the slippery grass before the verge ended. With a dozen or so feet to spare, it finally bounced to a stop, the engine stalling. He took a deep breath and let it out noisily, cursing and swearing at the maniacal driver. As he opened the door to assess the situation and clear his head, his heart skipped a beat.

The SUV had stopped on the verge thirty feet behind him. Two men were walking purposefully toward him, and by the looks on their faces they weren't about to tell him that his brake light wasn't working.

His mind flashed on Andrew's bruised and swollen face. Was Kingston about to get the same treatment? How had they found out about him? It had to be from Zandra Olson; there was nobody else. These and other questions flashed through his mind as the two drew closer.

Kingston recognized one of them as the driver of the Mercedes: the same shaved head, height, and build, only now he wore a leather bomber jacket and jeans. The other was foreign looking—Slavic, maybe—tall and square jawed.

They stopped a few feet away, and then, for a few seconds, simply stared at him. No words, no menacing gestures.

All at once, with lightning speed, a stinging backhand slammed into Kingston's cheek, setting him back on his heels. His hand went to his face and came away bloody.

"Your luck just ran out, Mr. Kingston," the man in the leather jacket snarled. Before Kingston could get out a word, the other man grasped his forearm with numbing force and started dragging him to the SUV.

"We're going for a little ride," he said with the trace of a foreign accent and a sadistic leer. Kingston knew it would be costly, and in the end futile, to put up a fight; these were professional thugs. Seconds later he was hustled into the backseat of the SUV, hands secured behind his back with a nylon cable tie, and the doors locked.

The man who'd struck Kingston walked to the Land Rover and got behind the wheel. He backed onto the road and drove off. The other man, now at the wheel of the SUV, made a U-turn and took off back in the direction of Coleshill.

By now, Kingston's was sure of their destination. Perversely, it appeared that he was about to get his wish: to find out who was living at Greyshill.

27

KINGSTON SAT ON the edge of a queen-size bed, staring out of tall windows that overlooked a garden of an acre or more. He'd spent the first few minutes in the bathroom, bathing his cheek, which had an angry three-inch gash on it from a ring on the bald man's hand. It was superficial, but still painful. A fencing scar might not look all that bad, he thought optimistically.

The sight of the garden took his mind off the stinging discomfort. The foreground was all lawn, with a checkerboard pattern of fresh mower marks. On either side, high brick walls were backdrop to deep flower beds containing shrubs—roses, of course—and the requisite perennials. At the lower end was a green-surfaced tennis court. On the opposite side, a large wall-enclosed kitchen garden included what appeared to be a chicken run and rows of beehives, backed by a stand of towering copper beech trees. Beyond, in the distance, were green pastures white-speckled with grazing sheep. This peaceful and innocuous-looking setting was a sharp contrast to the serious and potentially threatening situation he faced.

There was no doubt that this was Greyshill. He'd recognized the two white pillars on the way in. When the house had first come into sight, it was far beyond anything he'd expected. By his reckoning, it was certainly classified as of architectural and/or historic interest, early 1800s. In addition to the sprawling two-story white-brick house, with its gray slate roof and wisteria-draped porte cochère and walls, several outbuildings ringed a circular courtyard large enough to park at least thirty cars. These he guessed to be a small guesthouse, stables, and various workshops. Greyshill reeked gentility, scrupulous taste, and a great deal of money.

On arrival, he'd been relieved of his mobile, marched straight through the house and up a wide double-arched staircase to the spacious bedroom where he now sat pondering his precarious future. In those few seconds, he'd got to see enough of the interior to confirm his first impressions. Everything about the décor was pluperfect: inlaid marble flooring, room-size old Oriental carpets, superb antique furniture, and crystal chandeliers—clearly no expense had been spared.

An hour had passed; obviously whoever was calling the shots was in no hurry to deal with him. He'd had plenty of time to contemplate his plight, and he took cold comfort in knowing that, if nothing else, he might face the person or people who had arranged for Andrew's beating and perhaps had a hand in Brian Jennings's murder.

Despite the uncertainty of what lay ahead—now knowing what these people could do—he felt surprisingly sanguine about his prospects. The very worst-case scenario—one he preferred not to dwell on—was that they would dispose of him, making it appear to be an accident of some sort. That eventuality was unlikely, he hastily persuaded himself, because his captors would realize that others would know of his whereabouts as well as his reason for being in Coleshill. Given the opportunity, he would warn them that both Andrew and the police were aware of his activities, and if he wasn't back in London by the end of the day they would come looking for him at Greyshill.

Lying on the bed, head propped up on a silk pillow, staring at the intricate crown molding on the coved ceiling, he started to make a mental accounting of what had brought him to this dénouement: The events of the last few weeks that had started in Cheltenham with Letty McGuire and her missing mother had led him to Emma and to Reginald Payne, aka Brian Jennings, and now to Grace Williams and Greyshill.

And lurking around every corner, of course, was the damned rose.

Despite what he'd learned from Andy Harris and Darrell Kaminski, Kingston was nowhere near solving that riddle, either, though the likelihood that Jennings was implicated—solely or in part—now seemed overwhelming. His remarkable accomplishment with the garden at

Beechwood showed he was the only person in this entire affair with an expert knowledge of gardening—and roses.

His thoughts turned again to Grace. He wondered if she, too, was locked up in a room somewhere nearby. What exactly was her role was in this drama? How much had she known about the robbery? Why had she been carrying a gun? To avenge her brother's murder? And what about Sophie? He was lying on this bed because her story and how she'd told it had never raised the slightest doubt in his mind. For her to make it up would have been difficult or fiendishly clever. And why would she? Kingston supposed it was remotely possible that she'd been confused, distracted, or somehow mistaken that her mother had entered the house at Primrose Hill, never to come out. Or had Grace Williams entered expecting to stay for a while? For dinner or a meeting? There could be many reasons. Was it all part of a more Machiavellian scheme?

As Kingston pondered the imponderable, he heard a key turning in the door lock.

At last, it seemed, he was going to get some answers.

28

THE DOOR SWUNG open, and Kingston stood.

Facing him was the tall thug who'd driven off in the Land Rover. The man's expression was no different from their last encounter: surly and hostile, the only look he knew, Kingston suspected. He was now wearing a black suit with an open-neck silk shirt, causing Kingston an inward smile.

With one hand on the doorknob, he beckoned with the other for Kingston to come out, stepping aside to allow plenty of space between them. One side of his jacket was pulled aside just enough to reveal a holstered gun. Kingston took it as a not-so-subtle hint.

With the man close on his heels, they walked along the corridor, down the staircase, and across the spacious marble entry hall where, following curt instructions from behind, he entered a high-ceilinged drawing room–cum-library. It, too, had the stamp and sympathetic touches of a highly paid interior decorator: comfortable clublike furniture, laddered bookshelves across two paneled walls, a soft-hued Tabriz carpet covering most of the cherrywood floor, double French doors at one end, and a huge limestone fireplace at the other.

Kingston was surprised when his escort retreated, leaving him alone. He occupied himself for the next few minutes examining the library. Mixed in with historical works were books on politics, law, business management, social sciences, and biographies, mostly of notable British and foreign political figures. The remainder of the volumes appeared to have been supplied by the decorator as space fillers: used books by the yard.

Kingston crossed to the French doors that looked out onto a small cloisterlike garden with a center fountain, a teak Chippendale-style bench, and jasmine and other vines greening the high-walled surround. As he expected, the doors were locked. A gate set in the far wall was slightly ajar, with no greenery beyond. He had no idea which direction it faced but guessed that it led to the front of the house and the parking area.

He backtracked and sat in one of the leather chairs, picked up a copy of the *Spectator* from a stack of magazines on the coffee table, and started to read. Less than five minutes had passed when an almost imperceptible breeze wafted across the room. He was about to get up to see if someone had opened the doors to the garden, when he heard a rustle behind him. He stood and turned. Facing him, standing motionless inside the open French door twenty feet away, was a fashionably dressed, slender woman, holding a silk scarf and a book—a novel, by the looks of it. Backlit by the setting sun, it was hard to distinguish her features. He squinted for several seconds before it registered whom he was looking at.

Grace Williams.

"Dr. Kingston," she said, shaking her head slowly. "You shouldn't have come here."

She appeared oddly calm and self-possessed, her expression showing neither surprise nor concern.

"I didn't plan to, I can assure you. I was . . . uh . . . encouraged, shall we say," he said, gingerly touching his cheek.

"Yes. I saw you arrive. I'm sorry."

Kingston frowned. "Then perhaps you could explain. I'm confused. I was certain that you were being kept at the house in Primrose Hill against your will. Locked up. And here you are with free run of this place by the looks of it."

"Sophie. She put you up to it. I was worried about that—clever of her to follow me but a stupid mistake. It was an even bigger mistake on your part to listen to her," she said, as if she hadn't heard his question. "You realize you're in terrible danger here?"

"It had occurred to me. Why don't you just tell me what you're doing here and who owns this house?" he replied, trying not to show his impatience.

"I'm sorry for you, Doctor, I really am. You shouldn't have got mixed up in this business, but this is hardly the time or place to explain. It's too late for all that, I'm afraid," she said, tenseness creeping into her voice.

"Who are these people, Grace? Why won't you tell me?"

She crossed the room, stopping briefly halfway, resting a hand on the back of one of the leather chairs, and placing her scarf and book on the seat. "It doesn't matter anymore," she said, weariness in her voice. "Your showing up changes everything, but I'm just going to have to deal with it as best I can."

Kingston was starting to believe that he had made a huge mistake in trusting Sophie. Far from being a victim, it seemed Grace Williams had never been kidnapped or even endangered. Was she one of them? It seemed the only answer.

He was thinking of what to say or do next when the awkward silence was broken by the sound of car doors slamming shut, coming from the open French doors. Grace's demeanor changed abruptly.

"Your questions will soon be answered, Doctor. Your being here is unfortunate and inconvenient, but you brought it upon yourself, and I'm sorry I can't change that. I know you meant well. It's too late for explanations now, though. This is far more complicated than you think—far more serious and dangerous."

"Forget all that. It's irrelevant now. What about the gun? Do you still have it?"

"If you're thinking of making a run for it, forget it. You wouldn't even make it to the front door. These people don't need to find an excuse to kill you."

"So whose side are you on?" Kingston snapped.

"You're going to find out any—"

They both looked toward the creaking door as it swung open slowly.

An overweight, elderly man in a wheelchair appeared first—the person Kingston had seen at Primrose Hill. His thinning white hair was neatly combed, and his milky-blue, watery eyes chose to ignore them as he was wheeled into the room by the bald thug.

The man pointed toward the fireplace. "Over there will do," he said in a commanding voice that belied his feeble appearance. A few seconds later, satisfied with his positioning, he tilted his head to his bodyguard. "No need for you to stay, Victor. I'll call if I need you."

Now in visual command of the room, beefy, livid hands grasping the arms of the wheelchair, he took measure of Kingston and Williams, his teary eyes moving from one to the other like a judge about to don the black cap.

"Dr. Kingston," he rumbled, after a posturing silence. "First, perhaps you'll explain why you followed me from London and tried to obtain information about me and Greyshill, under false pretences and illicitly, from Sanderson's estate agents. You're an intelligent man. Surely you must know this type of deception is criminal and could lead to your facing charges."

Kingston nodded. "I've no doubt you can arrange for that. I also know that forcible abduction, physical assault, and imprisonment are indictable offenses."

"Not when it can be proved, beyond doubt, that you came here armed and with intent to do bodily harm to me and my staff," he shot back with a supercilious smile. "Your word against mine. Who do you think they're more likely to believe?"

"Please let's dispense with the lies and threats. Since you seem to know all about me, why don't you tell me who you are and, more important, why you think I pose a threat to you. You might also explain—"

"He's Allen Jay Hillier," Grace Williams interjected.

Kingston's eyes widened.

"You recognize the name, I see," she said. "Not a surprise. It's in the papers regularly. Allen is chairman of VirTex Group, Britain's fifteenth-biggest corporation. Along with a half dozen other companies, they own Alcor Pharmaceuticals, Symonds Biotech, and Metafor Systems. To salve his conscience, there's his charitable group, the philanthropic Hillier Foundation." She paused for breath. "Oh, I forgot to mention his majority stake in a Premier League football club and partnership in a

Formula One racing team. He's also a major political donor—both local and national—and is on the board of a half dozen other companies. In addition to this house and the one in London, he owns a villa in Cap Ferrat." She paused again. "Concise but accurate, I believe, is it not?"

Hillier said nothing. At first his expression had been one of modest approval, but it now betrayed a nervous uncertainty, wondering what she was leading up to.

"He's also a fraud, a former crime-syndicate operative, a murderer . . . and my former lover. Accurate, too, Allen?"

Kingston couldn't believe what he was hearing and watching. He scrutinized Hillier's face for a reaction, wondering how he would respond.

Hillier remained surprisingly calm. "What's got into you, Grace?" he asked. "Have I completely misjudged you? Surely this is not why you came to see me, to insult me and accuse me of these preposterous and unprovable crimes." He turned to Kingston. "Did you put her up to this? Have you two been working together all this time?"

Kingston shook his head. "It really doesn't matter, but for what it's worth, no, we haven't." Out of the corner of his eye, he noticed Grace bending, almost casually, to pick up her book from the leather chair. Hillier had noticed, too. In the midst of such a tense confrontation it seemed such an odd thing to do. Her action made sense when she she opened the book, reached inside and pulled out a handgun, and let the book tumble to the floor, exposing its hollowed-out center.

An eerie hush fell as Grace stood, feet apart, the gun leveled at Hillier with a two-handed grip. Kingston knew immediately that she knew how to use it.

"Put that damned thing down," Hillier snapped finally, as if it would do any good.

Grace stepped two paces closer. She was now fewer than ten feet from the man. "You're finished, Allen." Her voice was remarkably calm. "I've sent a long letter addressed to Nicholas Cooper, a reporter at the *Daily Mail*, telling him everything about you and your despicable past. There's no way now to stop it reaching its destination." She paused, as if to let it sink in, then continued, the black-barreled gun steady in her hand. "I must congratulate you, though. How you've managed to keep it a secret all these years is inconceivable, even if it meant removing people who stood in your way or threatened to expose you—my brother, for one. But soon the entire world will know who you really are and what you've done."

"You're mad," Hillier shouted. "You think I can't stop you?"

"Just try. You make the slightest move to call in your attack dogs, and you're dead. I know how to use this and, from here, I can put a bullet right between your eyes." She glanced at Kingston. "Same goes for you. Don't try anything stupid."

She looked back at Hillier. "Allen, I can live with my brother being a criminal and a robber, but unlike you, he never murdered anyone."

All at once—looking from Grace to Hillier, thinking about what she'd said and what he knew—everything clicked into place for Kingston.

He stared at Hillier. "You're the Manager. The one who put it all together—the mastermind behind the Great Highway Robbery."

A crooked smile crossed Hillier's lips.

"That's him," Grace said. "Enjoy your last few minutes of freedom, Allen, because you're about to be charged with multiple capital crimes."

"What do you want, Grace?" Hillier asked, showing remarkable composure. "This can all be worked out. You know as well I do that Brian Jennings, that pathetic brother of yours, was a criminal, an ungrateful swine, and a blackmailer."

Grace shook her head. "It won't wash, Allen. No more deals, no more lies, no more bribery—you've reached the end of the road. I should kill you right here and now. I'd be charged with murder, but it would be worth it. I don't have that much longer to live, anyway."

Hillier still wasn't flinching. "Go ahead, then. Pull the trigger." He stared at Grace Williams, eyes daring and unblinking. The room went deathly quiet, the tension so palpable that Kingston could hear the faintest ticking of a clock somewhere in the house.

"You can't, can you?" Hillier taunted.

"It would be so easy," she said, stretching out the last two words. "But then I wouldn't get the chance to see you brought to justice, to watch you suffer, to see you humiliated and disgraced in public." She lowered the gun in the direction of Hillier's paunch. "So you'd better listen carefully to what I'm going to say."

She gestured to Kingston with a nod, for him to move over to Hillier. "Dr. Kingston is going to wheel you out of here and I'll be right behind. This gun will be inches from the back of your head all the time. But first, get on that walkie-talkie thing of yours and tell Victor and that other brute to go to the courtyard, move the Land Rover away from the other cars, start it up, and leave the engine running with the driver's and front passenger doors open. If the tank is less than a quarter full, then use one of the other vehicles. Then tell them to make themselves scarce." She paused. "You understand?"

Hillier nodded almost imperceptibly.

"Dr. Kingston will take you through the French doors to the garden, out through the gate into the courtyard, and then to the car park. There you'll be left unharmed but where I can kill you with one shot if anything goes wrong. If I get as much as a whiff that one of your goons is trying to stop us, you'll be killed instantly."

Kingston was about to interject, mentioning his phone call to Andrew and adding that the police could arrive at any moment, but he realized it wasn't a good idea to warn Hillier.

Grace waved the gun at Hillier. "Call Victor now."

29

HILLIER DID AS he was told, and two minutes later, the trio emerged from the garden gate onto the perimeter of the gravel parking area. Some thirty feet ahead, stood the solitary Land Rover, with the two front doors open, as Grace had stipulated.

Before approaching the car, Kingston scanned the courtyard, its various buildings, and the other cars parked there, to make sure the area was deserted. All seemed secure, though he knew that Victor and his cohorts and perhaps others could easily be lurking out of sight nearby.

Two minutes later, Kingston was behind the wheel, putting on his seat belt, checking the fuel gauge, wondering what was keeping Grace, when he noticed she had had stepped several feet away, facing the three other cars parked close to the house but still able to keep a wary eye on Hillier. She raised the small gun, gripped it with both hands, and fired a rapid succession of shots—not one of them wasted—deflating the rear tires on each vehicle. In five seconds, the empty magazine was replaced with a full one from her pocket. She hurried to the car and sat beside him, slamming the door shut, winding down the window. There she rested her gun on the door ledge, leveled at Hillier, who sat in his wheelchair watching helplessly, alone, powerless, and brooding.

"Goodbye, Allen," she shouted over the rumble of the V-8 engine. "You'll never see me again." Closing the window, she withdrew the gun. Kingston slammed his door shut and the Land Rover skidded forward, scattering gravel from its spinning rear wheels. He eased off the pedal, and they moved briskly across the courtyard and down the long hedge-lined lane to the main road and freedom.

Kingston was thinking that it was taking them a long time to reach the road when a line of tall trees ahead signaled that they were almost there. Rounding what should surely be the last curve, his foot went instinctively to the brake. The feeling of relief and gratitude—to Grace in particular—that they'd escaped unharmed suddenly evaporated, replaced with a sinking feeling in his gut. He glanced at Grace. She'd seen it, too. The iron security gate at the end of the drive was closed.

Ten feet from the gate, hand brake on, Kingston jumped out to examine the gate, to see if there was a push-button opener. On his side there was nothing. On the other, visible through the railings, was a keypad. Grabbing the rails with both hands, he yanked the gate to and fro with all his strength to test its sturdiness, quickly concluding that it would be too dangerous to try to ram their way through. As he turned to get back in the car, he spotted a CCTV camera, and then another one, on tall poles hidden among the trees. "The bastard's watching us, too," he muttered under his breath.

He ran to the back of the car, remembering that Andrew had said there were tools stored in it. A cursory glance in the storage space told him there was nothing that would be of use, no sturdy rope or chains.

Time was becoming critical. Hillier knew that their only means of escape was blocked. And the option of attempting to scale the gate's high, sharp-pointed railings and take off by foot was no option at all. They'd already wasted two or three valuable minutes, but Grace was showing remarkable patience and composure, having said nothing but a loud expletive at seeing the closed gate.

Back behind the wheel, Kingston was about to do a hasty U-turn to find a place where they could go off-road across the fields, when a white van approached the gate from outside—no doubt a tradesman making a delivery. This stroke of luck could be their only chance. Kingston backed up and moved to one side of the lane to make room for the truck to come through the gate and pass. He was pinning his hopes on the chance that the time lapse between automatic opening and closing would allow him to slip through.

The driver entered the code in the keypad and, slowly, the gate opened. The van eased forward, but instead of passing the Rover as Kingston had expected, it stopped abruptly several feet away.

Its doors burst open and two men leapt out, running toward the stationary Rover. One was gripping a tire iron, the other a baseball bat.

Kingston jammed the gearshift into reverse and stomped on the accelerator. Instantly the vehicle hurtled backward, fishtailing crazily, gravel and dirt flying in all directions. He regained control, managing more by luck than skill to keep the car straight and not plow into the thick hedges on either side of the path.

Head and shoulders turned backward, eyes glued to the lane behind, he dared not turn to see if he was outpacing the men. Then, through the rear window, he saw Victor running toward them on the lane. He would certainly have a gun, and in a matter of seconds it could be all over. They would be either captured or dead.

Slowing so as not to narrow the gap between them and Victor more quickly, Kingston took his eyes off the rear window for a fraction of second and saw Grace leaning out the window, trying to steady herself against the lurching of the car, the gun trained on their attackers. A crack echoed across the fields, and the man closest fell to the ground, screaming, clutching his knee, the bat spinning out of his hand. Doubtless realizing that he could be next, the other stopped in his tracks, the tire iron dangling at his side.

There was no time for conversation. Kingston knew that if there was any chance of escaping, he would have to find a gap in the hedging where they could drive off into the fields, where the four-wheel-drive Rover could outrun just about anything else. Victor had slowed to a walk and now was fewer than fifty yards away.

"On your right!" Grace shouted. "A gate."

Kingston saw it just in time, skidding to a stop a few yards past it. He slipped into low gear and pressed his foot down, hard. The Rover leapt forward, smashed through the wooden gate and bounced crazily across a shallow gulley, eventually finding traction on the damp, grassy field, then picking up speed. A gunshot came from behind in the distance—Victor, now well out of range.

"Let's see if we can find a way out of this goddamned mess," Kingston said, glancing at Grace.

Andrew's old Rover took everything in stride, including deeply rutted, muddy stretches and a couple of marshy, flooded areas. Pressing forward, with no further signs of civilization, farms, lanes, even tractor tracks, they were now relying purely on luck to help them find a way out.

"Way over there, in the corner," Grace said, pointing. About a quarter mile away, a thin wisp of smoke was visible against a backdrop of dark trees.

"Looks promising." Kingston changed course as they crossed the corner of a recently plowed field, bouncing up and down.

Then he heard the sound.

The clattering noise was growing louder every second. At first he thought something was stuck in one of the car's wheels, but he quickly rejected that idea. The sound was reaching a crescendo when he realized what it was. He almost ducked instinctively as the black-and-yellow helicopter swooped over them with a deafening roar, no more than twenty-five feet off the ground. Kingston could feel the powerful downdraft through the steering wheel.

The pilot circled ahead tightly, revealing the word POLICE on the fuselage. He made a soft landing fifty feet away, giving Kingston plenty of time to come to a stop.

Kingston and Grace slumped in their seats. No words, just smiles of relief and a quick glance up to the heavens from Kingston as he got out of the car. One of the policemen aboard, wearing a bulletproof vest over a navy pullover with sergeant's stripes, was walking toward them. The other, holding a semiautomatic carbine in his lap, watched from the helicopter, its rotor blades turning idly.

"Better hide the gun," Kingston said to Grace.

Grace took it from the pocket in the door, wrapped it in her scarf, and quickly shoved it under the front seat.

"Dr. Kingston, I presume," the sergeant said with a trace of a smile.

Kingston nodded. "I can't tell you how glad we are to see you chaps."

"I'm Sergeant Wilkinson." He stooped to glance into the car. "The lady is Grace Williams, I take it?"

"She is."

"Well, I'm glad you're both in one piece. Now let's get you out of here." He turned and pointed toward the tiny column of smoke they'd seen. "Head over there. It's about four hundred yards. On the right, you'll see a farm gate." He paused, the smile back. "This time it might be good idea to open it, by the way. Beyond it is a lane that leads to the B846. Make a left—heading east—and when you reach the main road, turn right toward Amersham. We'd like you to go directly to Amersham police station, where you'll be asked to file an initial report. They're expecting you. The station is on King George Fifth Road, off Chiltern, near the railway station. In the meantime, we'll lead you across the field to the road, just in case," he said, and headed back to the helicopter.

Halfway there, he stopped and looked back.

"I forgot to mention, Doctor, there's a friend of yours waiting at Amersham. He's been very worried about you."

"Andrew," Kingston said. "Of course."

Wilkinson smiled. "Yes, Andrew. The desk sergeant said that he's been worried about his Land Rover, too," he added with a sly parting smile.

Kingston smiled, too, then shifted the Rover into gear once more.

30

KINGSTON LEFT THE rutted field, passed through the open wooden gate, and in minutes was on the road headed toward Amersham. Fifty feet above, the police helicopter made what Kingston took to be a farewell: a rolling wave and then a swoop upward with a loud clatter before disappearing among the low clouds.

For a long moment, neither spoke as Kingston shifted through the gears, picking up speed on the empty road ahead. He had a hundred questions to ask but didn't know where to start. Grace saved him the trouble.

"How far is Amersham?" she asked.

"I'm guessing five or six miles. Why?"

"We don't have much time, then."

He was about to ask what she was getting at when she cut him off.

"I owe you a huge thanks, an apology, and an explanation as well," she said, tugging her seat belt and shifting to face Kingston. "You saved my life back there and I'll never forget it. I just hope one day I'll have the chance to thank you in full. The apology is for deliberately misleading you, having got you into this mess in the first place, for lying to you when you and the policewoman came to Beechwood. It was stupid of me, but I was trying my damnedest to keep you out of it." She took a short breath. "I had to resort to that, otherwise it could have jeopardized my plan to deal with Hillier. It was all coming down in a matter of days. If I'd told you the truth, I had no idea what would have happened. You could have gone straight to the police, for all I knew."

Kingston had been avoiding eye contact, trying to keep her talking, but he took his eye off the road for a second to glance at her. He wasn't going to speak, but she raised a hand anyway, shaking it slowly.

"You don't have to say anything," she said. "I'd prefer you just listen so you know how this all came about. And, given what faces me, we may not get another chance. It's ironic that with everyone I've come in contact with since arriving in this country, I end up trusting you more than anyone else. I owe it to you to at least try to explain what led me here and why I did what I did today. I'm not making any excuses and I'm ready to accept the consequences, whatever they might be. I think you deserve to know the truth, though."

Kingston nodded. "I would like to hear it," he said, eyes back on the road.

"I knew all along about Brian," she said. "I knew about his friendship with Ronnie Butler, the robbery, and eventually what Allen Hillier's role was. I'll get to him in a moment, though." She paused to run her tongue over her lips.

"I didn't hear from Brian until three years after the robbery. He was hiding in the Welsh mountains. He told me that his new name was Reginald Payne and he was enjoying life on his 'little farm,' as he called it. He wanted me to track down Hillier for him. Later, when I went to visit him, he told me that Allen had converted half of his share of the stolen money and all of Butler's into diamonds."

"Diamonds?" Kingston barely stopped himself from slamming on the brakes. Grace's words brought Darrell Kaminski's story flooding back: the plot that Kaminski had overheard at Alcatraz.

"Yes, diamonds. That's what Allen did in those days—a lot of shady stuff. Brian knew Butler's plan was to hide the diamonds in a graveyard somewhere in the England but not where. Butler's plan was to go to the U.S. and start a new life under a new name and come back later, when the robbery was long forgotten, to retrieve the jewels. Hillier had supplied all the necessary papers, a U.S. passport, and passage on a freighter."

She waited while a Harley-Davidson in a hurry roared past them, too close for comfort. *Pay attention, Kingston chided himself—to the driving, as well as the story.*

She continued. "All that stuff about Brian being well-off, his success-ful business ventures, the house in the Chalfonts—it was all fiction. I vis-ited Brian in Wales once and a couple of times later at Beechwood—both from Canada, by the way. I really did live there for the last twenty-five years. Anyway, on what would be my last visit, I became concerned about his well-being. He was drinking a lot and I suspected drugs. Then I didn't hear from him for several years. In what turned out be our last phone conversation, he told me that he was not only in poor health but bad shape financially as well. He was planning to salvage what little he could from the sale of Beechwood—it was heavily mortgaged by then—and move to a state-run care home. I was in no position to help, not that I would've, anyway. Before we hung up, he threw me another curve—what he called 'the final atonement.' He said that if he died under suspicious circumstances, or was killed, I should immediately tell the authorities to investigate Allen Jay Hillier, the only person living who would want him silenced. When I asked why, what it was between him and Hillier that would provoke such an extreme statement, he clammed up."

Kingston glanced at her out of the corner of his eye, at the same time noting the AMERSHAM 2 KM sign ahead. At last it was all falling into place. The problem he faced now was that they were going to run out of time before he could get the whole story from Grace.

"What was your guess at the time?" he asked. "What was it between your brother and Hillier that would make him say that?"

She paused for a moment. "I didn't need to guess. I just knew, in my bones, that Brian had been blackmailing Hillier—and back there the son of a bitch confirmed it. You heard him."

Kingston nodded.

"Hillier." She shook her head. "The biggest mistake of my entire life. None of this would have happened if it weren't for him."

"You knew him a long time, though."

She sighed. "I did. I was seventeen when I first met him—before the robbery. It was at a nightclub in Soho. As he was leaving, he spot-ted Brian, who was at our table. To me Allen was Prince Charming. But Brian thought he was fawning over me and cautioned me to steer clear of him. I soon forgot all about it. Then I met him again, by chance, quite a few years later. At the time he owned a house in Kew and law offices on Kingsway. We dated for a while, and I learned how his empire had expanded in those several years. Eventually I moved in with him. By that time, he owned several businesses, was a director of others, and was well connected politically. I suspected that he also had connections with London's organized crime syndicates. It turned out that I was right."

In the rearview mirror, Kingston noticed that a blue-and-yellow striped police patrol car had slipped in behind them, maintaining its distance. That more or less ended his hope of buying a little more time in the police station parking lot.

Grace continued. "He was a complex man—charismatic, sophisticated, fiendishly clever one moment, callous and ruthless to anyone who crossed him or got in his way the next. Remember, he was a lawyer and knew how to evade the law and use it to his advantage. He never did his own dirty work. He had plenty of other people to do that. He was always squeaky clean." She looked away for the moment. "Going back to the blackmailing, it was obvious to me, knowing what I did, that Brian's threatening to divulge Hillier's role in the robbery would in itself be more than sufficient reason for extortion, and he knew he could count on Hillier paying up because he had far more to lose if it came to a showdown. A simple phone call to the police is all it would have taken to blow the lid off their secrets and put them both behind bars for a long time. Brian knew that his life was coming to an end, anyway. For Hillier, murder was the only answer. It wouldn't be the first time, either."

"He'd murdered someone else?"

This time she looked at him. "He arranged it. An American man."

Kingston frowned. "How did you learn that?"

"From a man I once knew. Hillier had hired him to do it."

Kingston was getting confused. It was all coming too fast.

"Surely he didn't admit to that," he said.

He didn't need to. He'd told me more than enough already—it was as plain as the nose on your face. A few days later it was in all the papers. The body was found in the Thames."

"You knew then that Hillier was responsible?"

"I was certain. But he didn't admit it, if that's what you're thinking."

"Can you tell me more about it? You'd better be quick, though," he said, seeing the AMERSHAM TOWN CENTRE sign on the roadside.

"It's complicated, but I'll try." She paused, thinking for a moment.

"It happened about a year after I moved in with Hillier. By accident, I overheard a conversation between him and another person, who I later learned was an American named Mark Slater. I could only get snatches of what they were saying, but it concerned some kind of deal. From what little I could gather, it involved a lot of money. A few days later, a man I hadn't seen in years showed up at the house. His name was Mike Dempsey. He was a creepy sort who kept pestering me to date him back then. It turned out to be a surprise in more ways than one."

"What did he want with Hillier—or you?"

Her answer was drowned out by two staccato siren blasts from the police car, now on their bumper. "Pull into the next entry on right," the crackling loudspeaker commanded.

"Looks like time's up," Grace said, pursing her lips. "We'll have to finish another time—if there is another time," she added, mustering a wan smile. She unbuckled her seat belt, took the gun from under the seat, and handed it to Kingston. "Here," was all she said.

They got out of the car. Kingston handed the gun to one of the policemen who were waiting. "You'd better have this," he said.

They walked together, followed by the policemen, who directed them toward a side door. "Thanks again, Lawrence," she said. "If nothing else, I hope you'll understand a little better now and won't be too harsh on me."

Kingston placed a hand on her shoulder and opened the door for her.

"Thanks," she replied, with another halfhearted smile.

"I've no idea what they might charge me with," he said, "but regardless of what happens from now on, I'll come and visit you as soon as they'll permit it. That's a promise."

"I'd appreciate it," she said.

He wished her good luck and gave her one last look, as they were escorted down separate corridors to make their statements and for whatever might follow. Although Kingston had many of the answers he needed, there were still many more questions to be asked.

31

KINGSTON GLANCED AT his watch: almost eleven P.M. He and Andrew had been at the Kings Arms Hotel in Old Amersham for the last two and a half hours. They had finished dinner and were sitting in comfortable, overstuffed chairs, with snifters of cognac, next to a brick and stone inglenook fireplace devoid of logs, in the six-hundred-year-old coaching inn's oak-beamed lounge.

At the police station, Kingston and Andrew had not met up until after Kingston was through with his interview. In the meantime, Andrew had taken it upon himself to make a dinner reservation and book two overnight rooms at the hotel, anticipating—correctly, as it turned out—that it could take a long time for Kingston to go through the rigmarole of making a formal statement. Not only that, checking his phone, he learned that a storm front was moving in over the Home Counties with forecasts of heavy rains and flooding. Added to that was the probability that Kingston would be knackered and surely starving after such a harrowing day and sleepless night. Kingston had needed no persuasion and was grateful for Andrew's thoughtful foresight and resourcefulness.

Kingston was tired. After a pint of bitters on arrival, a shared bottle of Pommard at dinner, and now the cognac, he could hardly keep his eyes open. All he could think about now was going upstairs, flopping down on the bed, closing his leaden eyes, and getting an uninterrupted night's sleep.

During the evening he'd given Andrew a blow-by-blow accounting of the events of the last eighteen hours. Fully expecting Andrew to lapse into his familiar I-told-you-so attitude, Kingston was surprised and thankful that Andrew showed more concern for his return to safety, his well-being, and what appeared to be a genuinely solicitous interest in what had occurred at Greyshill. Was this the beginning of a new Andrew? he wondered.

Grace Williams would be spending the night in Amersham, too— only she'd be under lock and key. At the station, after cooling his heels for a half hour, he'd been informed by the detective sergeant interviewing him that no formal charges had yet been filed against him and all that was required was his recorded statement describing the events of the afternoon as he remembered them. An hour and a half later, when he'd completed his statement and been told that he could leave, he inquired about Grace Williams. He was told that a verbal complaint had already been filed against her by Allen Jay Hillier, and that, because the incident had involved the use of a firearm, it was considered a "serious arrestable offense" and she would be held for twenty-four hours, longer if authorized by the chief superintendent. The Land Rover would also be impounded for now.

Kingston had wondered why Hillier hadn't included him in his charges, but after thinking on it he realized that Hillier would know that if he did, Kingston would countercharge with perhaps far more serious accusations: kidnapping with the use of deadly force, aggravated assault and false imprisonment, for starters. This Kingston planned to do, anyway, when the dust settled.

He had also called Emma to bring her up to date with the extraordinary events of the day. Contrary to expectations, she was remarkably sanguine, considering the gravity of the circumstances.

At last in bed, feeling the soporific effect of the beer, wine, and spirits, sleep didn't come as readily as expected. This was one night when the adage "fatigue is the best pillow" was the wrong prescription. Since closing his eyes, Kingston could not get Grace Williams out of his restive mind. Back in the library at Greyshill, and in the car, she had pulled back the curtains wide enough to reveal events and names of people in her past that started to explain some of the uncertainty and questions that had been plaguing and eluding him and Emma all these weeks.

Her explanation in the car had supplied him with a critical missing piece of the puzzle. Knowing now that Hillier had converted the stolen money into diamonds, that Butler and Jennings were close, and that Butler had, in all probability, fled to the U.S.—all that lent much more credence to Kingston's contention that Butler could have been the person who was instrumental in arranging for the acquisition of the Belmaris rose, that, somehow, he had ended up as an inmate in Alcatraz. But so much of what had happened was still unclear . . . He cracked open his eyes and glanced at the luminous dial of his watch on the nightstand: one thirty. *Enough.*

He turned over, hoping that sleeping on his other side might help. At least he wouldn't have to listen to his heartbeat.

And yet a few seconds later, the questions started to trickle back. What charges would be pressed against Grace Williams? What were the legal proceedings from now on? How long could she be detained before being granted bail? For that matter, would she be granted bail? That would depend entirely on the charges filed against her, he supposed— and what could those be? For a moment, he pulled the top sheet over his eyes in a futile attempt to will himself to sleep. He thought he'd succeeded, felt himself drifting away, when one last question flashed across his numb and jumbled mind, perhaps the most frustrating question of all, where this whole business had begun: What had happened to Letty's mother, Fiona McGuire?

He was no farther along with regard to that question than he'd been before the events at Greyshill.

He sighed, resigning himself to a long, sleepless night.

And, of course, a few minutes later, he was fast asleep.

32

THE NEXT FEW days were a waiting game for Kingston.

After they'd arrived back in London, Andrew had more or less disappeared. Either he'd decided to let Kingston stew for a few days or had gone off on another of his spur-of-the-moment trips—which was fine with Kingston; he welcomed the chance to be left alone for a while, to recuperate from his ordeal and gather his wits.

He had wasted no time calling Emma again. She'd read the newspapers and watched the TV news reports, glad that it wasn't a lot worse, and there was no indication of what Andrew had earlier described as her "dim view."

"I want a complete report, Lawrence," she'd said, "a full confession."

And for the next half hour Kingston had obliged.

Only after a twenty-minute question-and-answer period did she seem satisfied, expressing uncharacteristic sympathy for the ordeal that he'd suffered and inquiring about his still noticeably wounded cheek. He thanked her and quickly changed the subject by asking for her thoughts on what the immediate future might hold in store for Grace—the arrest process, the legal implications, what kind of charges she could be facing, how serious they could be, and how long she would likely remain in custody. Emma spoke briefly about the arrest procedure and bail, but as for the rest of his questions, she emphasized that she was a policewoman, "not Rumpole of the Bailey." It was the first time Kingston had cracked a smile in days.

The conversation was coming to a close when she brought up Letty's name and something she thought worth mentioning.

"How is she doing?" he asked.

"Very well. She always asks about you."

"Why don't I come with you on your next visit?"

"She'd really like that." Emma paused for a moment. "Last week she said something I found curious. It's straw grasping, but it could connect Fiona to Beechwood."

"Really?"

"It started with our talking about flowers and my mentioning our visit to the garden at Beechwood and how lovely it was. It must have stirred something in her subconscious, because she said she'd once had a foggy recollection of having visited a beautiful garden with her mum and a man when she was very little. I asked if she could remember anything special about it. And there was. She recalled a lake with flowers floating on it and a bridge crossing it. A bright red bridge."

"That is unusual. But it couldn't have been Beechwood. It only has what one would call a pond and no red bridge."

"I know. But to a four-year-old, a pond could resemble a lake."

"Good point."

"Didn't Grace Williams say that Jennings once owned a house in the Chalfonts? Maybe that had a pond."

"It never existed. Jennings's house in the Chalfonts, his money, investments, owning a successful business—it was all fiction cooked up by Grace, for our benefit."

"Why does that not surprise me?" She paused. "In any case, I would have thought red an unusual color for Jennings's kind of garden."

"Not really. Nikko bridges—an ancient design from Japan, many of which are sacred—are almost exclusively painted vermillion. They're not exactly two-a-penny in the UK, but I've seen a few. The loveliest I know is in the garden at Heale House in Wiltshire. It spans the river Avon, leading to a Japanese teahouse."

"Understandable why it could have been rooted in Letty's subconscious," Emma said.

"Colors, smells, and sounds—it's said they evoke the most powerful memories. But in her case, maybe we'll never know how."

Soon after that, the conversation ended with promises to meet again when Emma returned to London.

Both days since returning he'd left the flat at seven thirty and walked to Martin the newsagent on Sloane Avenue, three minutes away, to check the *Daily Mail*'s front page, to see if Grace's letter had reached the reporter yet. Still nothing.

His trip the next morning proved fruitless, as did the day following.

On the fifth day he began to get worried. It had now been almost a week since the incident. What had happened to Grace's letter? Had it been lost in the mail? Had it been received but been discarded as not credible? Had Hillier somehow managed to squash it? Had it even been mailed?

Kingston frowned. There was one way to find out. He picked up the phone.

"Hello?"

"Sophie. It's Dr. Kingston. Lawrence Kingston."

"Oh." She sounded surprised and, to his ears, a bit contrite. "Dr. Kingston, I apologize. I should have called you. But these have been difficult days. I'm sure you understand."

"They have, indeed." Much more difficult for me, he wanted to say. "You're holding up, though?"

"Yes, I am. I—I shouldn't have got you mixed up with this in the first place. I'm sorry."

"Don't apologize; you did the right thing. It might have turned out a lot worse for your mother if I hadn't."

"That's true, I'm sure."

"Have you spoken with her?"

"Yes. I went to see her yesterday."

"Good. How was she?"

"Surprisingly normal, actually. Not at all what I expected. She said that if I talked with you, to thank you again for everything you did, for saving her life. I'm not quite sure what she meant by that, though."

"Let's just say that trying to leave Hillier's place got a bit dicey. Much more than the papers would have you believe. We got lucky. Did she say how long they plan to keep her? What the charges are?"

"They first told her that one charge was for possessing a firearm with intent to cause violence. Another had something to do with trespassing, using threatening behavior, et cetera. I looked them up. They're both serious."

"You said 'they *first* told her.'"

"Those could change. Apparently there's a lot more to this whole thing than her waving a gun around threatening this man. I asked what she meant and all she said was that it was something to do with her and Hillier's past. She also said she came awfully close to pulling the trigger. 'A despicable murderous swine' was how she described him. I asked her if she meant that in the literal sense, and she said, 'Yes, you'll find out all about it soon enough.' I wasn't quite sure what she meant by that, either."

"I think I do," Kingston replied. "Sophie, one of the reasons I'm calling concerns a letter. Did your mother leave a letter with you to post?"

"She did."

"And did you send it?"

"Yes, of course. Why? Do you know what was in it?"

"I have a pretty good idea," he said. He told her what Grace had told him and Hillier at Greyshill, and said he expected the *Daily Mail* story to break any day now.

Sophie sighed. "I wish she had talked to me about all this. I had a feeling all along that whatever she'd been mixed up with back then was some kind of criminal activity that she was ashamed of, and rather than tell me face-to-face, she preferred that I found out secondhand—when it all finally came out in the papers."

"I imagine that it was simply too painful for her to have to explain and justify it to you, her daughter."

"I suppose," Sophie replied.

"For what it's worth, I don't think she went there to kill Hillier, Sophie. My theory—and it's just a theory—is that if what she knew about his past were to be made public, it would mean the end for him, utter ruin. That would give her much more satisfaction."

"I was really hoping you'd know more about this awful mess than what's been reported. I just hope to God she didn't commit some dreadful crime years ago and that that was why she left the country."

"I can't say, for sure, but I don't think that's the case."

"Typical of her, though—I'll find out after everyone else."

"Did your mother say if there's a likelihood of bail?"

"Not really. I asked if there was a chance she could be released anytime soon, and she said they were still waiting on that decision. Like the charges, everything, seemed to be in limbo. She did tell me that they'd taken a statement from Hillier, but, naturally, she wasn't privy to his version of what took place."

The call ended with Sophie promising to call back after she next spoke with her mother. She thanked Kingston for believing her when nobody else did and, in her words, "probably saving my mom from a far worse fate."

Kingston hung up hoping she was right. And wondering, still, what would happen with Grace's letter.

The next morning, he found out.

33

The *Daily Mail* headline:

Allen Jay Hillier, Mastermind of the Notorious Great Highway Robbery?

Fifty-six years later, Hillier's lover reveals all:
The 1957 crime, murder, and corruption

By Nicholas Cooper

THE NEWSPAPERS HAD been flying off the rack at Martin: Kingston got one of the last copies. He took it back to his flat where, timed perfectly, the kettle had just finished boiling for tea. At his usual breakfast—two poached eggs and toast with marmalade—he pored over the story.

Ten minutes later, he'd finished the article, mildly disappointed. Cooper had done a workmanlike job, but he'd focused only on the incident at Greyshill. It had all been described in considerably more detail than in previous reports, but he had been hoping Cooper would have got Grace to open up, would have probed beneath the surface to reveal her state of mind and the circumstances that led her to such an extreme decision.

There was no mention of Grace's letter, either, which disappointed him even more.

He was about to put the paper aside when he noticed a notation at the foot of the article: Today's report was the first of several, and the story would be serialized over the coming days. That explained everything. Undoubtedly there would be more about Hillier's crimes in future stories. Kingston realized, however, that he couldn't necessarily count on or wait for Cooper to reveal the things he needed to know. It was imperative that he talk to Grace himself. He should have done it days ago.

"You're losing it," he muttered to himself as he went to the living room and picked up the phone.

Directory Inquiries transferred his call to Amersham police station, and he spoke to an obliging Sergeant Evans, who was curt but informative. Yes, Grace Williams was still in custody. No, regulations did not permit her directly receiving incoming calls. Yes, she would be informed of Kingston's call. Yes, there was every reason to believe Ms. Williams would be able to call back within a reasonable span of time.

Sergeant Evans took Kingston's name, address, and phone number and bade him good day.

Kingston was relieved that Grace was still at Amersham. He took that as a good sign. Now all he could do was wait.

Early the next morning, Kingston had just returned to the kitchen with the *Times*, about to make tea, when the phone rang. It could be Emma, he thought. He was planning to call her to ask if she could try, through her contacts, to get more information about the status of Grace Williams's arrest: namely, how much longer she could be detained without being granted bail. He picked it up half expecting her cheery voice.

"Dr. Kingston? This is Grace Williams. I'm calling from Amersham police station."

For a moment he couldn't think how to answer without sounding as pleased as punch or, worse, nonchalant.

"Thank you for calling back," he said, with just enough sincerity to keep it from sounding like a cliché. "You're well?"

"Yes, I'm doing all right, thanks."

"When are they releasing you? They seem to have held you longer than normal without granting bail."

"I know. It's because of what they're calling extenuating circumstances. I've been told that it'll be resolved any day now, but the legal mumbo jumbo is holding it up. It has as much or more to do with my providing information proving that Hillier was the brains behind the robbery and was guilty of two murders as it has with what happened at Greyshill and my behavior there. That now seems to be a lesser issue, apparently. Particularly since I didn't threaten to harm or kill him—just pointed the damned thing. Anyway, my lawyer's dealing with it."

"That all sounds like good news, Grace," he said, realizing that it was the first time he'd addressed her by her first name.

"It is. The problem is, as with Reggie's murder, I don't have proof for the American man's, either—the one whose body was found in the river. But I've given the police and the CID all the information. It'll be up to them to come up with the evidence. Finding Mike Dempsey will be a big help in proving that."

"Right. I want to hear the rest of that story."

She paused, and he heard her draw a long breath. "It's far more complicated than you might think—which brings me to the point.

"If," she continued. "No—change that to *when* they release me, I plan to return to Canada as soon as possible. My attorney is close to putting Beechwood on the market, and once it's sold, it will sever my ties here." She paused again. "Doctor, the reason I'm telling you all this is that time is very short. I would like you to visit me before I leave, if you would? I feel an obligation to finish up where I left off with this wretched mess. Fill in the blanks for you as best I can."

"I'd like that as well, Grace. I'll come this afternoon, if that's not too soon."

"That would be good. Let's say two o'clock. I'll make sure you're on the visitor list."

"I'll be there, don't you worry."

Hanging up, he felt more ebullient, more optimistic than he had in weeks. If Emma were there, he would have given her a high five. Thinking back on how long the drive to Amersham had taken in the Land Rover, and what time he should leave, he picked up the newspaper, unfolded it, and scanned the headlines.

About to take a sip of tea, he held the cup suspended in midair.

Allen Jay Hillier, Possible Suicide

Police were called to the London residence of prominent businessman and philanthropist Allen Jay Hillier yesterday, after a staff member reported finding him dead in his bedroom. A brief statement made by his personal assistant, Jeremy Highsmith, confirmed the discovery, saying that evidence found in the bedroom and earlier statements by Hillier led the police to believe that he took his own life. They have not yet issued a formal statement, awaiting pathology findings from the Home Office.

Eight days ago police were summoned to Hillier's country residence in Buckinghamshire after receiving reports of gunfire. Two persons were taken into custody that day . . .

"Good grief," he muttered. "Grace has got her wish."

34

Bourne End, two days later

IT was seven o'clock in the evening at Andrew's house on the river, and though the sun was still high on the horizon, what could well have been one of the hottest the days of the year was about to become just another weather statistic. A soft breeze had picked up in the last half hour, teasing the leaves in the upper branches of the graceful weeping willows that straddled this peaceful stretch of the Thames.

For twenty minutes Kingston had been sitting alone on the lichen-splotched flagstone terrace that overlooked an uninterrupted expanse of lawn that sloped to the river, reflecting on this therapeutic vision. His handwritten notes and a near-empty glass of Macallan were on the table. Up until now, he'd picked up only the latter. He hadn't felt this ease and contentment for months, and he hoped it could linger, even if only for a little longer, before he had to deal with more serious, worldly matters wrought by greedy and pitiless men.

Emma was in the kitchen, helping Andrew put the finishing touches to dinner. Occasionally, Kingston could hear their laughter through the open French doors and windows—and not once in that time had he given a thought to the Great Highway Robbery, Greyshill, Beechwood, or even Alcatraz. This was even more noteworthy because that was why they were here in the first place: to discuss Kingston's final interview with Grace Williams.

That session, two days ago, had been an altogether depressing few hours. Though outwardly claiming to be satisfied by the turn of events,

Grace had showed signs of denial over Hillier's suicide, and her role in it. Kingston didn't know her well enough to be a true judge of her character, but perhaps she had gotten exactly what she wanted. Perhaps she was happy—though she certainly hadn't seemed that way to him.

Grace's lawyers were confident that if her case were to go to trial, it would end in an acquittal. The minute it was over, she and Sophie planned to return to Canada, each determined to forgive and forget and resume their lives. For Grace, in particular, things would never be the same, he knew. She was now internationally notorious, and the larger-than-life stories and photos of her years in the arms of Britain's most celebrated crime figure of the century, coupled with her brother's role in the robbery and his inauspicious end, had been front-page news every day. He had a feeling they would continue to be news for a long time to come.

At dinner, he did most of the talking, relating to Emma and Andrew what Grace had told him during their meeting at Amersham, and also his discussion with Sophie. After dessert, still with a lot more to discuss, they took their drinks into the airy living room, where Corbusier armchairs were arranged around a low travertine coffee table that squatted on pale bamboo flooring.

Kingston took a sip of wine and leaned back, stretching out his legs under the table.

"Wonderful meal, Andrew. Thank you."

"My pleasure. You should thank Emma, too—she was quite the sous-chef."

Kingston placed his glass on the table. "So where were we?"

Andrew frowned. "You were telling us what Grace told you about the conversation she overheard—the deal with the diamonds."

Kingston nodded. "Of course. Well, we know it was Hillier who had converted both Jennings and Butler's shares of the banknotes into diamonds. And we know that Jennings ended up penniless. But until now we had no idea what happened to Butler's diamonds—other than that he hid them. Now we do."

"Really?" Emma murmured.

Kingston nodded again. "Hillier rarely made mistakes. As Grace said, he covered his tracks by hiring people to do his dirty work and negotiate his deals. This time, however, he made a big error by hiring the wrong man. Hillier didn't know that the man—Mike Dempsey, whom I've already alluded to—was an old acquaintance of Grace's."

Kingston drew in a deep breath. "Here's what happened, according to Grace. A couple of days after she'd eavesdropped on Hillier's conversation with Mark Slater, the American chap, Dempsey showed up at the house to meet with Hillier. Grace was surprised because his was a face from the past. She'd met him—to her regret—several times when she was younger, before the robbery. He was a low-life lecher who hadn't changed much over the years—'just as obnoxious as ever,' were her words.

"By this time she'd figured out that something big was coming down, and she decided to exploit Dempsey's womanizing ways to find out what it was. Dempsey was still infatuated with her and more eager than ever to impress. A clandestine meeting in a local pub, a revealing dress, lots of charm, drinks—it didn't take long to loosen his tongue."

"Not quite the innocent, see-no-evil Grace we'd been led to believe," Andrew remarked.

"No question about that anymore. Back then I would imagine she could be quite a femme fatale." Kingston picked up the notes he'd made and thumbed through them. After a moment's checking, he looked up.

"Slater, the American, had contacted Hillier, saying that he was working on behalf of an unnamed client in the U.S. He claimed to possess a large quantity of diamonds, part of an estate, an inheritance to be passed on to the daughter of his client."

"The same diamonds?" Emma asked. "Those Hillier had given Butler in exchange for his share of the money from the robbery?"

"It seems so, yes," Kingston replied. "And when Slater mentioned that a daughter was the beneficiary and divulged the large quantity of diamonds involved, Hillier knew there could be no mistake—"

"He would likely have known about Butler's child, too, Fiona," Andrew completed the sentence.

"Exactly."

Emma took a pad from her purse, jotted a note, then looked up. "You're suggesting that Slater was either an ex-Alcatraz guard or con and Butler was doing time there? He was the 'client'?"

"I am." Kingston nodded. "So, seeing a golden opportunity, Hillier was all too eager to help. He promised to locate the mother and daughter—both of whom he claimed to know—and arrange for them to meet Slater to legally transfer the diamonds to Fiona McGuire, Fiona Doyle at that time. Hillier would certify the lawful exchange so that both parties had notarized legal documents to that effect.

"Hillier called Slater a few days later to say that he had located the mother, Caitlin Doyle, but the daughter, Fiona, was on holiday with friends. A lie, of course.

"But Hillier pulled it off. He informed Slater, truthfully, that legally the mother must represent the daughter, regardless—the child being a minor."

"Fiona was, what—six or seven at the time?" Emma asked.

"That's about right." He paused. "Here's where it gets complicated, though—devious, too. In the meantime, Hillier had hired a woman with acting experience, offering her a big payoff to pose as Caitlin. Provided with Caitlin's personal data, history, and forged IDs, and coached on the conspiracy, she accompanied Hillier to the meeting and the transaction was completed without a hitch. She handed the diamonds over to Hillier, and Slater walked away with legal documents that would prove to his client—Butler—that his wish had been fulfilled. And Bob's your uncle."

Andrew raised a hand. "A question?"

"Of course." Kingston was pleased and relieved that Andrew was (almost) back to his old self, taking an interest in Kingston's adventures.

"Wasn't the real Caitlin still alive?"

"She was, but according to Molly Collins, she was in and out of the hospital at that time. She died a few years later."

"So what about Slater's cut, his commission?" Emma asked.

"He'd already taken it, before even meeting with Hillier. Grace said that Slater had confided that information to Dempsey." Kingston paused. "And then—doubtless part of Hillier's plan all along—he had

Dempsey get rid of Slater. That was the reason for Dempsey being there in the first place."

"I'm curious," Andrew said. "Did she tell you where Butler had hidden the jewels?"

Kingston nodded. "He had buried them beneath a stone memorial in the courtyard floor of an old village church in Wiltshire."

"Ingenious hiding place," Andrew commented.

"How did Grace learn all this?" Emma asked.

"From Dempsey. She was not only surprised at how much he knew, but also his willingness to divulge what he'd obviously learned from Hillier, maybe Slater, too, though we'll never know. Not only that. As we know, two days after the transfer, Slater's unmarked body washed up on a bank of the Thames estuary—the police classified it 'an accidental drowning.' Dempsey never directly admitted having dealt with Slater, she said, but what he did tell her left very little doubt. He was still the same braggart."

"Interesting," Emma said. "Jennings's death was by drowning, too."

Kingston nodded. "The man's specialty, perhaps."

"Wouldn't it be easy to track Dempsey down?" Andrew asked.

"If he's still alive," she replied, hesitating. "You know, if Butler was sick, maybe dying, it might be possible to go through the U.S. Federal Bureau of Prisons archives and find out who in Alcatraz was hospitalized or near death at the time. That could give us the name he went by then."

"Something you could look into later, maybe, Emma?"

"I'll see what I can do," she said, making a note.

Andrew excused himself, saying coffee was ready and he'd be right back. In the meantime, Kingston and Emma continued chatting. After Andrew returned carrying a tray with a large cafetière, cups, and saucers. The coffee poured, he spoke first.

"What about the rose?" he asked. "How did that get to Alcatraz?"

"Well," Kingston said, "this is where we get into the realm of speculation and probability. But now our connection between Alcatraz and the robbery may help matters."

He paused and took a long sip of coffee, letting his eyes wander around the room, now softly lit by the lingering shafts of sun glinting off the beveled edges of the mirror over the fireplace.

"Let's start by assuming that it was Brian Jennings who shipped the rose to Alcatraz. Logically, it would have been at the request of somebody at the prison. If so, it can be narrowed down to one of five people: a prisoner, a guard, a secretary, a warden, or one of the privileged inmate gardeners. The least likely are the first two. In the case of the warden, we know he had a garden and, according to Kaminski, his secretary had quite a big say in things horticultural, so either could have been involved. That leaves an inmate gardener."

"You know more than any of us about the subtleties of these horticultural things, Lawrence. Whom do you think most likely?" Emma asked.

"Let me answer by first dealing with the only real physical clue we have about the rose mystery: the Graham Thomas book and its cryptic one-letter signature. All this time"—he paused, smiling at Emma—"I've speculated that the *R* could have stood for Reginald, and he had sent the book to someone on Alcatraz. But I now realize there could be another explanation I'd overlooked. I'm now convinced it's more likely the other way around: The suggestions in the book were made by someone on Alcatraz and sent to Jennings—to find the rose and ship the cuttings back." He smiled and pulled on his earlobe.

"I recognize that look," Andrew said. "What else?"

"Another tiny clue—and I should have figured it out sooner. In the lengthy back-page note—the description of the Belmaris rose, Emma—you'll remember that I described the person's writing ability as impressive; an excellent feeling for the language."

Emma nodded.

"At the time I was paying attention to the content and wasn't sufficiently alert to the style. But something kept nagging at me, so I recently reread the note. This time I immediately noticed the spelling of the word 'coloration' without the 'u' as we Brits spell it. In addition, there was 'inquiry' beginning with 'i' rather than 'e.' These spellings are used almost exclusively in the U.S"

Emma looked impressed. "So, do we have an *R* person on Alcatraz?"

"We do. The gardener who Kaminski referred to as highly intelligent, the inmate who'd worked for years on the gardens: Ryan Matthews. I think he was the one who made all those notes in the book."

"I'm confused," Andrew said. "Matthews sent the book to Jennings?"

Kingston shook his head. "No. Matthews wrote the notes, but I think it had to have been at Butler's request and it was he who sent it to Jennings in England—"

Emma, who had stopped making notes but had been listening intently, interrupted. "You seem to be pretty sure of yourself."

"When you think about it, Butler was the only one with something important to gain, and he was also the only person able to contact Jennings direct."

"I was going to ask about that," Andrew said. "How could they communicate?"

"I asked Andy Harris the same question. Letters between inmates and their families and their lawyers were permitted, but they were censored and retyped by guards to eliminate the possibility of secret messages conveyed either into or out of the prison. Apparently, prisoners had to submit a list of correspondents. In Butler's case, the only person he would be permitted to communicate with would have been, his girlfriend, Caitlin, because she was mother of his child."

"So Caitlin must have had a way to contact Jennings?" Emma said.

Kingston nodded. "He was Butler's best friend, so it stands to reason that Caitlin knew him, too. She would have likely known how to get in touch with Jennings, while he and Butler were on the run. My guess is that this would have been arranged prior to the robbery."

"So, contrary to the reports we read, she must have known something about Butler's role in the robbery."

Kingston nodded. It would seem so, Emma."

Andrew leaned back and looked up at the ceiling in feigned exasperation, then looked at Kingston, shaking his head. "I still can't possibly imagine an Alcatraz inmate trying to persuade a prison warden to grant special privileges simply in exchange for a rose—no matter how rare."

Kingston smiled. "I know. It seems far-fetched. So let me explain it a different way." For a moment, he stroked his chin, looking pensive. "Try to picture life on Alcatraz. Grim, bleak, hopeless day after day, on that rock of an island, in those cold stone cells . . ."

"Grim, for sure," Emma agreed. "Prisons do tend to be that way."

Kingston nodded. "Yes. Which is why Matthews was so thankful and at peace to be working in the gardens. It gave him the freedom to be outdoors for long periods of time—something to look forward to every day, something to live for. Any prisoner would give an arm and a leg to get garden privileges."

Kingston paused, glancing aside for a moment. "I think Butler saw the deal that Matthews had and decided he wanted it, too. He figured if he could get his hands on something that could persuade the warden or others to consider granting him special privileges—"

Emma was nodding. "Makes sense. Even to me, a brown thumb. What better gift for a warden, or the secretary, for that matter, whose personal interests were in gardening, beautifying the place? Can you imagine—the most sought after rose in the world on Alcatraz?"

"I think that was the case," Kingston said. "And once Butler told Matthews of his scheme, he would have been more than mildly enthusiastic about it, too. In fact Matthews would have had better motivation than any of them to acquire the rose. My guess is that he already had Graham Thomas's book in his possession. *Old Shrub Roses* was, and still is, required reading for gardeners."

Emma and Andrew were silent for a moment.

"All right," Andrew said, shaking his head, "I'm outvoted. It looks like you may have solved the mystery of the Alcatraz rose, after all."

"Well . . ." Kingston tried—with limited success—not to look smug. "A lot of it is supposition, but we do know that Butler's plan was to flee the country and go to America. It's reasonable to speculate that he succeeded and, once there, got mixed up with the wrong people—organized crime, possibly—then committed a serious felony and ended up if not in Alcatraz, then in another federal prison and was ultimately transferred to the island."

"I have a question," Emma said. "Where does Letty fit in to this? If at all."

"What happened to her mother, you mean?"

Emma nodded.

"I have some thoughts on that as well—again, not what one would call conclusive, I'm afraid," he said, picking up his notes and studying them.

After the pause, he looked up. "We know Fiona was born in 1956. But the one thing missing in all this—what we don't know—is if her mother, Caitlin, ever told her about her father, Butler. I'm proposing that she grew up as a Doyle and that she never learned about him and what he'd done. She believed what her mother had told her: that he'd died. Why wouldn't she? And, by the way, this is what the Collinses would have believed, all along. Anyway—for the record—Caitlin dies in 1968, and then, in 1991, thereabouts, Fiona meets Terry McGuire, a driver for a car parts company. A year later, they marry, and six years after that, Letty is born. A year after that, her father is killed in the accident, and six years after *that*, Fiona goes missing."

"Right," Emma said. "And at some point in that time, the book that Butler sent Jennings ends up in Fiona's possession."

"The question is how?" Kingston said, taking a last sip of coffee. "Now, when I talked to Grace—"

"Do you know if she had met Fiona?" Andrew asked.

Kingston shook his head. "I don't think so, but I did ask her if Brian had had any relationships, lady friends, during the years he'd been a fugitive. She did recall one instance. The two were having coffee one morning when she saw a mug—a china one, not one of those thick transport café ones—with dried lipstick on it. Jennings hastily replaced it with another. When she jokingly asked him about it, he mumbled what was obviously a cobbled-up excuse: It was from a woman who'd stopped by asking if she could use the phone. Her car had broken down and she wanted to call—"

"If you're trying to establish some kind of relationship between Jennings and Fiona, that's really reaching, if you ask me," Andrew said.

"Grace also mentioned finding a hairpin on the bathroom counter on another visit," Kingston added. "So whoever the woman was, it looks as though she visited more than once."

Emma shook her head slowly. "There may have been a woman. But as for her being Fiona, that's hardly what one would call hard evidence, Lawrence. In any case, there's a big age difference between them— twenty-plus years?"

Kingston nodded. "That's true. But I'm not implying they were having some kind of affair. All I'm suggesting is that if they knew each other, we not only have an explanation for how the book ended up where it did, we may also have an explanation for what happened to Fiona McGuire."

"What?" Andrew asked.

"All right, you two, let's back up here a little. *If* they met, we have only two choices: Either Fiona tracked down Jennings, or vice versa. If it were the former, she would have had to have known not only who he was but also, most likely, what her father had done."

"So what are you suggesting? I'm getting confused again," Andrew chipped in.

Emma was shaking her head. "To think that Fiona somehow found Jennings—one of the two Great Highway robbers still at large—when all of England's police force was unable to? That's hard to swallow."

"I agree," Kingston said. "That's why I proposed that Fiona was never aware of her father's crimes. I think Jennings found her. He was an old man, maybe wondering what had become of his best friend's daughter. Remember, it's highly likely that Butler had died by this time—and perhaps, even more important, Jennings was curious about what had become of Butler's share of the diamonds. That's more plausible, if you ask me. Remember, according to Grace, he was broke."

"It's still a reach," Emma said.

Kingston raised a hand. "All right. Let's just agree that they made contact, though. They would have so much in common. And if Fiona became a regular visitor to Beechwood—"

"That could explain how the book ended up with her," Andrew said.

"Precisely."

"We still have no proof that Fiona ever actually possessed the book or was ever at Beechwood," Emma said.

"Why not? We've agreed that the rose book was in Jennings's possession and we know it was on the bookshelf of Fiona's house. We've ruled out her husband Terry and her mother as having owned it—which leaves Fiona. What other explanation do we have?"

Emma frowned. Andrew was shaking his head now, too.

"Look," Kingston said, "we know that Jennings loved roses and had a magnificent garden. Say Fiona visited it—she could have easily fallen in love with the place, and it's reasonable to assume that he could have given her the book to educate or encourage her to learn more about the joys of gardening. For that matter, she might have asked if she could borrow it." He shrugged. "All I'm saying is that we're pretty sure he had the rose book, likely kept it for many years, and it ended up with Fiona. Can we at least agree on that?"

"Fine," Emma said, "we can agree on that. So tell me your theory, then—what happened to Fiona? Surely you're not suggesting that Jennings killed her?"

"No. That would be totally out of character. I believe her death must have been an accident. Something—I don't know what—must have happened, and she died before Jennings could get her to a hospital."

"C'mon, this is sheer speculation, Lawrence," Andrew interjected. "It's too convenient."

"If you remember, Andrew, I did qualify earlier that certain of these conclusions must depend on supposition and presumption."

"An accident at Beechwood, you mean?" Emma asked. "I see where you're going with this. He would have a body on his hands—"

"Exactly. Taking her injured but alive to a hospital is one thing. Calling the police and reporting that a friend has died accidentally on your property is another entirely. Jennings might never survive the ensuing investigation. I think he chose what he thought to be the lesser of two horrifying choices: disposing of the body himself."

Neither Emma nor Andrew seemed prepared to break the conspicuous silence that followed. As if on cue, the hallway tall clock chose that moment to strike the half hour.

"That's what I think is the most plausible explanation for her disappearance," Kingston said somberly. "That's why Missing Persons has no record, why it remained an unsolved mystery."

Andrew looked disconcerted. "Is that what you're proposing to tell Letty?"

"I think that the three of us should make that decision," Emma said.

"Of course." Kingston nodded. "Maybe another visit to Beechwood is in order. Not that I think we'll find anything."

Emma smiled. "Not unless the rose had decided to bloom again."

Andrew yawned. "Let's call it a night. My head's spinning. We can talk more about it in the morning."

It was agreed, promptly and without further discussion.

35

Kingston and Emma arrived at Beechwood two days later. Andrew had begged off to attend the last day of a vintage car show at Hampton Court, which had worked out well for all three of them. Kingston had been hoping to spend time alone with Emma.

At the front door they were greeted by a woman of ample girth with gray hair resembling fine-grade steel wool. She turned out to be none other than Thomas the gardener's wife. She announced with a sprinkling of authority that she was both housekeeper and custodian of the house in Grace's absence. Their having called ahead, she was aware that they had come to visit the garden to undertake a second search for a certain rose. It was obviously of no importance to her, so they'd been given free rein of the property, four acres in all, which, they assured her, shouldn't take too long.

Not that she seemed to care.

Under a blue sky furrowed with wispy cirrus, Kingston and Emma started their second tour of Brian Jennings's exceptional garden. To Kingston, this alone was worth the trip. Roses were less abundant, but still none vaguely resembling the size and color of the Belmaris climbing rose. After forty minutes, they had covered every inch of the garden, arriving at the farthest point from the house that now looked diminutive in the distance. Here, the garden ended at a low, twiggy hedge mostly of brambles, holly, and honeysuckle. Set in the hedge was a wooden stile beyond which stretched a grassy swath of land that ended about forty feet away at a line of beech trees.

Kingston walked up to the stile and glanced indifferently around the area. The only visible plant life were tufts of dandelions, thistle, cow parsley, and clumps of cheerful white-and-yellow ox-eye daisies. He was about to return to Emma when he glimpsed something white, the size of a book, on the grass close to the line of trees. He hopped over the stile expecting to find a scrap of cardboard or perhaps sun-bleached wood. Instead it was a small grayish slab with the name PEPPER crudely etched on it. Glancing left, he saw another twenty feet away. He walked over to it and found a similar slab, which upon inspection looked to have been made of concrete and bore the name SALT. Underneath was the date 1996.

It was Jennings's pet cemetery! Of course he would have had pets, Kingston realized. During the many years he'd lived alone, at Beechwood, he must have had many. This was borne out as he wandered the line of trees. He counted nine graves in all, randomly placed, presumably both dogs and cats. There was something irresistibly poignant about the scene. He had a mental image of a bereaved Jennings, a hardened criminal, carrying his dead pets to this quiet, out-of-the-way spot, to give them a proper resting place.

He was about to leave when he caught sight of another, slightly larger grave, a distance from the rest, under the dappled shade of one of the beeches. Maybe it was his imagination. His first thought was to ignore it, but his insatiable—and, to Andrew, exasperating—curiosity drew him to it. In a few seconds he was standing at the foot of another marker. Unlike the others, a small square had been chiseled off each of the four corners, to form a ragged cross.

Underneath the date 2003, separated by a scratched image of a rose, were the initials *FAB*.

"Emma!"

She glanced up.

"Something here you should see."

36

"I've got to hand it to you, Lawrence," Emma said, buckling her seat belt. "Your theory couldn't have been closer to the truth. The only question remaining is whether it really is Fiona's burial place."

One hand resting on the gearshift, Kingston glanced at her before driving off. "There weren't many other explanations, really. You're right, though. She might have been buried elsewhere on the property and the marker may just be a memorial. That's for the police to determine, now, though." He sat for a moment, the motor idling, staring through the windscreen, his mind elsewhere.

"Sixpence for your thoughts," she said, breaking the long silence.

"I was thinking about the date."

"The date? It was 2003, why? That's the year she went missing. It all fits."

"Something else happened in England that year: the worst natural disaster in three centuries."

Emma was frowning. "You've lost me."

"The Great Storm."

"Of course. Sorry, it didn't register. A lot of people were killed, it was catastrophic."

Kingston nodded. "Over a million trees were destroyed. I know that the National Trust properties alone lost more than three hundred and fifty thousand."

Emma's eyes widened. "The accident we were talking about—you're thinking Fiona could've lost her life in the storm? All those huge beech trees where we were standing—my God."

"It's just a guess," he said, shifting into first gear. "Though I have an idea how we might be able to learn more."

"Really?"

"Yes. I won't go into it now, but we'll know soon enough."

Emma smiled. "You know something, Lawrence? You sound more like Morse every day."

When they arrived in Middle Cheverell at one thirty, at least two dozen cars remained in the Rose & Thistle parking lot. Entering through the pub's open front door, past colorful, floral baskets, Kingston glanced around the bustling room and quickly spotted Clare Davenport at the bar going over papers with a young man who Kingston guessed to be a salesman. As Kingston and Emma approached, she looked up and beckoned them over, excusing herself to the salesman, who departed with a hasty farewell.

"Welcome back, Doctor," she said with a sunny smile.

"Glad to be here," Kingston said, turning to Emma. "Let me introduce you to Clare Davenport, proprietor. My friend, Emma Dixon."

"A pleasure to meet you, Emma," she said.

"You, too," Emma replied, nodding. "Your pub is charming."

"Thank you. Your table's ready, but don't let me hurry you if you'd like a drink first in the lounge."

"No, that's fine," Kingston said. "We'll have drinks at the table."

She explained that she had to attend a meeting and would join them in an hour or so, insisting they not leave before she returned. She waved over a waiter, who escorted Kingston and Emma to their table in the adjacent dining room.

The next hour was one of the most pleasant that Kingston had experienced in many months. A white-clothed table with a wildflower centerpiece, excellent pub cuisine, a bottle of Chassagne-Montrachet, and spirited conversation created an irresistible confection that suspended all sense of time.

The conversation opened with their speculating about the initials *FAB* on the stone marker. Emma had insisted that to conclude it was meant for Fiona, with only the first letter significant, was a leap too far.

Kingston disagreed, pointing out politely that it could be argued that Fiona's true name—the one on her birth certificate—was Fiona Butler, not Doyle—hence the B. Furthermore, he reasoned that Jennings, Butler's close friend, would more likely have chosen the name Butler than McGuire. As to the middle initial, he also had some theories—perhaps Jennings had wanted the stone to appear as that of another pet, hence the name Fab—or the most logical, that Fiona's middle name was Anne or Audrey, or whatever. That they could verify later. Or maybe, he granted, Emma was right, and the grave was not Fiona's at all.

They finally agreed that—unpleasant as it was—it was moot, since it would only ever be proved so with the discovery of human remains.

The waiter arrived with coffee and cleared the table.

Emma took a sip and looked at Kingston over the rim of her cup. "So what are you going to do now, Lawrence, now that this is all over?"

"I hadn't thought too much about it," he fibbed. "Resume my life of semiretirement, I suppose. How about you?"

She sighed. "Pretty much the same, I guess. Forced, in my case. We make quite a pair, don't we?"

"You miss police work, don't you?"

Her smile was wistful. "To be truthful, until I started collaborating with you, I didn't realize just how much. I'm really going to miss you—miss working with you." She paused for an instant. "I know I've been cynical at times, questioning your judgment, trying to rein you in, but I want you to know that I greatly admire your talents as a criminal investigator—let's face it, that's what you really are—and I have deep respect for you as a kind, thoughtful person, courageous, too—even taking into account a tendency to be stubborn and impetuous at times." She took another sip of coffee and smiled. "I know what you're thinking: I'm beginning to sound like Andrew. I mean what I said, though, even if it wasn't particularly well phrased. I'm not as talented in that department as you."

"Thank you, Emma. I must say, coming from you, I'm deeply touched and grateful for such sincere and lavish praise, though I'm not sure I deserve it. At the risk of sounding unduly sentimental, the coming days and weeks will be difficult for me, too. You're right, though, we are good partners, and I must admit that I've been secretly wishing for some time now that our inquiry wouldn't end. I'd even fantasized that we'd been engaged to solve another unsolved mystery." He grinned. "A cold case that has the police stumped."

Emma chuckled. "You're incorrigible. You're worse than I am."

Kingston's grin turned into laughter just as Clare Davenport appeared.

"I can see you two are enjoying yourselves," she said. "Good lunch?"

"Couldn't have been better," Kingston replied. Emma nodded in agreement.

"I think congratulations are in order," Clare said, pulling out a chair and sitting. "You two have become celebrities of sorts. Quite an achievement by all accounts."

Kingston shrugged. "We were just lamenting that it's all over. Our fifteen minutes of fame is ended, and we're two jaded retirees again."

"By the looks of you, it can't be all that bad."

Kingston smiled. "You're right. The ending could have been quite different. As a matter of fact, there's one last question that needs answering and it occurred to us, just today, actually, that you may be able to help."

Clare Davenport's penciled eyebrows shot up. "Me?"

"Yes. But first, a question: How long have you owned the Rose & Thistle?"

"My husband and I bought it in 1995."

"Good. Now I'm going to test your memory, if I may?"

"Go ahead."

"In 2003, a natural disaster struck the south of England, killing many people, felling millions of trees."

She nodded, her expression serious. "The Great Storm. It's impossible to forget. We were hit pretty hard down here."

"Do you recall whether the storm damaged Reginald Payne's house or property? Big trees destroyed?"

"Yes, it did. Many trees came down at Beechwood that day. Lots of houses suffered losses. It was reported in the paper with photographs. Part of his house was badly damaged when a tree crushed the roof. Reggie was okay, though." She paused. "I still can't get used to his real name, I'm sorry. Anyway, he wasn't injured. According to him at the time, it took almost a year to rebuild the rooms that were demolished."

Kingston looked at Emma. She met his gaze and simply gave a slight nod.

"Thank you, Clare," Kingston said. "You've been a great help."

And, he added silently to himself, you've helped change a young girl's life for the better.

Ten minutes later, walking side by side out the front door, Emma slipped her arm through Kingston's. For an instant, he thought he was elsewhere, long ago, at another place, in another life. As quickly as it appeared, the memory vanished. He said nothing, and they both kept walking. It all seemed so natural—so right. Words no longer seemed necessary as they made their way toward the car.

POSTSCRIPT

Three weeks later, Chelsea

THE LETTER THAT Kingston had been patiently awaiting finally arrived. He opened the envelope bearing the COUNTRY LIFE logo on the flap and, with guarded optimism, withdrew the one-page letter, noting another sheet of paper-clipped to it. He sat on the sofa to read it.

Dear Lawrence,

It was a pleasure to hear from you again after so long, though I have been follow-ing your exploits in the newspaper these past weeks, of course. I do hope that after your near miss in Staffordshire and now this last incident, you will start to consider a somewhat more passive pastime to satisfy your creative urges in the coming years.

The enclosed copy, from our 12 June, 2001, issue, should certainly settle the ques-tion you raised about Japanese Nikko-style bridges in Western gardens. Please keep in touch and let me know if you require further information on the subject.

With best wishes,
Julian Cartwright, Deputy Editor

As Kingston cast his eyes over the enclosed article, a wide smile spread across his face. Underneath a photo of a vermillion bridge span-ning a small lake was the caption:

Another splendid example of the sacred Japanese architectural feature in today's British gardens is this bridge in the exceptional private garden at Beechwood in Gloucestershire.

He put the article aside and stood, thinking of Letty. Her vague recollection could indeed have been based on fact—it was quite possible that she had visited the garden with her mother. For whatever reason, the bridge must have been destroyed, or moved in later years. Fiona McGuire had been at Beechwood. They were as close to closure as they would ever get.

He crossed the room, still smiling, and picked up the phone to tell Emma.

Acknowledgments

In part, the Alcatraz Rose is based on an event that took place on Alcatraz Island in 1989. That year, a group of Bay-Area rose aficionados from the Heritage Rose Group visited the island to search for and collect cuttings of old roses.

Two members of the tour, Gregg Lowery and Phillip Robinson, spotted an unusual rose in a weedy, overrun garden. Questioning its heritage, they took cuttings and cultivated the rose at their Sebastopol nursery at the time. Later, they identified it as the Bardou Job rose, among the rarest of about 100,000 known rose varieties and presumed to be extinct.

The deep red, climbing rose, was hybridized in 1887 in the Pyrénées-Orientales region of Southern France and named after Jean Bardou. Bardou's fortune came from manufacturing the famous JOB (his initials) cigarette papers. The rose is also recorded as once having been cultivated, 100 years ago, at St. Fagans Castle in Wales.

Over a span of 30 years, the two Heritage rose authorities, cultivated more the 3,000 old and rare roses at their garden in Sebastopol, California. The "Lowery-Robinson" collection is now owned and maintained by The Friends of Vintage Roses. Rosarians world-wide consider the collection to be one of the most comprehensive multiple-class collections of old roses ever assembled. (*thefriendsofvintageroses.org*)

Thanks for the inspiration Gregg. Without your discovery, I wouldn't have had a story.

While entirely fictitious, The Great Highway Robbery is based loosely on The Great Train Robbery (as described on Wikipedia), a similar grand robbery that took place in Buckinghamshire, England, in 1963. Belmaris Castle is modeled in part on Sudely Castle, Gloucestershire.

Britain's historic "Great Storm" occurred in 1987.

A very special thanks to Alcatraz historian, Chuck Stucker, son of a prison guard, who grew up on the island throughout his childhood. Chuck was beyond generous with his time, during numerous phone conversations and letters, and without his profound knowledge of all things Alcatraz—his verbal recollections, detailed information and descriptions of island during the prison years—my story would not have the same authenticity or accuracy.

Once again, kudos to the indispensible DC Claire Chandler, Hampshire Constabulary, for keeping me in conformance with U.K police procedural matters.

As in the past, I am deeply grateful and consider myself exceptionally fortunate to have had the support of my brilliant team of editors, advisors and copy checkers: my plot guru/editor, Dave Stern, the remarkable editing talents of Cynthia Merman, the meticulous John Joss, and horticulturist, Mike Hegerhorst. Lastly, my keenest two collaborators and critics: my wife, Suzie, who keeps me on the straight and narrow 'mystery' track, and long-time friend and author, Roger Dubin. Thank you all. Your collective guidance, encouragement and keen eyes have breathed life and substance into my story giving it that all-important final luster.

Last but by no means least, a heartfelt thanks to all my readers. Without you, there would be no Kingston and no future books. I will always remember that.

Made in the USA
Charleston, SC
09 December 2014